She's So Dead to Us

She's So Dead to Us

kieran scott

SIMON & SCHUSTER BFYR

New York   London   Toronto   Sydney

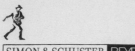

SIMON & SCHUSTER BFYR

An imprint of Simon & Schuster Children's Publishing Division

1230 Avenue of the Americas, New York, New York 10020

This book is a work of fiction. Any references to historical events, real people, or real locales are used fictitiously. Other names, characters, places, and incidents are products of the author's imagination, and any resemblance to actual events or locales or persons, living or dead, is entirely coincidental.

Copyright © 2010 by Kieran Viola

All rights reserved, including the right of reproduction in whole or in part in any form.

SIMON & SCHUSTER BFYR is a trademark of Simon & Schuster, Inc.

For information about special discounts for bulk purchases, please contact Simon & Schuster Special Sales at 1-866-506-1949 or business@simonandschuster.com.

The Simon & Schuster Speakers Bureau can bring authors to your live event. For more information or to book an event, contact the Simon & Schuster Speakers Bureau at 1-866-248-3049 or visit our website at www.simonspeakers.com.

Also available in a **SIMON & SCHUSTER** BFYR hardcover edition

Book design by Krista Vossen

The text for this book is set in Andrade.

Manufactured in the United States of America

First **SIMON & SCHUSTER** BFYR paperback edition April 2011

10 9 8 7 6 5 4 3 2 1

The Library of Congress has cataloged the hardcover edition as follows:

Scott, Kieran, 1974–

She's so dead to us / Kieran Scott. — 1st ed.

p. cm.

Summary: Told in two voices, high school juniors Allie, who now lives on the poor side of town, and Jake, the "Crestie" whose family bought her house, develop feelings for one another that are complicated by her former friends, his current ones, who refuse to forgive her for her father's bad investment that cost them all.

ISBN 978-1-4169-9951-5 (hardcover)

[1. Interpersonal relations—Fiction. 2. Social classes—Fiction. 3. High schools—Fiction. 4. Schools—Fiction. 5. Family life—New Jersey—Fiction. 6. New Jersey—Fiction.] I. Title. II. Title: She is so dead to us.

PZ7.S42643She 2010

[Fic]—dc22

2009046739

ISBN 978-1-4169-9952-2 (pbk)

ISBN 978-1-4169-9957-7 (eBook)

For Matt and Brady

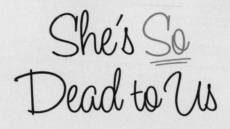

august

Oh. My. God. You are never going to believe who I just saw driving through town in a Subaru.

Who?

Ally. Ryan.

You're not serious.

Do I look like I'm laughing?

I heard she's been sunning herself on the French Riviera for the past two years, living off all our college funds.

No way. Her dad lost all that money.

My mom says they've been living in a trailer in West Virginia somewhere, like, under a bridge or something.

Oh my God. Did she look malnourished?

Her hair was kind of frizzy. . . .

I can't believe she's back. Does Chloe know?

Are you kidding? She sent a 911 text to the girls and they're already convening at Jump.

Unbelievable. Ally Ryan back in Orchard Hill.

I cannot wait for the first day of school.

ally

"So? What do you think?"

Hmm. What did I think? I had to take a moment to sort out an answer to that one. Here's what I came up with.

I thought that my ass hurt from sitting for four straight hours on the car ride from Maryland to New Jersey. I thought that the dingy gray condo in front of which I was now standing—discernible as my new home solely by the fact that the movers had propped the storm door open with a cinder block—was butthole hideous. Although, on the bright side, it was exactly the same butthole hideous as every other condominium on this particular block of the Orchard View condo complex, so at least it wasn't alone in its butthole hideousness. I thought that the last time I had been in Orchard Hill, about eighteen months ago, there had been a gorgeous apple orchard right where I was standing—an orchard that actually made sense of the name Orchard Hill—and that now it was gone. So not only was there no orchard anywhere near the Orchard View condominiums, but there was also no view, because we were at the bottom of the hill from which one would have viewed said orchard, back when said orchard existed.

Sigh.

I also thought—no, *knew*—that the way I answered this question would determine my mother's mood for the rest of the day. The rest of the week. Maybe the rest of the year.

So I smiled and said, "It's great, Mom."

Her tired, sad eyes brightened, and the tension disappeared from her smile. "Don't you think? And, honey, it's not forever.

I'm going to put half my paycheck away every week, and Danielle says that before we know it we'll be able to afford one of those cute little houses over by the library and . . ."

Danielle was Danielle Moore, mother of my old friend Shannen Moore and the only one of my mom's friends from Orchard Hill who still talked to her. Probably because she understood that wives and daughters should not be held responsible for the actions of husbands and fathers. Mrs. Moore was also the realtor who'd found us this lovely little condo in the first place. I reminded myself not to thank her when I saw her again.

I missed the rest of my mother's rambled promises because one of the movers—a round dude with too much facial hair— was walking by with my bike on his shoulder.

"Um . . . excuse me? Could I get that, please?" I asked, swallowing my aversion to strange men with pit stains.

He grunted and dropped my bike to the ground so hard that I swear I heard the suspension whimper. But at least it was my bike. If home is where the heart is, home had just arrived.

"Thanks."

He grunted again. I straddled my bike. Closed my hands around the well-worn rubber grips. There was plenty of dirt stuck up in the thick treads, and I was ready to add some more. Instantly, I felt about nine hundred percent better. Nine hundred percent more free.

"Ally, where're you going?" The light was already gone from Mom's eyes. "Don't you want to see your room?"

"I'll see it later. I'm going for a ride," I said.

"Where? I hope you're not thinking of—"

The movers slammed the truck door shut, muffling her

last words, but I knew what she had said. And we both knew that I was thinking of doing what she thought I was thinking of doing. There was no reason to confirm or deny. Without a backward glance, I rode through the gates at the front of the complex, hooked a left, and headed for town. It felt good to move. To breathe. To get the hell away from my mother and all her positive thinking. I love you, Mom, but things were not going to be the same now that we were "home." Things were never going to be the same.

But still, it was kind of good to be back. As I waited at the light at the bottom of Orchard Avenue, I couldn't believe it had been more than a year. The place looked exactly the same. Not one storefront had changed, and they all still had the same cheesy names that had cracked me up back in kindergarten. The Tortoise and the Hair Beauty Salon. Baby, It's Yours Kids' Clothing. Needle Me This Knitting Supply. Jump, Java, and Wail! Coffee Company. The proprietors of Orchard Hill lived for their cutesy plays on words, which just made the Starbucks and the Gap look all the more cold and austere with their been-there-done-that signage. The movie theater anchored the downtown shopping area, its old-school neon lights doused now, since the sun was still up, its marquee advertising the three latest and greatest indie movies of the month. The brick-faced post office was bustling with activity, and a few middle school guys were using its wheelchair ramp to show off their tricks. In Veterans' Park across the way, a group of girls were lying out in shorts and tanks, their tops folded up to expose the maximum amount of stomach. As soon as I saw them I stood up on the pedals, racing up the hill and under the train trestle toward the crest. I doubted I knew any of them—most of my former friends had huge backyards with pools if they wanted to lie out—but I wasn't ready to do the whole reunion thing yet. Which was hilarious, considering where I was headed.

I hesitated for a split second at the foot of Harvest Lane. What was I doing here, anyway? I hadn't seen this hill since February of my freshman year—the night my family and I had driven down it for what I'd thought was the last time, me staring out the back window of my dad's soon-to-be-repossessed BMW, trying to commit every detail to memory. I hadn't even called my friends to say good-bye. Hadn't texted. Hadn't e-mailed. Hadn't tweeted a less-than-140-character "See ya!" I'd been too confused, too scared, too embarrassed. And soon too much time had passed, and getting in touch felt awkward and humiliating and I just . . . never had. Now here I was, eighteen months later, wishing I could go back and smack my freshman self upside the head. Because if I had said good-bye, if I had kept in touch with any of them, it would have made moving back here so much easier. But how was I supposed to know my mother would one day get a job at Orchard Hill High? When we'd left, my parents had told me we were gone for good, and I'd believed them.

It wasn't my fault they didn't have a clue.

After spinning a couple of circles at the foot of the hill, I figured, what the hell? I'd come this far. If fate wanted me to bump into one of my old friends today, then let fate have her way. I turned, flipped my bike into first, and started the long climb. The late August sun beat down on my back, and sweat prickled my neck and underarms as I worked my bike uphill. There were no houses on this stretch of Harvest—the drop-off on my right was way too steep for building, the ridge on my left made of solid rock. As I came out of the trees, the view opened up and I glanced back over my shoulder to see New York City lying low and gray in the distance. In front of it, the town of Orchard Hill opened up like a pretty pop-up book at my feet. From this height I could see Orchard Avenue and all the little side streets crisscrossing it at various angles. Atop the hill on the far side of town was Orchard Hill High, where I'd be starting school in a few days, and at the foot of that hill, the Orchard View condos, where my mom was probably cursing my name right now. Beyond that were all the cute cookie-cutter houses on their gridlike streets and the strip mall with its Dunkin' Donuts and CVS and mom-and-pop pizza place and deli. At least we lived within walking distance of Munchkins and pizza. Always try to look at the bright side.

At the tip-top of Harvest I paused and put my feet down, breathing heavily and taking in the view. I'd been thinking about this moment the whole ride up from Maryland. But now that I was here, my heart fluttered with nerves. I swallowed hard and pretended I didn't feel it. Why should I be nervous? It wasn't like I was going to see anyone. It wasn't like it mattered. It was all in the past. I was a completely different person now. Smarter. Stronger. Better.

I took a deep breath and rode around the bend. Suddenly everything became crisply clear in front of me, as if I'd been looking through someone else's glasses for the whole ride up here and they'd finally fallen away. I leaned back on my bike and drank it all in. The tall, green trees forming a canopy of green, the hissing sound of the sprinklers spritzing the manicured lawns, the scent of barbecue wafting through the air from the backyard of one of the stately houses. Suddenly I was twelve years old again. Ten. Five. A little kid running from yard to yard, chasing fireflies with my friends, laughing and shouting and singing like no one could hear.

Home. I was finally, finally home.

I rode slowly, lazily, down the wide street, letting my front wheel weave in and out like I always did when I was a kid. The first house I came to was Faith's. It was all stone and brick and pointed roofs, like something out of a gothic novel, except that her little brothers' sleek, silver scooters were parked on the gravel path out front. The landscapers were out in full force, mowing and blowing and trimming and Weedwacking. There was one car in the driveway, a red Audi, which I didn't remember. But this was not surprising. Faith's mother got a new car every year, donating the old, barely driven one to charity as if she were doing it for the less fortunate and not just because she wanted her new-car-smell back. When I'd left, Faith was convinced she was destined for either Broadway or her own show on the Disney Channel. She was auditioning for some summer program at a theater in the city. I wondered, not for the first time, if she'd gotten in. If she'd taken her first step toward superstardom.

A little bit farther and I came to Shannen's place. Wide and white-faced and sprawling. The yard was unkempt, but it was otherwise the same as always. Two cars this time, and I heard music blasting from the general direction of Shannen's bedroom. I leaned down and pedaled as hard as I could until I'd gotten past the hedgerow and out of sight. The level of fear I felt at the thought of seeing her surprised me. What the hell was I going to do on the first day of school if I couldn't even handle the thought of Shannen Moore spotting me out her bedroom window? Drop dead of nervousness, apparently. I wondered how her family was doing these days. It had been almost two years since Shannen's older brother, Charlie, had run away. When I'd left, Shannen still thought it was her fault, and her parents weren't speaking to each other. Had things gotten any better since? Had Charlie ever come home?

At the corner was Hammond's place. It looked dead. Down the shore for the weekend, of course. No one spent more time at their shore house than Hammond's family. Sometimes they spent the whole summer, but they were probably back during the week now, since Hammond would have soccer practice. Everything revolved around Hammond's sports schedules, and his older brother, Liam's, back when he was in high school. I stood up on the pedals, trying to spot the secret path that cut through the tree line separating his backyard from my side one, but the full, green trees hid it from view.

The secret path. My heart pounded at the thought of the last time Hammond had used our shortcut, and I hooked a quick right onto Vista View Lane, scooting past the yellow DEAD END sign that both my mother and Chloe's mother had actually gone to borough hall to protest because it was so "unsightly." To my left was Chloe's place, and the thought of seeing her freaked me out even more than the thought of seeing Shannen. Did Chloe know? Had Hammond told her what happened that last time he'd come over? Were they still together? And if not, was I the reason?

I only knew one thing for sure: I was not ready to find out the answers to those questions. I laid into my pedals, putting Chloe's place behind me. And then, there it was. At the end of the cul-de-sac was my house. My home. The mansion where

I'd grown up. I'd assumed the gate would be closed, but it wasn't, and as soon as I saw the opening, I accelerated. I didn't even think. I just rode. Through the gates and up the hill of the driveway. At the top was the circle with the apple tree at the center, surrounded by little pink flowers and a stone border. My dad had taught me to ride my tricycle around that circle, and later my bike. All the scraped knees and tears and shouts of joy came flooding back out of nowhere. I rode around it once and everything unexpectedly blurred.

A set of shrubs had been planted under the library window. Someone else's bike tossed on the grass. New planters in front of the door with happy little marigolds dancing in the breeze. Not my house anymore. Not my home.

My gaze drifted to the right, to the row of evergreens that shrouded the view of the basketball court in the backyard. My dad had built it for me for my twelfth birthday—a state of the art outdoor court complete with scoreboard, bleachers, and a hand-painted sign that read RYAN ARENA. It was the best birthday of my life. All my friends were there, and Dad had jerseys made up for each of us with our last names emblazoned across the back. At my mother's insistence, the number was the same on each, because she knew that if, say, Chloe had been given number one everyone would think that meant I had chosen favorites—like she was my best friend. But my mother knew I hated putting labels on the group. They were all my best friends. Chloe, Shannen, Faith, Hammond, Trevor and Todd. We'd been together since kindergarten. Had never gone a week without seeing each other for a party or a practice or a music lesson or a charity event. In my opinion, we were practically related.

Which made the fact that I'd ditched this place without saying good-bye potentially unforgivable.

I wondered what my father would say if he could see me right now. "Chin up, bud," I heard him say in my ear. "No use dwelling on the past. What you do tomorrow and the next day and the day after that is what matters." Was that what he was doing out there right now, wherever he was? Forgetting about this place, about us? Starting a new future? Two weeks after he'd moved us out of Orchard Hill and in with my grandma in Baltimore, my dad simply disappeared. One night he was there, and the next morning he was gone. He hadn't left a note. Had canceled his cell. No one—not even my mother or his mother—knew where he was. Grandma had told me that my father was ashamed. That he couldn't handle being around us every day when he had hurt us so badly. That he'd probably come back when he felt himself worthy again. That was his way, she said.

But it made zero sense to me. Because his leaving hurt way worse than the fact that he'd lost all our money and our home. Way worse.

The thing was, my dad had always been there for me. He was the one thing I had that always made my equally privileged Crestie friends jealous. All our dads had these high-powered jobs in New York. Chloe's father owned a bunch of success-ful restaurants and was never around at night or on weekends. Shannen's dad practically ran this huge advertising firm and was always jetting off to LA or Chicago to oversee commer-cial shoots. Faith's father was a concert promoter, so he spent tons of time schmoozing superstars Faith never got to meet, which drove her totally insane. Hammond's father was the boss man at a cable news channel and spent half his time buying up smaller stations around the globe. The Stein twins' father did something in real estate that I never quite understood, but it meant spending lots of time in Florida and Texas. Basically, it was rare to spot any of their dads on the crest. But my father always did his best to make it to my basketball games and plays. He actually came to the hospital when Shannen and I crashed our bikes on a dare and broke various bones, while Shannen's father hadn't even called. My dad never missed a Christmas, always took my mom into Little Italy for Valentine's Day, helped me blow out my candles each birthday. Unlike the rest of the Crestie fathers, my dad had always been there.

Until he made some bad investments and lost everything. And not just for us. He'd lost a lot of my friends' parents' money, too. I'd never been clear on the details. All I knew was it meant we'd had to sell our house and cars and our shore house—and that we'd had to leave. I think that was part of the reason I hadn't been able to face calling any of my friends. What my dad did . . . it made me feel like an idiot. I'd thought he was so perfect—the greatest dad on the crest—and then he'd talked everyone's parents into some stupid risky investment and lost tons of their money. My dad, as it turned out, was a fake. A loser. And it made me feel like a loser too.

My mom was always telling me that my dad hadn't done it on purpose. After all, if he'd known that stock was going to tank, he wouldn't have put all our money into it as well as some of our friends'. She said he'd simply messed up. But he'd messed up so big-time that my life had been completely turned upside down.

So yeah, I was angry. But not so angry that I'd never get over it. At least, I would have. If he hadn't bailed on us.

The tears that had blurred my vision started to sting. I placed my feet on the stone and took a breath. I had not come here to cry. I was not going to cry.

I heard a noise behind me. The unmistakable sound of a window sliding open. My feet hit the pedals.

"What the hell are you doing?"

My fight-or-flight reflex was overruled by curiosity. I had to see who was living in my house. I looked over my shoulder. The first thing I thought was, *That's my room.* The second? *Who are you and why are you not on television?*

The guy who lived in my room was shirtless. He folded his bare, tan arms on the windowsill and gave me an arch look. His hair was wet, as if he'd just come in from a swim, and his eyes danced as he looked down at me. He had the most perfect shoulders I'd ever seen, and his biceps bulged as he settled in. An athlete. Definitely. A possibly naked male athlete of the highest hotness order. And he was living in my room.

"Are you lost?" he said.

He was amused. One of those guys who was so confident in himself and his position that even the appearance of a scraggly-looking girl trespassing on his property presented nothing more than an opportunity to tease.

I turned my bike around to face him, still straddling it, just in case I needed to make a quick getaway.

"You're in my room," I said.

He laughed, and I felt it inside my chest. My toes curled inside my beat-up Converse. "Oh, really?"

"Yep."

He looked over his shoulder. "So, that's your jockstrap on the floor."

I grimaced. "Okay, I've known you for two seconds, and already that's too much information."

His smile widened. "How is this your room?"

"I used to live here," I told him, swallowing a lump that suddenly popped up in my throat. "I moved a couple of years ago."

Now he was intrigued. He shifted position and looked me up and down. "Prove it."

"Okay. Go look inside the closet, above the door. I used to write down my box scores up there."

"What sport?"

"Basketball."

He narrowed his eyes but went. The second he was gone I noticed that my hands hurt. I released the grip on my handlebars and looked at my palms. Dozens of tiny red lines had been pressed into them from the rubber. I'd been holding on for dear life. He came back.

"You scored forty points in the state championship?"

"JV championship," I clarified modestly.

"If I had stats like that, they'd be spray painted on the walls."

"My dad," I told him. "He was always lecturing on being a team player. Didn't want me to get all me, me, me about it, so I had to hide it."

Which, considering how things had turned out, was pretty ironic.

He disappeared. Suddenly a basketball was hurtling toward my head. I reached up and plucked it out of the air with both hands before it could break my nose.

"Thanks for the warning!" I shouted, my heart in my throat.

He pulled on a maroon and gold T-shirt. Orchard Hill soccer. Of course. "I gotta see these skills," he said. "I'm coming down."

My palms started to sweat all over the ball. Who was this guy? If he was on soccer, he obviously knew Hammond. Was he friends with Chloe and them as well? Who was I kidding? Of course he was. He lived on the crest. Suddenly my brain was flying three steps ahead. He was definitely going to tell them I was here. Then everyone would be talking about me. What would they tell him? What would he think? He was just coming out the front door—tall . . . very tall . . . taller than me, even— when my cell phone trilled.

I considered not answering, but my mother would freak. I tucked the basketball between my hip and forearm and fumbled the phone from the pocket of my jeans.

"Hey," I said.

"Ally, I really need you back here," she said. "They want to know where to put your furniture, and we have to get something for dinner. Where are you?"

I looked at the hot boy who was standing in front of me expectantly with his perfect calves and ready smile and the lightest blue eyes I'd ever seen, the house that wasn't my house looming behind him.

"I'm on my way," I said.

His face fell.

I closed the phone and tossed him the ball. "I gotta go."

"Wait," he protested.

"What?"

Wow. Way to sound belligerent, Ally.

"If you used to live here, then you must know the crew," he said, taking a few steps toward me, passing the ball back and forth from hand to hand.

The crew? Seriously? "Um, the crew?"

"Hammond, Chloe, Shannen, Faith, the Idiot Twins," he said, rolling a hand around.

I laughed. The Idiot Twins. It was our nickname for Trevor and Todd Stein, local daredevils. Hadn't heard that one in a while.

"Yeah, I don't know who came up with that name, but it fits," he said with a smile.

"I did," I told him.

His eyebrows shot up. "Yeah?"

"There was this whole thing where Trevor and Todd rigged up a homemade bungee cord and tried to bungee jump off their jungle gym," I said, narrowing my eyes. "Let's just say the results weren't pretty."

He laughed. "Is that why Trevor's nose is like that?"

"Yep."

"Nice." He nodded, dribbling the ball. "I must mock them endlessly about that later." He looked me in the eyes, and my knees went a tad weak. Just from eye contact. "So, you coined the Idiot Twins. Nice work."

"Thank you," I said, bowing my head slightly.

"There's a party the night before school starts. At Connor Shale's house."

Connor Shale. The boy who'd shoved his tongue down my throat in Shannen's tree house the summer between eighth and ninth grade while his parents played Mexican train dominoes with mine on the patio down below. I'd been too polite to shove him off me and had let the heinousness go on for at least two minutes until, thankfully, Hammond Ross had appeared at the top of the rope ladder and laughed until Connor finally stopped. Then I'd practically fallen the ten feet to the ground trying to get away. My first kiss. Not my finest moment. Even more unfortunate? I'd only kissed one other guy since.

"You should come," Bedroom Boy said.

I experienced an unpleasant twisting in my lower gut. It was amazing how casual it was for him. Like he wasn't inviting me into the very scene I had both dreaded and looked forward to with a mixture of excitement, apprehension, and abject fear for so long.

But it was kind of nice that he wanted me there. And wasn't this a good sign, anyway? Clearly my friends hadn't been slandering me all over the place for the past eighteen months. If they had, he never would have invited me to a party with them. Right?

"Um, yeah. Maybe," I said. My phone trilled again. "I really gotta go."

"Oh, come on. Just one game?"

"Rain check," I told him, turning and peddling away.

"I'm holding you to that!" he shouted.

It wasn't until I was halfway down Harvest Lane that I realized I'd never even gotten his name.

jake

"Am I running some kind of geriatric summer camp here?" Coach shouted. "Let's hustle!"

I didn't hustle. I looked at Hammond and he rolled his eyes. I hate laps. If you're going to make us run distance, at least let us out on the streets. What am I, some kind of lab rat scampering in circles for your block of cheese? Upperclassmen, at least, shouldn't have to do this shit. It was so fucking hot out. And my brain was fried. And I still had three hours of practice ahead of me and back-to-school shopping with my mom tonight and all I could think about was the girl who used to live in my room.

The girl was hot. Not, like, model hot, but hot. I like a girl who dresses down. Who doesn't need all those bows and doilies and jewelry and crap—'cause she knows she's hot without it. And the ponytail? That sealed it. She even had those little curls behind her ear just, like, touching her neck. . . . Shit. So effing sexy. All night, I couldn't stop thinking about her. I mean, she used to sleep in my room. How could I not think about that?

"Dude, that's ten," Hammond said, smacking me in the chest with the back of his hand.

"Thank God."

We grabbed paper cups full of water and dropped down on the grass to watch the stragglers.

"Jonah! Pick it up!" I shouted at my brother. Just to be a dick. He was a freshman, and all freshmen and varsity virgins get hazed. He shot me an annoyed look but sprinted the last turn. Hammond laughed and crushed his cup before tossing it onto the ground.

"Look at that little fucker," he said, nodding at David Drake, who had finished ahead of us and was now running stairs on the bleachers, for no apparent reason. "He doesn't watch out, he's gonna get a kick in the head."

"Maybe he's on something," I suggested, not at all serious.

Last year David Drake had been the most pathetic player on JV. This year he'd added at least ten pounds of muscle and had shown some respectable skill on the field. It was obvious he'd been working his ass off all summer, which I respect. Not everyone cares that much. I know I don't. But Drake didn't live on the crest, and he still had the balls to play soccer, which around here was a Crestie sport. So that meant Hammond didn't like him.

Which brought up a question. Where was the new-old girl living? As far as I knew, none of the Crestie families had moved this summer. I glanced sideways at Hammond. "What do you know about the girl who used to live in my house?" I asked.

Hammond's head whipped up so fast I heard a crack. "What about her?"

"Who is she?" I asked. "Were you, like, friends with her?"

"Why? What do you know?"

I stared at him. Why was he so tense all of a sudden? "She came over yesterday," I said. "Guess she wanted to see her old place or something."

"Shut the fuck up. You *saw* Ally Ryan?" Hammond shifted position. He reminded me of a dog waiting for a treat. A pit bull–German shepherd mix. The kind of dog that would take the Milk-Bone out of your hand and then bite your fingers off just for fun.

"Yeah," I said. Ally Ryan. Her name was Ally Ryan. AllyRyanAllyRyanAllyRyan. "Wait. Ally Ryan. I've heard that name before."

"She comes up every once in a while," Hammond said.

Right. Now I remembered. She was the girl in the picture in Shannen's room. The one of a whole mess of Crestie girls taken at the country club pool in, like, sixth grade. I'd asked Shannen about her once, and she hadn't wanted to talk about her. Interesting.

"Dude. How did she look?" Hammond asked.

I didn't like his tone. He was practically licking his chops. "Fine. Good. Whatever. I don't know what she looked like before."

"Is she hot?" Hammond asked.

I lifted a shoulder. "She's all right."

Hammond eyed me for a long moment. I stared straight ahead at the field, where the coaches were lining up cones for drills. My face was burning. I hoped I was already red from running so Hammond wouldn't realize why.

"Dude, you don't want to go there," Hammond said.

I sucked down the rest of my water. "Who said I was going anywhere?"

"Good. Because Ally Ryan is, like, enemy number one."

"What? What does that even mean?" I asked.

"Short version? Two years ago her father screwed all our families out of a load of money and then left town," Hammond said. "We were all friends before that. You know, Sunday dinners and all that shit."

"She comes to Sunday dinners?" I asked. I dreaded the stupid Sunday dinner tradition. My mother had campaigned for over a year to get my family invited to them, and once we were in I still had no idea why. It was all so fake, the crest families gathering once a week for a homemade five-course meal like we were one, big, happy family. We didn't even know these people existed two years ago, but now all of a sudden my mother's happiness hinged on whether or not Mrs. Appleby approved of her banana crème pie or whether Mrs. Kirkpatrick broke her vegan rule for Mom's roast. I had an okay time with my friends, but the formal setting always made everyone act like tools, like Faith flirting with the wait staff or Shannen trying to sneak alcohol between courses or the Idiot Twins, well, being themselves, only ten times louder. I was constantly counting the seconds until dessert was cleared and we could bail. But I had a feeling I could tolerate Sunday nights a lot better if Ally were there.

"*Came*. Past tense, dude," Hammond said. "Look, everyone hates the Ryans. Her dad is the reason Shannen's father is on a permanent bender. He's the reason I have no college money and Liam had to take out freaking student loans. Trevor and Todd lost their *house* because of him."

"That's why they live at their grandparents'?" I asked.

"Yep."

Huh. I'd wondered why the Idiot Twins and their parents lived in the Enclave. It was this exclusive condo neighborhood on the crest where most of the places were owned by Crestie grandparents who only visited on the holidays. The Steins lived there year round, and every once in a while their grand-parents would come back and squeeze in. They seemed to like it, though. Nana and Pop were like superheroes to those dudes.

"Wait. But Shannen always says her dad's been sloshed her whole life."

"Maybe, but he got really bad when Charlie split, and then he went off the reservation after Ally's dad lost all their savings," Hammond said, his jaw clenched. "Stopped going to work, lost his job. . . . That's why he's 'consulting' now," he said, rolling his eyes and adding air quotes. We both knew Mr. Moore hardly ever left their house. If he was an advertising consultant, he wasn't doing very well at it.

"Whoa." I was surprised Shannen hadn't told me that part.

She was basically my best friend and usually told me everything. But then, maybe this was why she hadn't wanted to talk about Ally the one time I'd asked.

"No shit," Hammond said. "Chloe's dad's the only one who didn't get screwed when the Ryans skipped town. Guess he was the only one smart enough not to invest with the guy." He ripped up some blades of grass and threw them at his feet. "Trust me. We're all better off if Ally Ryan stays far, *far* away."

"Wow. Crazy," I said.

Probably not the best idea to invite her to Shale's party, then. I wasn't even sure why I'd done it. Usually I didn't invite anyone anywhere. Especially when it wasn't my party to begin with. I just go with the flow. Don't rock the boat. But I don't know. I think I'd just wanted to make sure I'd see her again. Of course if I'd thought about it for two seconds, I would have realized I'd be seeing her in school. Every day. But whatever. Maybe she wouldn't show up. I mean, if she was at all aware of how everyone felt about her, she'd be stupid not to stay home. Either way, not my problem.

Coach blew his whistle. "Let's go! Break time's over!"

"The girls are going to shit when they hear you talked to Ally Ryan," Hammond said as he stood up. "You coming?"

"Yeah." I got up and tossed my cup in the garbage can, then stooped to pick up Hammond's and tossed that, too. I wanted to know more, but I wasn't about to press for details. If I had learned one thing since moving to this town, it was that the people on the crest had their own way of doing things. They had their theme parties and their group vacations. They had their cheesy little traditions and their pack mentality, as my dad called it. And they also had their opinions. And hardly any of them made sense. At least, not to me.

"Hey, guys," David Drake said as he jogged to catch up with us. He bounced back and forth from foot to foot, juggling his soccer ball. He had this self-satisfied look on his face. The kid was showing off his energy level. Maybe later I should take him aside and give him a few pointers about not coming off like a pathetic, needy loser.

"Fuck off, Drake," Hammond said, slapping his ball away. It rolled across the field and onto the track on the far side, where the cheerleaders were throwing each other around.

David chuckled. "Yeah, right. Good one."

This guy had no idea of the size of the hole he was digging for himself. I looked at Hammond and we laughed. David did, too. Like he was in on the joke. Dig, dig, dig.

"Line it up!" Coach called out.

We did. I made sure I was between Hammond and David so that Ham couldn't shove the kid over in the middle of a calf stretch.

"That dude is so getting hazed this weekend," Hammond said, almost loudly enough for David to hear.

I bent over to stretch out. Ally Ryan's face flashed in my mind, and I squashed it. I wasn't about to hook up with some chick all my friends hated. Even if them hating her made no sense. It wasn't worth the drama. I was just going to have to start fantasizing about someone else. Luckily I'd heard some marys from Blessed Heart Academy were going to show up at Shale's. Blessed Heart girls were hot. I needed distraction from Ally Ryan.

Done and done.

ally

Right. So this was a bad idea. I felt it the moment I stepped up to the imposing double doors of Connor Shale's sprawling ranch-style house at the very back edge of the crest. The homes were newer here. More modern than the classic mansions my family and friends had grown up in. And Connor's was practically all windows. Floor to ceiling, back to front. How anyone got any privacy in this place was beyond me. The house was tucked away in the thick woods that formed the barrier between the crest and the Garden State Parkway a couple of miles off, but if you got past the trees, you could see everything.

Like Chloe Appleby standing in the center of the sunken living room, surrounded by Shannen Moore, Faith Kirkpatrick, and a half dozen other Crestie girls, both younger and older. Like the backyard beyond, where the Idiot Twins had hooked up some kind of zipline over the pool, from which they were now swinging like monkeys from two opposing trees. As I watched, the two of them collided in midair. There was a groan. A splash. Then a cheer. Which meant, I supposed, that they had lived.

And then there was Bedroom Boy, who was pressed up against the far wall, a girl in a barely there minidress slobbering all over him. Well, then. I guess he hadn't invited me here because he actually wanted to see me or anything.

I took a breath to quell the disappointment in my chest. This was not about Bedroom Boy. This was about seeing my lifelong best friends for the first time in a year and a half. I reached for the door, but my nerves took hold and atrophied my arm. I

couldn't do this. Wait, yes I could. I had to. If I didn't see them
now, I'd see them at school tomorrow. And then our encounter
might happen in front of my mom. Which would just make it
that much more intense. Besides, if I stood out here one second longer, someone was going to notice me, and then I'd have
to go in but I'd already be mortified because they'd have seen
me hesitating. This was a total nightmare. I held my breath,
pushed open the door, and stepped inside.

"Ally?"

The voice came from behind. I whirled around to find
Hammond Ross standing there all Long Beach Island tan in a
colorful Billabong T-shirt and destroyed cargo shorts. He was
just as blond as ever, but taller, broader, less doofy-boy and
more hot-guy. Also, he didn't look unhappy to see me. Which
kind of made sense, but also kind of didn't.

"Hammond. Hey."

His eyes flicked past me toward Chloe and the rest of them.
Checking to see if they'd noticed him talking to me. My nervousness mounted.

"What're you doing here?" he asked, wrapping me up in a
brief hug.

So I guess they hadn't noticed us yet.

"I—"

"Wait." He pulled back, looking suddenly nervous. "You're
not gonna tell anyone about—"

"Oh. My. God. She's. Here."

I would have recognized Faith's voice even if it hadn't
been louder than every other one in the room. I moved from
Hammond and the wide-open foyer into the even wider-open
living room, where all my former friends had turned around

to face me. Bedroom Boy somehow lost his hanger-on as he stepped away from the wall. He hovered a bit behind the rest of them, pushing his hands sheepishly into the pockets of his chino shorts. Even though he'd just been hooking up with some drunken frosh and obviously didn't care one iota about me, my heart was not unaffected at the sight of him standing there with his hair all coiffed, a royal blue Polo shirt hugging his muscles just so. But it was more distracted by the fact that I was here. I was home. With my friends.

"Hey, guys," I said, lifting a hand awkwardly.

Hammond closed the door behind me and went directly to Chloe's side. So I guessed they were still together. There was a prolonged moment of silence as the periphery people moved discreetly away, staying close enough of course to keep an eye on the impending drama. I tried not to ponder what it meant that my friends hadn't all rushed forward to hug me. Instead, I took them in. Chloe Appleby in her white sundress and coral sweater, her light brown hair pulled back in an eyelet band. Her posture was as perfect as ever, her discerning green eyes assessing me as if I were the new girl in town rather than the girl she'd known since nanny care. Shannen had cut bangs in her dark hair, and they practically covered her eyes. She was wearing skinny jeans and a black T-shirt with a studded belt, looking like some kind of badass supermodel. And then there was Faith. Faith had changed more than anyone. Gone were the cutesy tank tops and wild blond curls and natural skin. She was now wearing a cowl-necked tank top over microshorts and high-heeled sandals, her hair straightened and her face so perfectly painted it was practically airbrushed. Gone also was the friendly, open face. She had a scowl on like nothing I'd ever seen before.

"You have got to be kidding me," Faith said. "What are you doing here, *Norm*? Because I know no one invited you."

Norm. That was the nickname we Cresties had for the kids from the other, "normal" side of town. Which I guess was me now, technically. It wasn't pretty, but there it was. My eyes automatically flicked to Bedroom Boy. He flushed and looked away. Perfect. I loved a guy with no spine.

"I just wanted to see you guys," I told her.

My brain struggled to reconcile this bitchy socialite with the cherubic Hannah Montana fan I'd left behind less than two years ago.

"How are you?"

"Oh, please," Faith said. "Like you care?"

"Faith," Chloe scolded. That was Chloe. Always making sure that no situation grew too awkward or unpleasant. I had news for her. I was already feeling plenty awkward.

"No! No way!" Faith said, incredulous. "You know the only reason she's here is because she wants us to take pity on her. She thinks she can be, like, rich by association or something."

My skin stung as if I'd just endured a full-body slap. She couldn't have been more wrong.

"Like we're really going to be your friend again after your dad *stole* from our families?" Faith said, turning on me again with narrowed eyes.

"Stole?" I repeated, baffled. "He didn't steal anything. Is that what you guys think? He—"

"Oh, please! So that's why my parents can't retire and Shannen's mom had to sell their shore house and get a job and Hammond has no trust fund?" Faith said, crossing her skinny little arms across her skinny little chest. "Did you know the

Zeldinas and the Fallons had to move away and the Steins had to take over their grandparents' place? They lost their *homes* thanks to you."

I swallowed hard. I knew my family had been hit hard by my dad's mistake, but no one had ever told me exactly what it had meant for everyone else. Trust funds, retirements, and homes just gone? I had no idea.

Okay, Ally. Deep breath. You didn't do this to them. Your dad did. They can't really take it out on you.

"And don't even get me started on what you did to Chloe," Faith added before I could speak.

Gravity reversed itself. I looked at Chloe. She couldn't know, could she? Faith didn't mean—

"All right. That's enough," Shannen interrupted, speaking up finally.

Faith was dumbfounded. "Shannen, you're not gonna let her—"

"Faith, please," Chloe implored. "I don't want to make a scene."

"Too late," someone in the crowd muttered, earning a round of uncomfortable laughter.

"It's okay," Shannen said. "Everyone, just chill."

Shannen stepped in front of me. The girl who used to challenge me to swim races and paint my toenails in rainbow colors and name stars with me at sleepovers in the backyard. The girl I'd comforted on the worst night of her life. The one whose deepest secrets I kept locked away in the bottom of my heart.

"You need to go," she said. "Now."

My heart couldn't take this. "Shannen, I—"

"Faith's right. Take a look around. You don't belong here."

27

Her dark eyes flicked over my Old Navy shorts and well-worn shoes in distaste. I felt sick. My friends were really going to reject me because of what my dad did? Because I wasn't wearing the latest label? I looked around, desperate for someone to tell me this was a joke—to take my side. Chloe looked sad, almost sorry, before she trained her eyes on the floor. Bedroom Boy, meanwhile, stared right back at me, his jaw clenched with something unspoken, his blue eyes almost pleading. For what? For me to go? Or for me to never have come?

Right then, the back door slid open, letting in shouts and squeals and splashes from the backyard. In tromped the Stein twins in their almost matching Hawaiian-print bathing suits, dripping pool water all over the pristine wood floors. They had identical red welts forming on their foreheads. Not that either of them seemed to care.

"Yo! Where's the chips and dips?" Trevor shouted.

Todd stopped in his tracks. "Dude. Who died?" Then he saw me and his eyes lit up. "Ally Ryan!" He loped over and gave me a huge, wet bear hug, his soaked brown hair dripping all over my shoulders. "You're lookin' smokin' as ever! Where you been, girl?"

Trevor came over and hugged me too, turning me into the filling inside an Idiot Twin sandwich. The force of their hugs brought tears to my eyes. I'd missed them. All of them. Even the Idiot Twins. But clearly, only these two doofs had missed me.

"I have to go," I mumbled, extricating myself from their clammy grasp and ducking away so that no one could see my eyes.

"Wait, what?" Trevor said.

"You just got here! We're gonna have chips and dips!" Todd added.

I would have laughed if I hadn't been so miserable. On my way out the door I almost barreled over some punk-looking chick with blond hair who had just walked in—right in time to see my ignominious exit. I sputtered an apology, then almost tripped again when I realized she was Annie Johnston, Faith's best friend. Another one with a completely new look. In any other scenario I would have stopped to say hi, but she probably hated me as much as Faith did. I slipped by her and ran for the edge of the jam-packed driveway, where I'd stashed my bike under the thick border of evergreen trees.

My legs pumped the pedals with all their might as I raced away from Connor's house, my breath coming short and shallow, until I reached Harvest Lane. There I placed my feet on the ground and glanced back over my shoulder in the direction of Vista View. Somewhere back there behind the trees was my old house. My old life. The life that I, apparently, could never go back to.

I was never going to lie out under the sun with Chloe again or ride bikes with Shannen or put on fake concerts with Faith or climb trees with Hammond and the twins. I was never going to kiss Bedroom Boy under the bleachers after a soccer game. Never going to see him waiting for me after class or searching for me in the caf or standing in a tux under the domed ceiling of the country club ballroom.

Not that I had been daydreaming about those things for the last two days. Not at all. Clearly it was time for me to officially grow up. I turned my back on Vista View and rode on.

My mother was going to die when she heard what had

happened tonight. All she wanted was to move home and reclaim her old friends, her old life. That was all she wanted for the both of us. Well, it appeared that, for one of us at least, that was not going to happen.

God, I hated my father. How could he do this to us? To them? How could he lose all their money, move us out of a town we loved, and then just drop us? Just disappear without a word, without an explanation? Where the hell *was* he? Was he ever going to come back? Was he ever going to try to rectify what he'd done?

I tipped my front wheel down the hill at the top of Harvest and took my feet off the pedals, just letting myself fly. Letting the wind clear my head and tug a few tears from the corners of my eyes. At the bottom I almost forgot to stop. Almost flew directly into the two-way traffic on Orchard Avenue. But as soon as I saw the cars whizzing by, my brain snapped back into focus. I hit the brakes hard and yanked my wheel to the left, stopping two inches away from the brick wall of the bagel shop at the corner. My chest heaved. My heart raced. My pores oozed hot sweat into my clothes. And only one word came into my mind.

No.

Just like that, I knew. I knew my mother would never find out about tonight. She didn't need to know I'd pathetically reached out to them and been brutally rejected. Clearly, my new life in Orchard Hill was going to be just that—a new life. I didn't need the Cresties. I felt, suddenly, foolish for ever thinking I did. Somehow I'd survived the last year and a half without them. I could survive the next two. And so what if

Bedroom Boy hadn't defended my honor back there? I could handle myself. Sort of. At least, I would. From now on.

I turned my bike down Orchard Avenue and headed for my new home. Faith was right. I was a Norm now. It was time to start living like one.

Did you guys hear what happened at Connor Shale's house last night? It is so intense.

What?

> *Faith Kirkpatrick completely bitched out Ally Ryan.*

>> *Wait a minute. The Ally Ryan? She's back?*

Where have you been? I've been tweeting about this for days.

>> *Wait. You were invited to Connor Shale's house?*

Um, no. What am I, sleeping with the guy? Please. Annie told me.

Annie Johnston? How did she get in?

> *Oh, she goes to all the Crestie parties. She's, like, obsessed with Faith Kirkpatrick or something. Ever since Faith dumped her at that Spring Fling dance freshman year?*

Oh my God! Yeah! Remember that?

Wait, Faith's a lesbian?

> *No, you loser! They were just friends. Faith was, like, the only Crestie who ever even acknowledged us. Until she turned to the dark side.*

And Ally.

Ally what?

> *Ally was always cool to us too.*

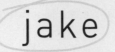

jake

"I'd better get eighth-period study hall," Shannen said, yawning hugely. She stopped at the bottom of the steps to the junior/senior entrance and looked up at the school. It was sort of intimidating. The first time I saw it I thought it was some huge church. It was all red brick and had towers at the corners. The one right above us held the clock that hadn't worked since before I moved here. We sometimes snuck up there at lunch and tossed soda bottles and doughnuts off it to watch them explode. The Idiot Twins had once even peed off it. Gross, but kind of funny.

"Why? It's not like you can leave campus," Faith said as she checked her reflection in a tiny mirror for the fourteen thousandth time that morning. She clicked it closed and sighed. "Seniors get all the perks."

"Yeah, but I can sleep," Shannen said, taking the steps two at a time. "By eighth I am definitely gonna need a snooze."

"Unless I get study hall too," I said.

Shannen grinned. "Of course. Then we'll be having some fun."

We knocked fists as Faith rolled her eyes at us. "Just try not to destroy any school property. My mom's *this close* to not letting me hang out with you guys anymore after the whole founder-clown incident."

Shannen and I laughed. Over the summer we'd been bored one night and she'd decided we should dress up the town hall statue of the two Orchard Hill founders as clowns. We'd gotten caught, of course, since the Orchard Hill police station is inside borough hall. But we'd had a killer time getting as far as we had.

Out of the corner of my eye I saw Ally Ryan waiting at the bottom of the hill on the other side of Orchard Avenue, at the corner of the OVC complex, which was where she lived now—according to all the rumors I'd heard last night after she'd left the party. She was wearing jeans and a white top with buttons and short sleeves. Her hair was down. It looked nice down. Standing next to her was her mother. At least, I figured it was her mother. They looked a lot alike. Except that as they crossed the street toward the school, her mom actually seemed happy to be there.

I felt bad about what happened at Connor's last night. The way the girls had kind of humiliated Ally. And about how I hadn't said anything. I wanted to talk to her about it. I had no idea what I was going to say, but I hoped it would come to me soon.

"So what the hell happened last night with that Ally girl?" I asked. We were all climbing the steps together, and the girls stopped as soon as I asked.

"What do you mean? You were there," Faith said.

"I know, but I mean . . . what did she do to Chloe that was so bad?" I asked.

Faith and Shannen exchanged a look. "It's complicated," Shannen said, tossing her dark hair over her shoulder.

I saw at least ten guys take notice of her because of that one gesture. Shannen's dad was tall, athletic, and Irish. Her mom was skinny, petite, and Chinese. Apparently the two countries had to get together more often, because they had pretty much spawned the hottest girl in North America and every guy at OHH was grateful.

"Girls," I said, rolling my eyes. I looked back at Ally and her mom again. They were heading toward the faculty entrance around the corner. Shannen and Faith hadn't seen them yet.

"You coming?" Shannen asked.

"I'll catch up."

They exchanged another look —always needing to check the other's reaction to everything—and then kept walking. I jogged around the corner to the front of the school, sticking close to the building, and was waiting against the outer wall when Ally and her mom got to the stairs. I clutched the strap on my backpack and waited for Ally to see me. When she did she almost tripped, then looked away. I knew it. She hated me now. The girl I couldn't stop thinking about hated my guts. I took a few steps toward her so she couldn't ignore me.

"Hey," I said.

Both she and her mom paused. "Hello," her mother said.

"Hi, Mrs. Ryan. I'm Jake Graydon," I said. Whenever I was around parents, my manners kicked right in. "Ally and I met the other day at—"

"A party," Ally interrupted.

I looked at her, confused.

"You went to a party?" Ally's mother said. "When?"

"Last night. Just for a little while. It's a long story," Ally said.

"You went out to a party and didn't tell me?" her mother asked.

Great. Now I'd gotten her in trouble. This was not going well.

"Mom!" Ally said through her teeth.

"Where was this party?" her mother asked, hand on hip.

"At Connor Shale's," I said, trying to help.

Ally's mother's face lit up, and I felt momentarily satisfied. Until I saw the look of death Ally shot me. What? What had I done now?

"You went to Connor's house? How is he? How's his mom?" Mrs. Ryan asked.

"Mom, aren't we going to be late?" Ally said pointedly.

Ally's mother sighed, but she seemed happy, still. "Yes, I suppose we are. Nice meeting you, Jake."

They started to walk inside through the faculty doors. Which, I guess, meant Ally's mom was faculty. That would explain the spiral-bound teacher's ledger thing she had under her arm. That must suck. Having your mom work at your school.

"Actually, could I just speak to Ally for a sec?" I asked. Her mom seemed both surprised and somehow impressed that I wasn't giving up. "It'll only be a second, I swear."

Ally heaved a sigh. "I'll be right in, Mom."

"Okay," her mother said. Then she shot me a suspicious look. "But if I don't see you in the office in five minutes I'm sending out a search party."

Funny. I kind of liked her mom.

"So, Jake Graydon, huh?" Ally said. "Nice to meet you, I guess."

Suddenly I felt nervous. I never felt nervous around girls. Except Shannen sometimes. And that was for an entirely different reason—because half the time I was with her we were doing stuff that could get us in trouble. "Yeah, so last night kind of sucked," I said with a smile.

"You were there? Could have fooled me."

She reached around me for the door, and I had to sort of sidestep to block her way. I hesitated for a second. Where had that move come from? I didn't think I'd ever tried to block a girl from walking away in my life. But, then, she'd caught me off guard. I'd been expecting her to laugh and blush and say, "Don't worry about it." That was what most girls would have done.

"Look, I wanted to say something, but what could I say? I don't know what happened between you guys before I moved here."

She looked me dead in the eye. Another thing most girls didn't do. We both knew it was a cop-out. I'd been up all night thinking about all the things I could have said or done. Told Faith to back off. Cracked a joke. Just gotten Ally out of there. All night I'd been pissed that I hadn't done those things. And now I felt a surge of anger over being called on it. It was bad enough that I was pissed at myself, but who was she to be mad at me?

"What? I barely even know you," I said. "I mean, all I do know is that you used to live in my house and you used to be friends with my friends, yet somehow I'm responsible for defending you?"

Ally paused. She looked at her feet and laughed. "You're right."

I blinked. Stood up straighter. "I am?"

"Of course you are," she said, lifting her face. "I've never needed a knight in shining armor before and I don't need one now."

"Okay. So can we just—"

"And you're right about something else," she said.

I paused, annoyed at being cut off. "What?"

"We don't know each other. And I think we should keep it that way."

Then she turned and strode inside, letting the door slam in my face.

For a long moment, I couldn't even move. Girls didn't walk away from me. Ever. I couldn't believe she wouldn't let me apologize. What was she, too good for me or something? A pair of teachers approached, clutching their Starbucks coffee cups, and I turned on my heel and stormed back across the grass toward the junior/senior entrance. Fine. Whatever. Let her be a bitch about it if she wanted to. We'd pretend we'd never even met each other. It would make everything a whole lot easier, anyway.

ally

The activities board was exactly as I remembered it: a huge magnetic wipe-board right outside the principal's office, papered with sign-up sheets for the various clubs and activities synonymous with the beginning of the school year. Fall drama tryouts (Faith's name was already scrawled across the top of the list), the *Acorn* (student news website), Interact Club, SADD, the Green Team, Hiking Club, and on and on. I yanked a pen from my messenger bag and scribbled my name on the Backslappers list, trying not to look at the other names jotted above it. Chloe Appleby, Shannen Moore, Faith Kirkpatrick, and a dozen other familiar Crestie names.

I was not going to let them intimidate me out of doing what I wanted to do, and I'd loved being a backslapper my freshman year. I underlined my name, capped my pen, and turned around.

"Um, no."

Faith was standing right there, completely overdressed for school in a black minidress. Walking up behind her were Shannen and Chloe. Shannen looked at the list and balked.

"Backslappers? Really, Ally?" she said with a frown. "Wouldn't you be more comfortable doing something with your people?"

My face burned at what she thought was an insult. "I'll be fine, thanks. And since when do I have people?"

"We're just thinking of your happiness," Chloe said, lifting her shoulders. "Backslappers is a Crestie club."

"And *you*," Faith said, scrunching her nose, "are no longer a Crestie."

"They're right," Shannen said with a faux-sympathetic sigh. "Backslappers could get . . . awkward for you."

"There's no rule that only people who live on the crest can join Backslappers," I said, hoping they didn't notice that my knees were shaking.

"There doesn't have to be a rule. *We* don't want you there," Faith said bitchily. I was starting to wonder if she ever said anything *un*bitchily anymore. Didn't she remember that I was the one who had taken her under my wing? If it wasn't for me, she wouldn't even be friends with Shannen and Chloe, yet now she was the one trying harder than any of them to make sure I was left out. The irony was painful.

"Whatever. I'm bored with this conversation," Shannen said, putting her hands on Faith's slim shoulders and steering her away. "Let's leave the Norm alone."

I bristled at her use of the nickname. That was going to get old fast. As they walked away, Chloe shot me a look that I couldn't read in all my annoyance, embarrassment, and general sadness. I followed them at a safe distance into the caf.

All day I had suspected that people were watching me and whispering behind my back, and the cafeteria confirmed it. It was hard to explain away the gaping stares when they were coming at me from all angles at once. Keeping my chin up and avoiding direct eye contact with anyone, I moved quickly through the food line and paused at the door to the outdoor courtyard. It was sunny and gorgeous out and I longed to sit at one of the picnic tables under the shade of the thick maple trees, but the courtyard was Crestie territory. The Norms pretty much kept to the indoor cafeteria, except for the brave few who occasionally ventured to the tables near the garbage cans, along the periphery.

Hammond saw me through the window, salivating there like a loser, and started to lift his hand in a wave until he saw Chloe and the girls walking toward him. Then he blushed beet red, and I turned around and took the first seat I saw— at the very end of an empty table. To my right, nothing but freshmen. To my left, a group of pasty, black-clad kids who had obviously spent their summer watching and rewatching the first two seasons of *True Blood* in someone's basement. I recognized a few faces at the table across the aisle, but they were way too far away for me to consider getting up and going over there. Plus, what if they wanted to have nothing to do with me? What if the Crestie poison had trickled down to the Norms?

I took a huge bite of my turkey sandwich, resolving to eat as quickly as possible and spend the rest of the period with my face in a book, letting the rest of the world fade to white noise.

"Would you ever get a nipple ring?"

A tall, lanky guy with a buzz cut sat down to my right, dropping his tray and a *Time* magazine on the table. On the chair next to him he slapped down a guitar catalog and a soccer ball.

"Wha?" That's how surprised I was. I couldn't even finish the word.

"Don't mind him. He has a filtering problem."

Annie Johnston, Faith's BFF, sat down across from him. She was wearing a black T-shirt dress and purple-and-white striped tights. On her thumb was a black star tattoo. In her nose, a tiny diamond stud. I believe the last time I saw her she was wearing a Jonas Brothers T-shirt and pink glitter barrettes.

"There's an article in here about it, and I'm interested," the guy said, gesturing at his magazine. "So, would you?"

"No plans at present," I said. "But never say never."

"Good answer," he said, flashing an adorable, dimpled smile.

Annie whipped out a small, battered notebook with stickers all over the cover and jotted something down. I saw my name at the top of the page and angled for a better look, but she snapped it closed and shoved it back in her backpack. Weird.

"Um, hey, Annie," I said awkwardly. "How've you been?"

"Functioning. You?"

"Good, I guess," I replied hesitantly.

Wasn't this the girl who used to burst into select songs from *Wicked* in the middle of lunch? What was with the acerbic?

"This is David Drake," she said, gesturing with a potato chip.

"We were lab partners in eighth," he said.

I lit up in recognition. "Right! You never forget the person you cut up your first frog with."

He tilted his Gatorade bottle toward me, and I clicked it with my Snapple.

"That's funny," Annie stated, not sounding amused at all. It was more like she was making an anthropological observation. "You're funny."

"Um, thanks," I said.

"So, we came over here because we figure we should be friends now that you're back," David said.

I narrowed my eyes. "No offense, but . . . why, exactly?"

"Ever hear that saying 'the enemy of my enemy is my friend'?" Annie asked.

"No."

"It's a saying," she said, like she was trying to convince me.

"I believe you," I replied. "But what does it have to do with anything?"

"We hate the Cresties, the Cresties hate you," Annie said, lifting a hand. "Therefore, we should all be friends."

The lump in my stomach traveled up to my throat. David must have noticed something in my face.

"Not that anyone actually hates you," he said quickly.

"No. They actually do," Annie countered matter-of-factly.

"Annie," David said through his teeth.

"What?"

I couldn't take this conversation anymore. "No. It's fine. I just . . . I'm confused." I looked at Annie. "Weren't you at Shale's party last night?"

"I crash Crestie functions from time to time. For research," Annie replied. She took a swig of her milk and wiped her lip with the back of her hand.

"Research?" I asked.

"Yeah. They don't exactly like the Norms showing up, but if I don't bother them, they don't bother me. It's like a 'don't talk, don't talk back' policy. You, however, you talk back." She gave a short, almost proud, laugh.

"Not really. . . ."

"Listen, just so you know, if you ever want help steering clear of the Cresties, I have all their schedules on here." She whipped out her school-issued laptop, also covered in stickers, and opened it to reveal a spreadsheet of student schedules. Yes, all the students at Orchard Hill High were given their very own MacBook on their first day of school, for use throughout their academic careers at OHH. My own slightly-used-but-clean computer was currently nestled inside my messenger bag. I had a feeling the powers that be weren't going to appreciate Annie's decorations when she returned hers at the end of senior year. "I can help you map out Crestie-free routes to all your classes."

"Oookay," I said, taking a sip of iced tea. "Hey, Annie, I have a question. Why do you have all the Crestie schedules on your computer?" I asked in a joking tone.

"You're funny," she said again, narrowing her eyes at me. "I don't remember you being funny." She turned the screen forward and typed a few words. "I'm writing an exposé. Or a trashy novel. Haven't decided which yet. But either way I have to keep tabs on them at all times. That's why I go to their parties even though they don't want me there."

So that's what she meant by "research."

"Wow. That's . . . interesting. Is Faith helping you with that?" I asked.

She let out this noise that was, like, half cackle, half guffaw. "Um, no."

I looked at David. He shook his head ever so slightly like, *Don't go there.* I guess more had changed between Faith and Annie than their personal styles. Time for a new topic.

"You play?" I asked, nodding at David's soccer ball.

"Soccer or guitar?" he asked, pouring some protein powder into his Gatorade, capping it, and shaking it up. "Actually, it doesn't matter. I play both. And this year I have a new band and I plan to make varsity."

"Cool. Maybe I can be your backslapper."

"You're still doing Backslappers?" Annie asked incredulously.

I shrugged, ignoring the twinge of nerves in my shoulders. "Yeah. Why?"

"The Cresties own the Backslappers," David said. "Are you a sadist?"

"You're on soccer with them and you're still alive," I pointed out.

"Excellent point," David said, tipping his bottle again. "But I'm tough. I can take it."

"So can I," I replied, wishing I felt a tad more confident.

"I like a girl with guts," David said as Annie sighed audibly and made another note in her notebook. Which I was definitely going to have to get my hands on ASAP. "But when it comes to backslappers, I'm holding out for Shannen Moore."

He nodded toward the windows, and I turned to look at my old friend. She was sitting at the end of the Crestie table, chatting with Faith and Chloe in her skinny jeans and emerald tank top, those long bangs once again covering her eyes. Jake, Hammond, and the Idiot Twins were watching something on one of their laptops, yucking it up in that doofy way boys do when they're in a group. And yet, even being doofy, Jake was still annoyingly hot.

"He's been in love with her for-ev-er," Annie said edgily.

"I would *kill* for her to backslap me," David said.

"I'll slap you right now," Annie offered.

I laughed, wondering if Shannen would ever even give David Drake the time of day. Maybe, if the ice ever melted with the Cresties—if they ever realized it was my dad, not me, who had screwed them over—I could try to hook them up sometime. But even as the idea occurred to me it seemed inconceivable that Shannen and I would ever be close again. My spirits sagged.

I had started to turn back to the table when my eyes caught Jake's. He stopped laughing. Our gazes locked for a long, intense moment during which all oxygen disappeared from the caf. He blinked first, and I blushed and turned my back on him. Great. Now he probably thought I was ogling him. Jerk. I couldn't believe that lame attempt at an apology he'd made that morning. Like, what? I was going to swoon and kiss his feet for acknowledging me after the complete diss of the night before? Maybe if he'd been at all genuine—if he'd said anything true rather than getting all defensive—I might have cared. But that? That was crap. Clearly he was that hot guy who got all the girls but had the depth of a puddle. *So* not what I needed right now.

No. From now on I was steering clear of Jake Graydon, in thoughts and deeds. Besides, if I so much as flirted with him, my friends would probably think I was trying to use him to get to them, and I wasn't about to give them the satisfaction. No way, no how.

No matter how long my residual blush lasted.

ally

The first Backslappers meeting was held in the bleachers alongside the soccer field, where David, Jake, Hammond, and the rest of the team were huddled around the coach on the sidelines. This was my first time up at the field since I'd been back, and I suddenly flashed on a memory of a gorgeous fall day back in freshman year when Chloe, Shannen, Faith, and I had spent an hour jogging around the track after school, pretending we were exercising, when really we were checking out the hot junior and senior boys on the soccer team. Every time we caught one of them looking we'd up our speed and ridiculously overexaggerate our conversation to show them just how oblivious to them we were. In hindsight I'm sure they were all laughing at us. Faith had been totally in love with this junior named Mike Mancinelli at the time, so when practice was finished, I'd gone over and talked to him for her. I'd always found it easier to talk to guys when I was doing it for my friends rather than for myself. Mike had been kind of a jerk, giving me some line about how he'd take Faith out if I came along, so I'd told him off, much to the amusement of his friends, and then we'd all taken Faith to Scoops to drown her sorrows in peanut butter fudge ice cream.

The memory made me feel sad, so I trudged over to a bench near the back of the growing crowd and hunkered down. Chloe, Shannen, and Faith were already seated in the front row, chatting happily. Had they all forgotten about the stuff we used to do together—all the fun we used to have? Why did it mean so much to me and nothing to them?

It was a gray day and breezy, so I'd worn my Hancock East basketball sweatshirt from my school in Baltimore, which drew confused and irritated looks from every girl who settled in around me. Note to self: When joining a school-spirit club, it's best not to baffle the natives with the name and colors of another school.

"All right, everyone! Let's get this meeting started!"

The girl calling us to order was Trista Strickler, Crestie senior and major joiner. Even back when I was a freshman and she was a sophomore, she'd been either a member or president of at least half a dozen clubs. She had red curly hair held back by a Burberry headband, and a smattering of freckles across her upturned nose. Her sweatshirt was the proper colors: maroon with her name embroidered in gold on the left breast. On the back was the Orchard Hill High tiger in midpounce.

"I have the sign-up sheet right here," Trista said, holding up her clipboard. "The first thing we need to do is assign a player to each of you. Anyone have any special requests?"

Instantly two-dozen hands shot into the air. Trista laughed. "Okay, let's start at the top left. Name?"

"Melissa Waner," the brace-faced girl said. Her friends giggled.

"Melissa Waner, sophomore." Trista checked her off. "Who do you like?"

"Jake Graydon," Melissa said. More giggles. Much louder this time.

"No way. Jake's mine," Shannen said.

"But I wanted Jake!" Faith added with a pout. "There's no way I'm getting stuck with someone with back hair. Oh God! Or backne!"

"Please. Jake's my best friend. I call him," Shannen said.

Was that true? Were Jake and Shannen best friends? Was she just BFF with whoever lived in that room? The thought made me smirk past a sudden slice of envy. But was I jealous of Jake because he got to hang with Shannen, or Shannen because she got to hang with Jake? I decided I didn't want to think about it.

"He's my friend too." Faith's bottom lip jutted out even farther.

"Wait a minute. I called him first," Melissa Waner said bravely. "Jake's mine."

I rolled my eyes and leaned back on my elbows, waiting for the shrieking and hair pulling to start.

"All right, all right!" Trista shouted, holding up her hands. "I had a feeling something like this might happen, so I've come prepared." She fished a plastic baggie with a bunch of pink paper scraps inside out of her backpack. "I've written each player's name down on one piece of paper."

"We're going to draw names from a hat?" Chloe asked.

"Actually, we're going to draw names from a bag," Trista corrected. "Seniors first, then juniors, and so on. Everyone, please come down here and line up in class order."

They all jumped up like someone had just offered free manicures. I trudged down the bleachers after them and slid into line behind Chloe, who inched forward as if my B.O. were offending her. I felt an almost physical need to talk to her—to pull her aside and explain—but now was not the time.

The three seniors picked their names, and it was now Faith's turn. She chose Jeff Levitt, who was apparently backne free, because she gave an overly dramatic sigh of relief as she read his name.

Shannen was up. She unfolded her paper. "Hammond Ross!" She turned around and handed the slip to Chloe, who took it happily and slipped from line.

"Wait! No trading!" Trista said.

"But Trista! It's Hammond," Chloe said, her green eyes wide.

Trista's brow knitted as she mentally debated whether to stick to her all-important rules or give Chloe what she wanted. "Okay, fine. Shannen can pick again."

Chloe, as always, won. And no one even batted an eyelash. Shannen reached into the bag again, unfolded her paper, and sighed.

"Josh Schwartz."

"Oooh. The captain. Big responsibility," Trista trilled.

Shannen forced a smile but was clearly not happy. So much for David's fantasy of having Shannen's slaps all over his back.

"And you are?" Trista asked as I stepped forward.

"Nobody," Faith said before I could answer, earning herself a few laughs. Shannen smirked. Chloe smoothed the front of her OHH polo shirt and looked away.

"Ally Ryan," I answered.

Trista checked off my name. "Go ahead and pick."

I reached into the bag, repeating "David Drake" over and over and over again in my mind. The team roster had been posted that morning and David had celebrated like a maniac when he found his name under VARSITY STARTERS. If he couldn't have Shannen, I had to believe I was the next best option. I unfolded my scrap of paper and my vision actually blurred.

"Who is it?" Trista asked, her pen poised.

I swallowed hard. "Jake Graydon."

Of course.

There were disappointed groans throughout the crowd. A couple of girls actually bailed from the line. Chloe, Shannen, and Faith looked as if they were about to shove me over the railing and onto the track. I took a seat a few rows behind them, slumped down, and looked out at the field, where the guys were lining up for a penalty-kick drill. Jake's perfect calf muscles flexed as he moved his weight from foot to foot. I wondered what he would think about having me as his backslapper.

"Okay, ladies! Everyone has their man," Trista said happily, once the line had dwindled. "Our first big event will be next Friday, the day of the opening game. You'll be decorating your player's locker and baking him a little something to leave inside. Feel free to leave him an inspirational note as well, or a poem or whatever moves you. Be creative. I know last year one of our girls left a mix of heart-pumping songs to listen to pregame, and the player really loved that."

"That was me," Chloe said, raising a hand to shoulder level and preening. A bunch of the girls looked at each other knowingly, like, *Who else could it have been?*

"We'll meet here briefly on Thursday, when I'll hand out locker numbers and combinations, and then we'll have the run of the halls until six o'clock, so you'll have plenty of time to decorate," Trista continued. "It's your first chance to really show your player what kind of backslapper you're going to be, so do it up!"

A few of the girls clapped, and everyone started gabbing at once. Shannen and Faith got up to talk to Trista, and as Chloe was still gathering her things, I saw my chance. I clomped down the bleachers and dropped in front of her.

"Can I talk to you?"

Chloe glanced over her shoulder at Shannen and Faith. "About what?" she asked quietly.

I blinked. Did she really have to ask?

"About . . . you know," I said, finding it hard to form the actual words. "The thing Faith mentioned at Connor's that night?"

Chloe's cheeks turned pink and she looked at her shoes. "Oh, that. She was just being melodramatic. You know Faith."

Okay. Now I was totally confused.

"Well, it *was* kind of a big deal," I said, tucking my hands into the front pocket of my sweatshirt.

"Please. It was almost a year ago. And it was just a party," Chloe said. Then she rolled her eyes. "I mean, I know I always made a huge deal about how important my sweet sixteen was, but I get why you didn't come. Really. It's all good."

My mouth sort of hung open. What the hell was she talking about?

"Wait. You invited me to your sweet sixteen?" I asked.

Now it was her turn to be confused. Her brow knitted and she crossed her arms over her chest. "Yeah. Isn't that what . . . I mean, that's what Faith was talking about. How you never RSVP'ed? I was upset at the time, but—"

"Hey, girls!" Faith interrupted brightly. My brain was still struggling to catch up as she and Shannen joined us. "My mom's waiting in the parking lot. We're all going to Riverside to get dresses for the Harvest Ball. Wanna come, Ally?"

My eyes darted to her face. I knew she was messing with me, but somehow my heart still flipped in hope.

"Oh, wait! The shoestring that is your budget couldn't even lace up one of my Gucci boots," she added, tilting her head so that her blond hair tumbled over her shoulder.

Shannen laughed, but Chloe simply looked pained. There was only one explanation for all the confusion of the past two minutes: Chloe didn't know. That night at Connor's, when Faith had mentioned what I "did to Chloe," she'd been talking about this infraction against manners I'd apparently committed by not RSVP-ing to Chloe's sweet sixteen—a party to which I'd never received an invitation. That was confusing enough, but I could deal with that later. The more important point was that Chloe didn't know. And also, from the looks she kept shooting me, she wasn't one hundred percent down with the evil ostracizing of Ally Ryan. Ironic, considering she was the only one here I'd actually betrayed.

I was starting to feel dizzy. And sick. And maybe just a bit hopeful. If Chloe wanted to be friends again . . . maybe there was a slim chance I could get things back to the way they were.

"Come on," Faith said, hooking her arm around Chloe's shoulder. "We have to go warn Jake to expect some low-budge decorations and Costco brownies this year." She snorted a laugh. "Later, Norm!"

I glared at her back as they sauntered off. She may have gotten a couple of zingers in, but she was wrong about one thing: Jake was going to get the most kick-ass locker decorations in history. Over the weekend Annie had helped me land a job at CVS, where she worked, and I would spend my entire first paycheck on Jake if it would prove to Faith and the rest of them that I could still be a good backslapper.

I took a deep breath and leaned against the front railing on the bleachers as the girls hit the soccer field sideline to chat with Hammond, Jake, and some of their teammates. My heart was still pounding over the realization of my near miss. I'd almost apologized to Chloe for what had happened with Hammond all those months ago, and she hadn't even known about it. If I had gotten out the words, if she'd found out that way, I may have lost her forever. But now I had a chance to be friends with her again. All because I'd been too chicken to just say it.

How lucky was I? I mean, maybe Chloe didn't need to know. It hadn't meant anything, after all. At least, not to me. I'd been emotional and confused and scared and sad. And clearly she and Hammond were still together. What would be the point of telling her and screwing up her relationship? Of alienating the one person who seemed to be happy—or at least not angry— that I was back?

I swallowed the lump of guilt that had formed in my throat and decided it was for the best. I was just going to have to continue to keep my deepest, darkest secret. I'm not just doing it for me, I told myself. I'm doing it for all of us.

jake

The Friday of the first soccer game, colorful leaves had fallen all over the walkways at school, and for the first time it really felt like fall—all crisp and clear and windy. Inside, the team's lockers were decorated. I always thought it was stupid, having a whole club with the sole purpose of fawning all over us. But it wasn't just soccer. We had the backslappers, and the football team had the cheerleaders. Next week there would be a huge pep rally for them and their lockers would be decorated too. That was how we did things here at OHH. We were all about the spirit.

Besides, this day meant cupcakes for breakfast. And a hot girl waiting by my locker. And this year, that girl was going to be Ally Ryan.

My friends were all sympathetic that penniless Ally was in charge of my decorations, but I didn't give a crap about the size of the posters. I just thought it was awesome that Miss Holier Than Thou had to show me the love. I kind of looked forward to lording it over her.

Also, it meant I was going to get to talk to her again.

When I turned down the hallway toward my locker, I almost tripped. I looked over my shoulder to make sure this wasn't a joke. A few people were staring, but that was about it.

The entire hall was decorated. Streamers across the ceiling, attached to the wall over my locker and fanning out in all directions. There were at least ten posters with my name on them. Glitter and sequins and stars everywhere. Mini soccer balls dangled from my locker door, which was surrounded by balloons, and my name had been spelled out in letters decorated with the black-and-white soccer ball pattern. I opened my locker door carefully, and confetti exploded in my face. I was still spitting it off my lips when I smelled the chocolate. Piled inside on the floor were half a dozen cellophane-covered paper plates. Brownies, cookies, cupcakes, lemon squares, blondies, doughnut holes. More dessert than one person could eat in a week. A big yellow card was propped on the shelf with my books.

Jake Graydon kicks! Good luck in the game tonight, Tiger! Your backslapper, Ally.

For some reason, my palms were sweating. I couldn't believe she'd done this. That she'd gone all out like this. It must have cost her a fortune and she'd done it all for me. The girls were going to shit. Hammond was going to *shit*.

"You like it?"

I turned around. Ally stood in the center of the hall in a tight maroon T-shirt and denim skirt. And she was giving me the eye. I knew it. I knew she wanted me. Maybe that bitchy act the first day of school had just been a reaction to Shale's party. But now . . . I looked her up and down. It was like a whole new her.

"It's awesome," I said, placing the card back in the locker and slamming the door shut.

"Cool," she said. And smiled. "I spent my entire paycheck on it. And I baked all that stuff myself. It did not come from Costco."

I glanced toward the back of the school. "Do you wanna go and, like, talk or something?"

A little wrinkle popped up over her nose. "Um, sure."

"Come on."

We walked down the hall and out the back door. No one was around. I nudged her arm and pressed her up against the wall.

"What're you doing?" she asked.

"Thanking you," I said.

I was half a millimeter from her lips when she ducked away. My forehead hit the rough brick wall.

"Ow! Fuck." I brought my fingertips to my scratched skull.

"What the hell?" she spat. "God! Maybe whoever was your backslapper last year slapped more than your back, but I was just doing my job."

My heart felt sick as my brain tried to catch up. "But I thought—"

"What? That because I went all out on your locker that I was, like, in love with you or something?" Ally said, looking me up and down in disgust. "Get over yourself." She yanked open the door and strode inside. The slam made my head throb even worse.

I leaned back against the wall and touched the bump above my nose again, checking my fingertips for blood. There wasn't any. "Fuck me," I muttered under my breath, kicking at the ground.

So much for that.

ally

"Graydon! Get off the field! Now!"

Jake cursed under his breath and stormed past Coach Martz. I flushed with heat as he passed me by, his eyes on his muddy cleats, sweat soaking his hair and the collar of his shirt. He shrugged Shannen off as she made a move for him and slammed his open hand into a stack of paper cups on the water table, sending them flying. I swallowed hard and clutched my own arms.

It was the third match of the year, and the team's top scorer, Jake Graydon, was not on his game.

"Ally," Trista sang in my ear. "It's about time for you to start acting like a backslapper."

In the first two games I hadn't so much as talked to Jake, let alone slapped his admittedly sexy back, and Trista had definitely noticed. I wondered if she'd still be on my case if I told her that he tried to maul me behind the school on the morning of the first game. Jackass.

"Drake! Sub in for Graydon!" Coach shouted.

My heart leapt.

"Seriously?" David said, popping up off the bench.

"No. I'm practicing my stand-up routine," Coach spat. "Yes, seriously! Sub in!"

"Go, David!" I shouted, slapping his shoulder as he jogged by.

"Yeah, David! Kick ass!" Annie screeched from the bleachers.

We shared a smile before she got back to taking Crestie behavioral notes on her laptop. David hadn't seen much game time before, and never in the first half. Now he was biting back a grin as he took the field.

"That's great, Ally, but I didn't mean for him," Trista said, nudging my elbow. "Jake is your responsibility. Go! Pep talk the boy!"

She practically shoved me toward the bench. Jake sat at the end, his elbows pressed into his thighs, his hands clenched into fists against his forehead, his right leg bouncing up and down. I knew how he felt. We'd all had bad games when we just couldn't get anything right. But did I really want to boost Mr. Ego? The guy who was so cocky he thought a few posters meant I wanted to taste his tongue? Maybe he needed some humbling.

"Jake! Dude! It's all right, man! You'll get 'em next time!" Trevor shouted from the top bleacher.

"Jake, Jake, Jake! Jake, Jake, Jake!" Todd chanted, trying to get the crowd into it. "Jake, Jake, Jake!"

I rolled my eyes at them. Didn't they know they were just making it worse?

"Oh, no worries, man! Look! Here comes your backslapper to save the day!" Trevor joked loudly, standing up and pointing at me.

"Ally Ryan to the rescue! Woot!" Todd added, raising the roof.

I would have knocked their skulls together, but I had a feeling that had already happened to them too many times. It was probably the whole reason they were like that.

Jake, meanwhile, spotted me and dropped back against the bench, shaking his head. Like I was some huge, pointless disappointment. A waste of a backslapper. Was that what he thought?

Suddenly, Shannen's hand fell on my arm. "You're not really going over there."

My adrenaline rose in my veins. "I'm his backslapper."

"I'll do it. He doesn't even know who you are," she said snidely.

I glanced past her shoulder at Jake. So he still hadn't told anyone we'd met. That Crestie code was as strong as a gag order. I pried my arm from her grip.

"Thanks, but don't worry about us," I said. "We'll be fine."

I knew that calling me and Jake "us" and "we" would piss her off—show her that her exclusionary tactics were lost on me—and I was right. Her nostrils flared as I walked over to the bench and sat down next to him.

"What is it with you?" I demanded

His eyes narrowed. "What?"

"What's your problem?" I asked, turning my knees toward him.

He glanced at Chloe, Shannen, and Faith, who were hovering just on the edge of earshot, and leaned in. "Look, I'm sorry I tried to kiss you, okay?" he whispered through his teeth. "Obviously I was wrong. But I don't really think that right now is—"

"I'm not talking about that! I'm talking about the game!" I replied, blushing.

"What the hell are you doing out there?"

"Excuse me?" he blurted.

"Missing passes, giving them easy steals. I thought you were the star of this team!"

I tried to ignore the obnoxious, annoyed glares of my former friends. This was not about them right now.

"Dude, that guy is all over me!" Jake protested, throwing his hand out. "Did you see that illegal tackle? He should have gotten a yellow card for that. It's not my fault if the refs are freaking blind."

"Oh, wah, wah, wah," I replied sarcastically, tilting my head back and forth. "Poor Jake's getting defended. Are you gonna cry about it now?"

A few people in the stands laughed, Annie harder than most. Jake, meanwhile, blazed red with anger.

"Um, Ally?" Trista said, appearing behind us. "This isn't exactly what I meant."

"I'm not crying about it," Jake snapped.

"Oh, no? That's what it sounds like to me," I shot back.

He stood up and faced me. "I can run circles around that guy."

I pressed my lips together to keep from smiling. "Oh, so all of a sudden you're a player?" I said dubiously, standing up to look him in the eye.

"More of a player than you'll ever be," he shot back. Was it just me, or was he trying not to smile now too?

"Oh, yeah?"

"Yeah!"

"Then why don't you try proving it?" I demanded.

"Fine!" he shouted.

"Fine!" I replied.

Suddenly, he grinned. To my surprise, he leaned toward my ear. "You're pretty good at this." Then he smiled at me again before jogging over to Coach and pleading his case to be put back in the game.

"Wow. Nice work, Ally," Trista said as she walked by. "I think I underestimated you."

I turned around, grinning over both the praise and the lingering buzz of flirtation, and found Shannen staring me down through narrowed eyes. Clearly I had somehow crossed her imaginary Crestie line, and she didn't like it at all.

jake

"Nice tits, Dorkus," Hammond said, clapping David Drake on the back.

David gave us a tolerant look. Impressive, considering he was wearing a huge bra on the outside of his soccer jersey and that the bra was stuffed with rancid sweat socks from the locker room's lost and found. He also had red lipstick on his lips and blue eyeliner around his eyes, plus a purple wig one of my teammates had borrowed from his little sister.

All Hammond's idea. All his way of putting Drake in his place for taking my spot on the field. Which I was pissed about, but it wasn't exactly his fault. Still, I guess it was better than the kick in the head Hammond was always threatening to give him.

"Can I get you anything, sirs?" David asked us bitterly.

"I could use a beer," Hammond said as I tried not to laugh.

"I'm right on top of that, sir," he said.

As soon as he was gone, Hammond and I both doubled over. "I'm a genius, dude," Hammond said, smacking my hand, front and back. "The newbies look hilarious."

"Yep," I agreed with a nod. Once Hammond had come up with the idea to haze Drake, I'd insisted we make all the other new players dress up too. That was only fair. At least this way David wasn't in it alone.

"So, dude, you figured out who you're taking to the Harvest Ball yet?" Hammond asked me, taking out his BlackBerry to check his messages.

I automatically glanced across Hammond's game room at Ally. A few people were starting to dance in the open space between the pool table and the arcade games, but she was hanging out by the wall, talking to Tommy Kopp. I was surprised she'd shown. Usually Norms didn't come to these parties. But then, usually there were no Norm backslappers, either. She looked hot in her frayed jeans and OHH soccer T-shirt, her hair pulled up in a ponytail. The only question was, why the hell was she talking to Tommy Kopp? That guy had breath like a garbage dump and a face to match.

"Dude. Don't go there," he said. "Haven't we had this conversation already?"

I tore my eyes away. "What? I don't even know what you're talking about."

"Good. Because Ally Ryan is off-limits," Hammond said, pocketing his phone again.

"I know, man. Please. I'm not about spoiled goods."

I felt guilty even as I said it.

"Spoiled goods." He laughed shortly and slapped my chest with the back of his hand. "I'm totally using that."

Shit, I hoped not. The thing was, I bet Ally Ryan could have made the boring-ass school dance at least semitolerable. The crap she'd pulled before the half tonight had been semicheesy, but it had worked. My head had been all over the place—my mom's obsession with getting me an SAT tutor, my dad's threat to take away my Xbox and cable if I didn't get my grades up, that girl from Friday night who would not stop freaking calling me—and Ally's antics had gotten it back in the game. "Anyway, I'm weighing my options. You?"

"Ha ha. You're hilarious, man," he said. His eyes flicked toward Ally. Or maybe he was just looking for Chloe. "Chloe already picked out my suit and my shoes."

"Nice," I chided, nudging him with my elbow. "She fit you for the leash yet?"

"Hammond!" Chloe called out from her spot behind the bar. Since we were at his place, she'd taken over as hostess. "We need more ice. Do you have more ice?"

"Duty calls, man," Hammond said, rushing off.

I laughed and looked over at Ally again. My heart did that catching thing it had only ever done since she'd moved here. She was watching me. No. We were now watching each other. Screw Hammond and his warnings. I had to talk to this girl. What she'd done at the game was unexpected, to say the least. Especially after everything. What did it mean? Had she forgiven me for the almost-kiss thing? I had to know.

"Hey," I said, joining her.

She didn't look at me. "Hey."

"I'm surprised you came," I said.

Her eyes flashed. "Not you, too."

"Not me too what?" I asked.

"This whole no-Norms thing?" she said.

"No. That's not what I meant." My face was getting hot. "I don't think you *shouldn't* be here. I mean—"

"Good. Because this is a party for the soccer team and the backslappers, and I am a backslapper, in case you haven't noticed."

I sighed. Two seconds of conversation, and I'd already stuck my foot in it deep. "Can we talk about something else?"

"Sure. Brilliant hazing," she said. "Not cavemanish at all."

My jaw clenched, but I let it roll off my back. "This is nothing. Last year they made me and Hammond jump up and down on a trampoline in our underwear for three hours just because we were the only sophomores to make varsity."

"Oh, so you think this is better?" Ally asked.

"Believe me. It's better."

My face burned even hotter at the memory of every hot senior girl at OHH laughing at me while I tried to keep my junk from bouncing around in their faces. This was far better than that. I wanted to tell her that I was the one who kept her little friend David from being alone in drag, but it sounded too much like a pathetic plea, so I didn't. But why was she friends with that guy, anyway? Every day I had to watch them eat lunch together, and he was always cracking her up even though he isn't remotely funny. It was so annoying that he got to hang out with her and no one even cared. Meanwhile I was standing here feeling conspicuous for saying two words in her vicinity. I took a sip of my beer and tried not to look at my friends. But they were starting to notice.

"Why do you have to be so tense all the time?" I asked her. "It's a party."

She rolled her eyes and shoved a pretzel in her mouth. I sighed and looked where she was looking. Dorkus Drake was trying to talk to Shannen, who was only half acknowledging him—doing that tight smile thing she does when she wants someone to leave her alone but isn't in the mood to humiliate them. As I watched, she looked up at me, then at Ally, like WTH?

Snagged.

"That'll be the day," I said, turning to the side to avoid further eye contact with Shannen.

"What? You don't see it?" Ally asked.

"Shannen Moore and Dorkus Drake? Uh, no." I downed the rest of my beer and placed it on the bar. "The guy's a total loser."

Ally bristled. "That *loser* was one of two people who lowered themselves to talk to me on the first day of school."

"Hey. I talked to you," I reminded her. "You just didn't want to talk to me."

She blinked. I had her. Ha. But then her eyes narrowed. "Excuse me. I'm going to go hang out with my friend now." She stood up straight, dusted some salt off her fingers, and strode across the room, where she tugged Drake away from Shannen.

Two seconds later, she and Dorkus were slow dancing. They both looked ridiculous—him in his outfit, her with his boobs in her face. She stared at me over his shoulder, like she was trying to prove some point. Whatever. Like her walking away from me to dance with a dork was going to piss me off? And now Shannen was weaving her way through the crowd and around the pool table toward me like she was out for blood. Great. Now

I was going to get the third degree over talking to Ally Ryan, when all she'd done was completely blow me off. Sometimes it sucked being best friends with a girl who had such serious opinions about everything. I turned around, grabbed Lacey Goodman by the wrist, and dragged her through the door into the theater room. When I glanced back, Shannen had frozen in her tracks, and as the door was closing, I saw Ally stop dancing and stare at me.

Mission accomplished.

"Hey, Jake. I didn't even think you noticed I was here," Lacey said, backing into the velvet-covered wall. Only the can lights over the screen were on, and I could barely see her in the dim glow.

"I noticed," I said.

Even though I hadn't really. When I went to kiss her she kissed me right back. No arguments, no ducking away. Easy.

I didn't need Ally Ryan. I could have any girl, anytime. No strings. No guilt. No judging stares. And that was the way I liked it.

ally

On stage, David Drake was kinda hot. Well, not on stage really. It was more a cleared-out corner of Annie's wood-paneled basement. But there was a spotlight on him and his band. And ten freshmen woo-woo girls screaming in his face. He was wearing a long-sleeved, gray waffle shirt under a black Doors T-shirt, distressed jeans, and a beanie cap, all of which worked for him. And he had the whole wide-stance guitar-playing thing down like nobody's business.

"He's awesome!" I shouted to Annie, who was bobbing her head in a noncommittal way to the beat. She was wearing a sleeveless, plaid wool dress with a lace top underneath and knee-high boots. Something no one else in the room could have pulled off but that looked perfect on her. It made my plain-old jeans and striped T-shirt look seriously blah in comparison.

"Not bad," she said, lifting one shoulder.

Not bad was an understatement. Everyone loved the music, and the people-watching was a perfect distraction to keep me from obsessing about last night's party. The one at Hammond's. The one where none of my old friends had acknowledged my existence, David had gotten hazed, and Jake had ended up fooling around with some sophomore in the home theater.

Who was that girl? Was she his girlfriend or just some random hook-up? I glanced at Annie and thought about asking her. She, after all, knew all there was to know about the Cresties. She'd obviously know if Jake had a new girlfriend. But if I asked, she'd want to know why I cared, and that would open up a whole can of worms I did not want to deal with.

Someone stepped on my foot and muttered an apology, bringing me back to the now. My face burned even though no one here knew what I'd been thinking. So much for distraction. Controlled Chaos finished their song with a crash of drums and a peal from the guitar. Everyone in the packed basement cheered and whistled, lifting their cups.

"Whooo! Yeah, David!" I shouted, clapping my hands above my head.

"Thank you! We are Controlled Chaos!" David said into the microphone. Then he flung it on the ground, causing a loud wail of feedback, and loped out into the crowd. A few girls hugged him, and he slapped hands with some of his friends as he worked his way over to us.

"Hey, David! That was incredible!" I gushed.

He hooked his thumbs into the pockets of his jeans, all casual. "Yeah. Thanks for coming."

I blinked. This was not the excitable David I had come to know and was starting to like.

"Dude. Drop the rock-star act. You know you're freaking out over all the groupies," Annie said, shoving his shoulder.

David held his too-cool expression one second longer, then doubled over and snorted a laugh. "I know! Isn't this insane?" he whispered to us. "That girl over there asked me to sign her bra!"

"Wow. Not bad for a first gig," I joked as he leaned up against the wall next to me.

"Are you gonna do it?" Annie asked, taking a swig of her soda.

David's eyes widened. "Are you kidding? She's in my youth group at church. I think that would buy me a ticket directly to hell." I laughed, and David studied me with narrowed eyes. "I'm glad you came."

"Are you surprised?" I asked.

"No," he said quickly, glancing at Annie. "Well, yeah. I mean, we just weren't sure you would. Since it's a Norm party and all."

My throat tightened, and I looked down at my cup for a second. For days I had actually gone back and forth over whether or not to come. I hadn't been to a party on this side of town since I was in Brownies, and I'd been worried that Annie's friends wouldn't want me here. But so far, no one had given me a second glance. Unlike the two Crestie parties I'd attended where I'd been just about as welcome as the Orchard Hill police.

"Well, the Cresties don't exactly want me around anymore—"

"Oh, so you're just here by default," Annie said, an edge to her joking tone.

"No! It's not that. I'm just saying . . ."

I looked around at the couple of dozen people milling around the basement. A few girls had whipped out an old Mouse Trap board game and were attempting to put it together. A couple of guys in the corner were firing up the ancient Xbox on the even more ancient TV. Everyone seemed to be having a good time, and I felt relaxed. The way you're supposed to feel at a party. Even though my old friends probably would have either laughed or heaved if they could see what constituted a party on this side of town.

"I'm having fun," I said finally. "This is way better than any Crestie thing I've been to."

Annie grinned. "Way better."

"Oh, but come on!" David said sarcastically. "They have bars and pools and bathrooms with two sinks!"

"Ah, but the company here is of a much higher quality," I said with a smile. "Norms are far cooler than Cresties."

"I'll drink to that," Annie said, raising her plastic cup.

"I would too, but I don't have anything to drink," David added.

Annie and I laughed and clicked our cups together. "So, Ally, since you're such a Norm now, do you want to come over tomorrow and help me and David with the Fall Festival? I'm in serious need of volunteers."

Annie had mentioned the Fall Fest before. It was a fund-raiser she organized every year to raise money for the underfunded arts programs at school. Apparently most of our extracurricular cash went to the athletic teams.

"You should totally come," David said. "She promised me free pizza."

"Oh, well, if there's free pizza, I'm in," I said.

"There's the most beautiful girl in the room!" Logan Pincus, the burly, curly-haired drummer from David's band, came loping over and threw his arms around Annie, lifting her off the ground in a sideways bear hug. She rolled her eyes, and her whole body stiffened. David pressed his lips together as if to keep from laughing.

"Logan? Remember our chat about personal space?" Annie said.

He replaced her on the ground. "Right. Sorry."

Annie took a step back as Logan shoved his huge hands under his arms. "So? What do you think? We rocked, right? Didn't we rock?"

"Come on, Annie. You've gotta admit we rocked," David said, rubbing his hands together.

The two guys exchanged a conspiratorial look, and I got the distinct feeling there was something going on here that I didn't know about.

"I don't know. I think we should ask Ally," Annie said, looking at me pleadingly. "Ally? Do you think they rocked?"

I stared back at her. Clearly there was a right answer to this question, but I had no idea what it was. The two guys watched me expectantly. What was I going to say? That they didn't rock their first gig?

"Um, yeah. They totally rocked," I said.

Annie groaned, leaning backward. David and Logan bounced up and down so boisterously the bookshelves along the walls started to shake.

"We're going to the Harvest Ba-*all!*" Logan sang, grabbing Annie and dancing her around. "We're going to the Harvest Ba-*all!*"

"Thanks a lot!" Annie said to me, her head lolling around as Logan manhandled her.

"What just happened?" I asked David with a laugh.

"Logan's been asking Annie to every dance for the past two years, and she always says no, but last week they made a deal that if we rocked our first gig, she'd go with him," David explained. "You just sealed it."

"Oh. Oops." I bit my lip and smiled an apology as Logan twirled Annie past us toward the far wall. The other party-goers scrambled out of their way to keep from getting their toes crushed. "Sorry, Annie!"

"You're going to make this up to me!" she shouted back. "Tomorrow you're on glitter duty!"

"Glitter duty?" I asked David.

"She loves to have glittery signs for the Harvest Fest but hates dealing with glitter," he replied. He looped his arm around my shoulders and gave me a squeeze. "Aren't you so glad we crashed your table on the first day of school?"

I rolled my eyes as he headed off to the bookshelf that was serving as a makeshift bar. Someone turned up the music, and a few of the freshmen girls started to dance with the other members of David's band. As the party swelled around me, my heart fluttered with excitement. The truth was, I couldn't have been happier that Annie and David had crashed my table that first day. And I was psyched that Annie had invited me over to hang out with her and David tomorrow. For the first time, I was starting to believe that I could make new friends in Orchard Hill. That I could have a life here.

A life that was Crestie free.

You guys! I think Jake Graydon is going to ask me to the Harvest Ball!

Why would you think that?

Well, you know, after Friday night . . . plus he totally just smiled at me in the hall.

Well, I heard he already asked Lacey Goodman.

What? Lacey? Why?

She's Lacey Goodman. Do you really have to ask?

Ew. Really?

No. Lacey's going with Chris Harrington. I heard Jake was gonna ask Cori Ranger.

But Cori doesn't even hook up!

She didn't used to. Before she met Jake at Josh Schwartz's Saturday.

I think I'm gonna throw up.

Don't worry. You still have a chance.

You think?

It's Jake Graydon. Pretty soon he's going to have worked his way through the entire school and he'll have to make a second round.

jake

The door to my room opened and I dropped my Xbox controller and lifted my Physics text onto my lap. Then I saw it was Shannen and let the book slide to the floor.

"Nice try, Graydon, but even your mom would've caught that one," she said.

"Everything okay?" I asked. Usually when Shannen came barreling into my room unannounced, it was because her dad was on a bender and she needed to escape. "Your dad?"

"Oh, he did the 'come home and pass out' thing tonight. I'm just bored." She shoved her hands under my arms from behind to lift me up. "Come on. Hammond and the Idiot Twins are downstairs harassing your brother, and Chloe's in the car."

I shut off the TV. "The car?"

She shot me a wicked look over her shoulder. None of us had our licenses, but that never stopped Shannen when she had a plan. And when Shannen had a plan, it usually meant a good time.

I followed her down the stairs at a jog and into the kitchen, where Jonah sat at the counter trying to do his algebra homework. The Idiot Twins were sandwiching him between them, shouting numbers in his ears so he couldn't concentrate, while Hammond stood across the room, throwing popcorn from our popcorn machine at all three of them. The popcorn machine was right next to our sundae bar. Mom had it all installed over the summer in an attempt to turn our house into party central. She loved it when my friends were around.

"Quit it," Jonah complained, trying not to whine. He elbowed the twins on either side, but they clung to him as Hammond laughed.

"Dude. Not cool." I grabbed the back of his polo shirt to drag him out of there. With my free hand I slapped Trevor on the back. "Let's go."

Hammond launched one more shot at Jonah, and Todd gave my brother a world-class noogie as we walked out. Still, Jonah somehow managed to snatch the popcorn out of the air and eat it.

"Nice," I said to him.

He grinned in reply. "Quit letting those assholes into our house."

"I'll see what I can do."

The side door opened before we could escape, and my mom walked in wearing her tennis whites. She'd been over at Chloe's house playing against Mrs. Appleby. There was sweat on her chest below her diamond pendant, but her strawberry blond hair looked perfectly poofy as always.

"Hello, Shannen . . . boys," she sang, swinging her racket. "Jake." Her eyes flicked toward the door. "Where are you going?"

"Out," I replied.

"Have you done your homework?" she asked.

"Yes," I lied.

"Jake." She already seemed exasperated. "We made a deal at the beginning of the year, remember? If you want to go to Fordham like your father, you have to get your grades up."

"Mom," I said through my teeth, "I swear."

"We're just going out for ice cream, Mrs. Graydon," Shannen piped up. "Everyone's gonna be there."

I held back a smile. My mother was all about grades, but she was even more about looking like the cool mom in front of my friends, and Shannen knew it. It was totally lame, but I had used it to my advantage more than once.

"All right, all right," my mother said. Suddenly it was no big deal. "Have fun. There's always tomorrow for homework."

"Thanks," I said. "Let's go."

"Ice cream! Sweet! I didn't know we were going for ice cream!" Todd cheered, jumping up and down with his hands on Hammond's shoulders.

"Dude, take some Ritalin," Hammond groused.

We all laughed as we piled through the double doors. Shannen's mother's Land Rover was in the driveway, and Chloe waved at us from the backseat.

"Nice work," I said to Shannen, giving her a shove. "Way to play my mom."

"Oh, please. If I hadn't done it, you would," she said, shoving me back. "Here, you guys. Help me get this in the truck."

She bent at the waist and wrapped her arms around the legs of the lawn jockey that stood at the foot of the stairs. The twins clapped their hands in unison, rubbed them together, then crouched down without so much as a question.

"Um, why?" I asked, crossing my arms over my chest.

She rolled her eyes up at me. "You hate this thing, don't you?"

I did. It had been there when we moved in, and I'd always thought it was the ugliest thing ever, but my mother loved it. She thought it made us look wealthy or something. As if the eight-bedroom house with resort-style pool, full outdoor basketball court, completely stocked library, and gym didn't cover that already.

"Yeah," I replied.

"So help me get it in the car."

Hammond and I shrugged. The thing was way heavier than it looked, and it was a struggle for all five of us to lift it over the rear bumper and into the trunk. We laid it down on its side and it stared out at me, holding its lantern like an accusing finger.

"Sorry, dude. I'm sure you're going to a far better place," I said. Shannen slammed the door and we got in the car.

"Where're we going?" I asked.

"That's for me and Chloe to know," Shannen replied, her eyes sparkling.

As always. Chloe, who was sitting on Hammond's lap, sighed.

"Wait. We're *not* going for ice cream?" Trevor asked.

Todd slapped him on the back of the head.

"Where's Faith?" I asked, glancing over my shoulder at Hammond.

"She's working with her vocal coach," Chloe answered. "But she made me promise we'd take pictures."

"Pictures, huh? This is gonna be *good*," Trevor said.

"You guys have no idea," Shannen said, smiling at Chloe in the rearview.

I pushed the button on the automatic window, letting the cool fall air whip my face. Shannen accelerated down the hill at Harvest Lane and hooked a left toward town.

"Are we going to leave him in the park?" Hammond asked.

"Nope."

Shannen zoomed past Van Houten Square at the center of the shopping area. A bunch of kids we knew were hanging around outside Jump, the local coffee place. They shot us quizzical looks when they saw Shannen behind the wheel.

"Are we going to the club?" Trevor asked.

"No."

"The farm," Hammond said. "Are we putting him in the pumpkin patch?"

"No. No way. Trevor's scared of the pumpkin patch at night," Todd said, leaning forward in his seat.

"The pumpkins have eyes," Trevor said ominously.

"Don't worry, you freak. We're not going to the farm."

"Oh! The new annex?" Todd said, bouncing up and down. He gripped the back of Shannen's headrest with both hands. "Oh, dude! Are we sinking him to the bottom of the pool?"

The annex was this monstrous addition being built onto our school to house the new Olympic-size pool. The swim team had always used the country club's indoor facility, but by this winter we were going to have our own pool in which to dominate the division. Just like we had last year.

Shannen tilted her head, like this was something she might consider. "No."

"Oh, wait. I know where we're going," I said, feeling triumphant at having figured Shannen out. "We're going to Coach Harrison's house." Shannen had been pissed at Coach Harrison ever since she quit her job at the high school to coach basketball at one of the state schools. Maybe it was redemption time.

"How does that make any sense?" Shannen asked.

"I guess it doesn't," I replied. But how did any of this make sense? Who would make sense as the recipient of my mom's ugly-ass lawn jockey?

She slammed on the brakes at the stoplight at the bottom of the hill. An Orchard Hill police cruiser rolled past us, and I held my breath. The cop glanced up at Shannen and blinked, but he kept driving. The light turned green and we bucked forward.

"You're really not going to tell us where—"

The words died in my mouth as Shannen turned right, the tires squealing, and raced past the sign for the Orchard View Condominiums. My question had just been answered. We were going to Ally Ryan's house. A hard stone formed inside my gut. I looked over my shoulder at Hammond. He stared out the window, his nostrils flared.

"Welcome to the OVC, baby!" Trevor cackled.

"Shannen, what're we doing?" I asked.

She squinted at the quaint street signs and made a sudden right, so late that she almost ran over the opposite curb. "It's perfect. Mrs. Ryan bought this thing at an antiques auction for, like, a zillion dollars when we were in fourth grade. It was, like, her pride and joy. We're just returning it to its rightful owner."

No, you're not. You're taunting Ally. Reminding her that she no longer lives in the house she grew up in. That she no longer belongs. "I don't know about this."

"It's just a prank," Shannen said. "Why do you care? Do you like her or something?" She glanced over at me, flicking her bangs from her eyes like a challenge.

"No." I stared straight ahead. "It's just . . . isn't this kind of, I don't know, childish?"

"God. Lighten up," Shannen said. "This is it."

Shannen put the car in park, perpendicular to two other cars in their assigned spots, but kept the engine running. She jumped out and left the door yawning open as she popped the trunk. The Idiot Twins scrambled right out, already laughing under their breath. Jerks. I knew they liked Ally too, but they never said no to anything. Chloe hopped out of the backseat after them. She smoothed her skirt and opened the lens on her camera.

"Are you marys gonna help or what?" Shannen asked.

I looked back at Hammond again. Neither of us moved. I was surprised. This was the kind of jackassery he was normally totally up for. But then, so was I. And I hadn't moved yet either.

"You can't back out on us," Shannen hissed. "We can't move this thing on our own."

"Shit," Hammond said under his breath. He shoved his door open and got out. "Jake. Let's go."

I swallowed hard. I should just get out of the car and help them. If I didn't, I'd never hear the end of it.

"What's your problem?" Shannen asked, coming to my window. "What happened to Up the Stakes Jake? This is nothing compared with some of the crap we've pulled."

The half-wits behind the car started to try to remove the ten-ton statue themselves. There was a bang and a tumble, and Todd let out a string of curses worthy of a New York cab driver stuck in traffic at the Puerto Rican Day Parade. Chloe shushed them and giggled. A flash popped.

I glanced up at the windows on the row of identical condos, wondering which was Ally's. If she looked out right now, she would see this. All of us out here being juvenile delinquent losers.

"Jake? Hello? What's the problem? You don't even know the girl," Shannen said. "What, she's such an incredible back-slapper you've developed some kind of soft spot for her?"

Sometimes every word out of Shannen's mouth sounded like a judgment.

"No," I said.

"Then let's go already!" She yanked open my door and watched me expectantly.

Shannen was going to do this anyway, that much I knew. The best thing was to get it over with and get us all out of here as quickly as possible. Before Ally could see us. Before she could see I had anything to do with it. Before all her opinions of me could be confirmed.

"All right, all right," I said. "Let's do this."

It took about thirty seconds of grunting and sweaty-handed shifting to deposit the lawn jockey on the small square of cement outside Ally's front door. Right in front of the obviously new and obviously cheap welcome mat, which was decorated with happy strands of sunflowers. Next to it were two small pumpkins waiting to be carved. I felt like I was going to hurl.

"Remember how Ally's dad used to have a whole truckload of pumpkins delivered to their house?" Chloe whispered. She was looking down at the pumpkins too, the camera hanging from a string around her wrist. She glanced at Shannen wistfully. "And we'd all come over to carve them the night before Halloween?"

Shannen rolled her eyes, but I could tell she wasn't unaffected by the memory.

"Pumpkin gut fight!" Trevor and Todd shouted way too loudly.

"Dudes! Shut it!" Hammond whispered, which made them double over laughing.

"Are you sure you want to do this?" Chloe asked.

Finally Do-the-Right-Thing Appleby had arrived.

"Chloe! Come on!" Shannen hissed. "This was practically your idea."

"I just said I bet her mom misses the lawn jockey," Chloe said, wide-eyed. "I didn't mean we should bring it over here! I mean, look how sad it looks."

We all stared down at the lawn jockey. It was so massive it took up almost the entire step. Suddenly a light flicked on overhead.

"Shit!" the Idiot Twins whispered in unison, and ran.

Chloe was right on their heels, carefully but quickly picking her way down the steps. Hammond, Shannen, and I froze.

"Let's get out of here," I hissed, my heart in my throat.

"Wait. There's one more thing," Shannen said. And she rang the doorbell.

"Dammit!"

Shannen laughed and sprinted for the car. Hammond launched himself face-first into the backseat. My gut stone was now choking all air supply as I fumbled with the handle and ducked inside. Shannen hit the gas and peeled out. Hammond kept repeating "shit, shit, shit" over and over and over again while Chloe hid her face in her hands and the Idiot Twins whooped and cheered. I told myself not to look back. That it was a huge mistake to look back. But I did anyway.

I looked back to find Ally Ryan's stricken face staring after me.

ally

"Hey, guys! Thank you so much for coming!" Annie clutched my arm in one hand, David's in the other. "I was worried there wouldn't be anyone here!"

I glanced around the baseball field, which had been completely taken over by the Fall Festival. For the past two weeks— ever since that first "glitter Sunday"—David and I had spent

a lot of our free time helping her with publicity and planning. We'd wheedled free ad space out of the local papers,
decided not to put the hot chocolate stand right next to the
popcorn stand because it would just cause stomachaches, and
made several other crucial decisions involving pricing, porta-
potties, and decorations. The three of us had a lot of fun, and
I'd thought that David and I had put in a ton of work, but now
I realized that Annie had done a lot more. This event was huge.
There were rides, game booths, food vendors, and even a few
wandering jugglers, and it seemed like every kid from the Norm
side of town was dropping cash in the hopes of winning lame
prizes. The autumn sun shone down on the crowd, and a light
breeze tossed colorful fallen leaves across our feet. Everywhere
I looked there were the telltale decorations of fall: pumpkins,
hay bales, bunches of Indian corn. Somewhere behind us, a
bell tolled and a bunch of people cheered.

"Yeah. This place would be dead without us," I joked.

"I know, but these people are all freaks," Annie said, releas-
ing us.

David laughed, placing his hands in the front pocket of his
oversized OHH soccer sweatshirt. "I thought the artsy people
were your people."

Annie blinked and tugged down on the brim of her gray
plaid fedora as she looked around. "They are. But that doesn't
mean they're not freaks," she joked.

"She's right, you know." Faith Kirkpatrick walked up behind
us. The very sound of her voice made my shoulders clench.
"And I happen to think you two fit right in."

She was wearing a tight black turtleneck and black pants,
a glittering pink star drawn at the corner of her left eye. Her

blond hair was slicked back in a ponytail, and a Chanel purse dangled from the crook of her arm. Just looking at her standing there all high and mighty made me want to punch something. Was she in the car that night when Jake and the Idiot Twins and some unknown driver had left our old lawn jockey on our front step? Had she seen where I was living now? Was that why she had that particularly amused smirk on?

I hated myself for even going there. Hated myself for feeling ashamed that she and the others had seen how far my mom and I had fallen. I should have been—and really was—more pissed about the fact that my mother had cried over their stupid prank. That she'd been forced to spend hours on the phone with the condo board—whose strict exterior decorating codes we'd unknowingly violated—over the weekend trying to explain that it wasn't ours.

"What are you doing here?" I asked.

"Mrs. Thompson was somehow convinced that the drama club's presence should be mandatory. Thanks a lot for that," she said, sneering at Annie. "So I'm doing face painting. Want a goatee? It would be an improvement."

My face flushed with heat.

"Or you, Annie? I could do a whole white face thing," she said, waving a hand in front of Annie's face. "Might actually camo the zits for once."

Annie opened her mouth to respond, but I beat her to it.

"Enough! When the hell did you become such a psychotic bitch?" I blurted.

Faith's jaw dropped as David guffawed. A few people around us turned to stare as they walked by, their candy apples momentarily forgotten. Maybe what I'd said sounded harsh, but Faith deserved it. Annie was a nice person—a person who had welcomed me back here even though we'd never been that close, a person who'd helped me get a job and hung out with me at school and invited me to her house even though no one else wanted to be seen with me. She didn't deserve to be torn down by her former best friend.

"What? Speechless? Don't have an answer?" I asked, crossing my arms over my chest. "Because I'm curious. Do you remember the actual date and time of your supervillain transformation? Was there a scorpion sting involved? A toxic spill? Or maybe you were the victim of one of those organ-snatching rings. They drugged you and you woke up in a tub full of ice with no heart?"

"Screw you, Ally," Faith said, narrowing her eyes.

"Right back at ya, Faith."

I couldn't believe that Faith Kirkpatrick and I were snipping at each other. She was supposed to be a sweetheart, a church-goer, the person who saw the good in everyone. When exactly had her soul turned black?

"Okay, okay, let's walk before this gets ugly." David looped his arm through mine and yanked me away from Faith. Annie followed after us, stunned.

"You have a mean streak, Ally Ryan," she said. "Not that I don't approve."

"She deserved it," I exclaimed, throwing out my hands as we approached the hot chocolate booth. "You guys, seriously. What the hell happened to Faith? She used to be Miss Congeniality, and now she's like Jigsaw on crack."

"It happened in February of freshman year," Annie said, holding on to her hat as the wind kicked up. "Right around when you moved away, now that I think about it. One day she's perfectly normal, the next she's mocking Becca Gray's Hello Kitty binder and screaming at me at Spring Fling about how I'm a loser with no friends."

"Really?" I said, swallowing hard.

"Yep."

We inched forward on the line, but my mind was not on hot chocolate. Suddenly, it all made sense. All Faith had ever wanted was for Chloe and Shannen to accept her, but they'd only hung out with her because of me. Once I was gone, she must have been desperate to hang on to them. Desperate enough to drop her few Norm friends and do it in a way that would impress the Cresties. Like bitching Annie out in public and mocking Becca to her face for something Chloe and Shannen thought was lame.

It was my fault. My leaving had turned Faith to the dark side. God. No wonder everyone around here hated me. I had never realized how much my dad's actions and their consequences had affected everyone. Even Annie. Suddenly this hot gush of anger surged through me and my jaw clenched. I wished he was there right now just so I could tell him to his face how much he'd messed up my life. But he wasn't. And wherever he was, he was happily oblivious to all the misery he'd left behind—which just pissed me off even more. It was so not fair. He should be the one suffering, not me. He'd screwed over our friends, torn us from our home, and then left us without explanation, and my mom and I were the ones who had to deal with it all.

"Oh my God. Shannen Moore," David said under his breath.

I didn't even realize my fingers had curled into fists until he spoke, bringing me back to the now, and they unclenched. Sure enough, Shannen was cutting purposefully across the field, headed straight for Faith's booth. My heart dropped at the sight of her. I knew she had to be involved in the lawn jockey debacle. "Prank" was her middle name. I'd learned some of my best stuff from her. But everything we'd ever done had been harmless—swapping people's front porch jack-o-lanterns the day before Halloween, rearranging all of Chloe's mom's books in the library, stealing the ladder from Hammond's boys-only tree house while he and the Idiot Twins were still up there (and returning it three hours later when they were starving and really had to pee). We'd never done anything overtly cruel to anyone, least of all each other.

"God, why don't you just say hello to her? Or even better, ask her to the Harvest Ball like you've been whining about doing for three years?" Annie suggested, holding down the pleated skirt of her jumper-style dress as the wind kicked up again. "This is getting pathetic already."

"No." He shook his head. But then his eyes suddenly filled with hope. "You think I should?" he asked me.

I didn't. Not even a little bit. Shannen may have had a tough exterior when I knew her before, but these days that exterior was also frozen over by a thick layer of ice. But who was I to rain on anyone's lifelong crush parade? I knew better than anyone that Shannen had her good qualities. She just hadn't been exhibiting any of them lately.

"Sure. Go for it," I said, crossing my fingers behind my back in hope.

David was buoyed by my tentative confidence. He stepped out of line and cleared his throat. "Hey, Shannen."

She paused. Her eyes flicked over him, then me. "What?"

"Um, yeah, I was just wondering. . . . Do you have a date for the Harvest Ball?" he asked in a rush.

I sent Shannen telepathic messages. Please just don't humiliate him. Please, please, please be the kind person I know you're capable of being.

"Actually, I do," she said. Then miraculously she gave him a kind smile. "But thanks for asking."

Then she glanced at me quickly, turned, and walked away. For that split second it was as if we were friends again. As if she understood me. As if she cared about someone other than herself. Something other than her insular clique.

"Ouch," David said.

"Bitch," Annie added under her breath. She whipped her notebook out of her pocket and furiously started making notes.

"Sorry." I patted him on the back. "It could have been worse, right? I mean, she already had a date, so . . . you were just . . . too late."

"Yeah, right," David said, looking at the ground as the line inched forward. He leaned down and plucked a small leaf from the laces of his Skechers, then shredded it into tiny pieces. "She doesn't like me. She's never gonna like me. I should just get over it already."

"I know! Why don't you two go to the ball together?" Annie suggested, so excited by the idea she bent at the knees and brought her pad and pen to her mouth in her fists.

David and I looked at each other. "Uh . . ."

"Come on, please? Someone has to be my Logan Pincus buffer," Annie begged. "If you guys are there together, then you can both buffer me."

"I don't know. I wasn't even planning on going," I said.

"Come on, Ally! Please?" Annie begged. "It's your fault I have to go with the guy in the first place. You owe me!"

I sighed as David looked at me. "We could look at it as community service."

"Datebuffers-dot-org?" I joked, tilting my head.

David laughed and let the tiny pieces of his leaf flutter away on the breeze. "Let's do it."

I hesitated for just a second but didn't even give myself a chance to think about why. It wasn't as if anyone else was an option anyway. Especially not now.

"Sure. Why not?" I said. "It'll be fun."

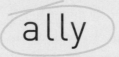

ally

Jake Graydon was staring at me. He was cocked back in a chair in his blue suit and dark orange tie, some sophomore girl in a low-cut dress nibbling on his neck, and he was staring at me. Why? Why was he looking at me like I was the gravy and he was the biscuit? Had we not locked eyes just the other night in the OVC parking lot when he was making his getaway? Did he not know that I knew he was an asshole of the first order?

"Would you ever marry outside your religion?" David asked me.

I tore my eyes away from Jake and looked at David. His arms were around my waist, and mine were around his neck as we slow danced under the disco ball at the center of the gym floor. In all the Jakesession (my new term for my quite unhealthy and completely inexplicable Jake obsession), I'd forgotten what we were doing here.

"Are you making an offer or just asking one of your non sequitur questions?" I joked.

David frowned in thought, turning me in a slow circle. He looked adorable in his gray suit and blue tie, all clean shaven and gleaming from aftershave.

"The latter. Wait. I always get that wrong. Is it the latter or the former . . . ? Whatever. The non sequitur one," he said. "What are you, anyway? Religionwise."

"Evangelical. But honestly, it's never been a big thing with my family, so I guess I would marry outside my religion," I said. "But it would be weird if my husband didn't want to celebrate Christmas."

"I'm with you. Anyone messes with my eggnog habit and I'll bust their ass," David joked.

I laughed. We'd turned in a full circle, and my gaze went directly to Jake again. I wished he wasn't here. I was having a perfectly nice time with David, Annie, and Logan—both of whom were sitting at a nearby table while Annie took copious notes on Crestie behavior—until Jake had arrived fashionably late with his latest victim. Ever since then I'd known exactly where he was at any given moment, and I'd been nothing but tense.

What the hell was my problem? Practically all I thought about was Jake. Half the time I fantasized about bumping into him in the hall and ripping into him for the lawn jockey prank. Telling him about how my mom had called some junk-hauling place, and they'd said it would cost two hundred bucks to pick the thing up and dispose of it because it was so heavy. Two hundred dollars! Money we did not have. Didn't he realize that his actions had consequences? In my fantasy he would be chagrined into speechlessness and I'd walk away all triumphant while he hung his head in shame.

The other half of the time the very same fantasy ended up with him grabbing my arm as I tried to walk away, pulling me to him, and kissing me half to death.

I was in serious need of some therapy.

"So, I have a question," David said.

We'd turned so that Jake was no longer in my line of sight. Slight reprieve. "Let me guess. Would I ever name my first born after a planet?" I joked.

"Close," David said. "Would you go out with me?"

I stepped on my own foot and sort of slid sideways. "Wait. What?" My heart was pounding a mile a minute. He had to be kidding. He was kidding. Right?

He looked around, dropping his arms from my waist. "Um . . . do you really need me to say it again?" he asked, his smile beseeching and adorable.

I swallowed hard. He was serious. "I thought you liked Shannen."

David shrugged one shoulder. "That was stupid," he said. "That was, like, the unattainable stupid crush. But you . . ." His Adam's apple bobbed as he looked at me, his gaze steady. "You're, like, extremely cool. Pretty much any guy in this room would kill to have a girlfriend like you."

My heart melted into warm mush. Could he possibly be any sweeter? What *girl* in this room wouldn't kill to have a cute guy say that to her? I took a deep breath and considered David. Sweet, fun, adorable David, who was growing more uncertain and vulnerable by the second. What was stopping me from saying yes?

"Hey."

We both turned. Jake Graydon stood in front of us, jacket unbuttoned, hands slipped casually into his pockets. Hotter than any normal person had the right to be.

"Um, hi," David said ironically. Not that Jake would get the tone, considering he had no idea what he'd just walked in on. "What's up?"

Jake gave David a baffled look. "Uh, actually, I came over to see if I could, you know, cut in or whatever."

I snorted a laugh. "Yeah, right."

Jake colored slightly. "What?"

"No, you cannot cut in," I said slowly. A thrill skittered over my shoulders. He was finally giving me my chance to reject him. To make him feel the way I'd felt when I saw him peeling off from my house with the Idiot Twins cackling in the backseat. I still had no idea which one of his friends was driving the car, but it didn't matter. Jake had been there, defiling my home, rubbing my downfall in my face. And now he was asking me to dance?

"But I—"

David slipped in front of me, facing off with Jake. "She said no thanks. You can walk away now."

My heart fluttered. David was defending my honor. But as much as I appreciated the gesture, I wasn't about to let him speak for me.

"I've got this, David," I said, stepping around him. I looked up at Jake, lifting my chin. Annie and Logan were suddenly there at our side, as if a brawl were about to break out and they were ready to throw down. "I'll dance with you," I told him, "after you give me the two-hundred dollars you owe me."

His brow knitted. "What?"

"Two hundred dollars. That's what it's going to cost to have the lawn jockey you and your friends left on my doorstep hauled away." I folded my arms over my green H&M dress—the one I'd bought for last year's Holiday Dance in Baltimore. The good thing about moving to a new school? All your clothes are brand new again. And even if it cost one tenth the amount of Faith's black strapless, I still thought I looked pretty good in it. "I assume you have the cash."

Jake blanched. "I . . ."

"No? I'll take a check," I said obnoxiously. "I *do* know where you live in case it bounces." I held out my hand flat, waiting.

"I didn't know," Jake said. He looked away. "I didn't think it'd be that big a deal."

I narrowed my eyes as my heart started to soften. It was so Jakesessed it wanted to take that meager nothing of an apology and run with it. But I wouldn't let it. My brain had some pride, even if my heart didn't.

"Come on, David. I'm over this dance," I said, taking his hand. "Let's get out of here."

Confused, David followed me toward the door nonetheless. Jake, much to my surprise, came after us.

"Wait." His hand was on my arm. I turned around. "Look, I'm . . . I'm sorry, okay?" he said quietly. "We shouldn't have done it. But it's not like it was my idea—"

"No? Then whose was it? Tell me so I can ask *them* for the cash," I said.

Jake looked away again, his handsome face turning a deeper shade of red.

"Fine. I'll expect the money in the morning."

I twisted around on my heel and walked off, David, Annie, and Logan jogging to catch up.

"Are we really leaving?" David asked. "Should I get the coats?"

"Yeah. I mean, if it's okay with you guys," I said. "This is lame anyway, right? I say we hit the diner."

"I'm all over that," Logan said. He smacked David in the chest with the back of his meaty hand. "Let's go."

The two of them loped off toward the lobby, where the makeshift coat rack had been placed. I kept moving for the door, wanting to put as much space between me and Jake as possible.

"Okay. That was weird," Annie said, clutching her notebook in one hand, her pumpkin-shaped purse in the other.

"What?" I asked, both fuming and exulting. I'd finally gotten to tell him off, but somehow, I was still pissed.

"In all the months I've been documenting Jake's every move, I've never seen him (a) go after a girl who's walking away from him or (b) apologize for anything."

I paused with my hand on the metal door. "Really?"

"Really," she said, whipping the notebook open to jot something down. "Clearly you've had some kind of positive effect on Jake Graydon."

I swallowed hard and looked across the room at him. He was rejoining his friends and his date, as if nothing had happened. Apparently it wasn't a *huge* effect.

"Here you go, milady," David said, holding out my mom's black wool coat to me.

"Thank you." I slipped my bare arms into the warm sleeves.

"Let's go. I'm starved," Logan said, shoving open the door and barreling through it ahead of Annie. She rolled her eyes and went after him before it could slam in her face. As hard as he'd worked to win this first date, he wasn't exactly gunning for a second.

"Um . . . shall we?" David said, tilting his head.

"Yeah," I replied. My stomach was clenching and unclenching as I remembered what we'd been talking about before we were so rudely interrupted. Jake was clearly a jerk, and David was clearly his polar opposite. Maybe the key to breaking the Jakesession was to replace it with something else. Something real. Someone who actually cared about me.

"Hey, David," I said.

His eyebrows rose. "Yeah?"

"The answer to your question is yes," I said.

His grin lit the entire room. He took a sliding, sideways step toward me. "Yeah?"

I grinned back. "Yeah."

David slipped one arm around my back. "Cool."

Then he leaned in and kissed me, his lips warm and soft, his eyelashes tickling my cheek. When he pulled away, I smiled. There may not have been fireworks, but it was nice. Part of me had to wonder if Jake had seen *that*, too, but I forced myself not to look over at him. From now on, I only had eyes for David Drake. I was a Norm, I was going to date a Norm, and I was going to forget all about the lame-ass Cresties and their evil pranks.

"Come on," David said, taking my hand. "Let's catch up with them before Logan eats his dad's car."

I laughed as he held the door open for me and I slipped out

into the cool night. At that moment, there was no doubt in my mind that I had just made the right decision.

ally

Twenty-three down . . . formerly trendy berry. Formerly trendy berry ending with an *i*. What kind of berry ended with an *i*? Why could I not get this?

"Done!"

Annie smacked the "ring for service" bell atop the CVS counter and threw her hands up.

"You are not done." I lifted my head. My neck hurt from straining over *Ultimate Crosswords* for the past half hour. Annie turned her book around and showed me her puzzle. Every single box was filled in. I looked down at my pathetic excuse for a crossword board. It was maybe half done. If I was being nice to myself.

"What's twenty-three down?" I whined.

She looked over her board. "Acai! That's the easiest one."

"I suck at this," I said, throwing my pencil down. Why had I even spent a dollar ninety-nine (minus discount) of my hard-earned money on that crappy book if she was going to beat me every time we challenged? I checked my watch and sighed. Ten minutes and I would be able to clock out. "Why is this place so dead?"

"Football game," Annie said, jumping up and coming down with her butt on the counter. She swung her legs over, grabbed a Reese's from the display underneath, and tore it open. "This side of town goes dead on game night. Now, if you were working at the *Apothecary*," she said, putting on a snotty tone and lifting her nose, "you'd be seriously busy."

The Apothecary was an old-school pharmacy and makeup outlet on the Crestie side of town. I used to accompany my mother there once a week to pick up "essentials" like La Mer skin cream, Estée Lauder eye gel, and cooling pedicure socks shipped in from Italy. None of which could be afforded now. I wondered what my former friends would think if they saw the current state of my mom's makeup bag. These days it was Avon and Olay all the way.

"Right. Norms play football, Cresties play soccer," I said, rolling my eyes. I walked around the counter and joined her, eyeing the candy selection. "Speaking of Cresties, you'll never believe what happened this morning."

"Wait!" Annie ran around the counter again, shoving an entire peanut butter cup in her mouth, and extracted her notebook from her bag. She poised her pencil over it and looked up at me like an expectant cub reporter out of a Superman cartoon. "Okay, go!"

I casually picked up a tube of Mentos and put it down. "When I went outside for my morning bike ride, the lawn jockey was gone."

"*Really?*" she said, in a leading way that made my heart pound. She bent and scribbled vehemently in her book.

"What're you writing?" I asked, standing on my toes to try to see. She shielded the page with her hand like a little kid who didn't want her test paper copied.

"Just that maybe Jake Graydon is human after all," she said.

I blushed and looked away, setting about reorganizing the battery carousel, which did not need reorganizing. I had figured it was him. Of course it was him. But it was nice to have someone else confirm the suspicion.

"So, you and David," Annie said behind me. "That's . . . interesting."

My stomach flipped, and I swallowed back a wave of unpleasantness. "Why?" I asked, lifting a shoulder. When I turned around, I looked her right in the eye, but it took some effort. "I like David. He's sweet." I paused, searching for the right thing to say. "David is . . . good for me, you know? I think it's gonna be good."

Was I trying to convince her or me?

"Uh-huh," she said skeptically, shoving her pencil and notebook back in her bag. She extracted a dollar and rang up her peanut butter cups. "Just remember that when you're breaking his heart in a few weeks."

"Annie! I'm not gonna break his heart," I said, my own chest constricting.

"We'll see."

Before I could protest further, the door chime sounded and my mom walked in. She looked beautiful. Her hair was done up all fancy, and she was wearing more makeup than I'd seen her wear in months. Her eyes and her smile were both bright—genuine. Not forced or strained or tired. It was a nice change, even if I wasn't so psyched about the reason behind it.

Lately my mom and Mrs. Moore had been talking on the phone a lot—even though none of the other Crestie moms had stopped by or called since we'd been back—and every time my mom hung up with Mrs. Moore she'd ask me how Shannen was doing, like she was hoping all four of us could get together

or something. I'd always say "fine" and then change the subject or have to run to the bathroom or something, all so that
I wouldn't have to explain to my mom that her one friend's
daughter had no interest in hanging out with me anymore. It
had just started getting old when Mrs. Moore had floated the
idea of my mother going out on a blind date with this widower
from the crest named Gray Nathanson. Ever since then, Mom
had been more about preparing for Gray than badgering me
about Shannen. Tonight was the big night. Up until now, I had
somehow avoided thinking about it.

"Hey, hon!" my mother sang, her voice quavering with
excitement. She executed a turn, the skirt of her black cotton
dress twirling. "How do I look?"

"Amazing," I replied truthfully.

Annie whistled. "Smokin'."

"Why, thank you, Annie," my mom said, giving a slight bow.

The two of them had met a few days earlier when my mom
had come to visit me at work. Annie had been jamming down
the keys on her computer and muttering under her breath,
recording a rather heinous encounter with Chloe at the latest meeting of the *Acorn*, for which Annie wrote and Chloe
edited. Apparently Chloe's perfectionist nature did not gel
with Annie's freewheeling style, and everything Chloe said
was a criticism. Annie, it seemed, was not good at taking criticism. When she'd finished venting, she'd slammed the laptop
closed with a bang, looked up at my mom, and smiled beatifi-
cally, as if everything were completely normal. Back home
that night, when I'd asked what my mom had thought of
Annie, she had said my new friend was "intriguing." Couldn't
have said it better myself.

"I just wanted to stop by to make sure you're all set for dinner," my mom said. "You can nuke that pasta from last night, or there's some chicken in the freezer."

"Okay. I'll be fine," I told her, a lump forming in my throat. I knew what I was supposed to say, I just hadn't realized it was going to be so hard to say it. "Have fun, Mom," I managed to get out.

"Thanks, hon," she said, her smile widening. "We'll see how it goes."

Then she gave me a quick peck on the forehead and turned to wave at Annie. Instead she found a pack of mints hurtling toward her. My mother lifted her hand and snatched it out of the air. And people wonder where I get my athleticism and dexterity.

"What's this?" my mother asked.

"Just in case," Annie said with a wink. "They're on me."

"Thanks." Mom blushed, pocketed the mints, and walked out.

"Gross!" I said. I picked up my *Ultimate Crosswords* book and whipped it at her. Annie easily dodged out of the way.

"What? I just wanted her to be prepared!" Annie protested.

"That's it, I'm clocking out."

"But you have five more minutes!" Annie whined.

"They can dock me!"

My hands were shaking as I shed my blue-and-red CVS-issue polo, changed into a T-shirt, and typed my code into the computer in the break room. I couldn't believe my mom was going on a date. That she might even be kissing some random guy at the end of the night. The very thought made me gag, and my eyes stung with tears. My parents weren't even divorced yet. Not that it mattered. They would have been if my mom's lawyers had been able to track him down before our money ran out and she couldn't pay them anymore. Where was he? Unlike most of my friends' parents, my mom and dad had always been totally into each other. Kissing and hugging and holding hands. Going out on "dates" even though they'd been married almost twenty years. Couldn't he, I don't know, sense that the love of his life was moving on? Or had he never really cared about us at all? Because if he had, how could he just forget about us? Just leave without a single call or an e-mail or anything?

I took my anger out on the back door, shoving it open with a bang. The delivery area where trucks pulled in and out all day, unloading supplies to CVS and the stores in the strip mall—Stanzione's Pizza, Dunkin' Donuts, Hill Deli, and the dry cleaner—was deserted. A slight mist fell, tickling my skin, cooling it. My bike was locked up to a water drain next to the Dumpster, and it took me longer than usual to work the combination. When the chain finally fell free, I straddled my bike and rode toward the crest. This time I knew where I was going, and this time I had a clear agenda. I probably should have been heading over to David's house— dropping in on the guy I had just last night decided to focus on with all my energy—but that wasn't where I wanted to be. Not right now. Not in this mood. I had some stuff to work out, and sitting on a couch watching some lame DVD while awkwardly holding hands with my new BF was not going to cut it.

And besides, I wanted to know for sure. Had Jake taken the lawn jockey? Was Annie right? Had he suddenly become human on the very night I'd started going out with someone else?

I took the Harvest Lane hill at a sprint and arrived at my old house soaked with sweat and rain, my chest heaving up and down. I paused as I approached the front door. The lawn jockey was standing just off to the right of the bottom step. As if he'd never left.

Even though my finger was shaking, I managed to press the bell purposefully. Then I held my breath. A tall, wiry kid who was not Jake answered the door.

"Hey." He looked confused.

"Hey," I said. "Is Jake here?"

"Yeah. Hang on." He half closed the door. "Jake! Some girl!"

I heard the barreling feet on the stairs. The stairs down which I used to fly in my sleeping bag, pretending it was a bobsled course in the Olympics. Jake's feet were on my stairs. So bizarre. He slapped his brother on the back of the head as he arrived, then blushed when he saw it was me.

"Oh," he said. "Hey."

"Nice lawn jockey," I said. "New?"

He blushed so fast I thought his face might pop. "Sort of."

"I owe you a game," I said, peeling off my hoodie and tossing it over my shoulder. I tried not to care that my gray T-shirt was sticking to my skin at the base of my neck, under my arms, and at the center of my stomach.

He looked up at the sky. The misting had changed into steady drizzle. "It's raining."

"Oh, so you're a wuss," I said.

He gave me a look, then disappeared. Seconds later he was back, basketball in hand. He threw it at my chest. Hard. "Let's do this."

jake

"Did I mention I've never lost on this court?" Ally taunted, a smile on her dripping-wet face. Her hair clung to her forehead and neck, but she made no move to fix it. She stood up straight and held her arms out, palms up, the ball on her right hand. "I own this place." I could not believe she was going out with David Drake. How did a dorkus like David Drake get to go out with someone this cool?

"Yeah. You may have said that once or twice," I replied.

When we'd first come around the side of the house to the full-size, outdoor basketball court, I'd actually thought Ally might cry. The sign on the state-of-the-art scoreboard above the three-bench bleachers still read RYAN ARENA. Jonah and I had always thought Ryan was some dude. Apparently not. According to Ally, her dad had this court built for her on her twelfth birthday. And since then, she had dominated on it. Right up until a year and a half ago, when she'd moved out and I'd moved in.

"You ready?" she asked. "Because if you need to take a minute . . ."

"Bring it," I replied.

Ally's grin widened. She palmed the wet ball in her left hand, faked right, and went left. My feet slipped on the wet asphalt, and I went down. She got around me easily, considering I was on the ground, and hit a textbook layup. I pushed myself to my feet, cursing under my breath. There was a nice, wide scrape on my knee.

"That's fourteen to twelve," she said cockily, holding the

ball in one palm. "You sure you want to keep this up? Cuz you're about to lose to a gi-*irl*!" she sang.

I rolled my eyes, but inside my stomach was doing flips. This girl was definitely not like the others. There was no apology. No "Oh! You hurt yourself! Let's get you cleaned up!" Nothing.

"I'm sure," I said.

She bounced the ball to me. The rain was coming harder now, and we were both soaked through. Her T-shirt clung to her in all the right places. I had to get back to the game before my body started thinking for me.

"Twelve—fourteen," I said.

I dribbled from hand to hand. She bent at the waist, rocking back and forth on her hips, her eyes on mine. She had this look on her face like she knew she was going to win. Screw it. Basketball was not my game. There was a good chance I wasn't going to get around her. Might as well go through. I barreled straight ahead, slamming her shoulder with mine. As she went sprawling I realized that might have been kind of unnecessary. I hesitated before tossing the ball up, which gave her just enough of a window to spring off the ground, go vertical, and slap the ball away. It bounced toward the edge of the court, and by the time I figured out what had happened, she was shooting a perfect arcing shot over my head. It fell through the net with a slosh, spraying water everywhere.

"That's game!" Ally shouted, raising her arms.

I hung my head. Good thing it was raining. Otherwise Hammond or the Idiot Twins might have dropped by and witnessed this tragedy.

"Nice one," I said, reaching my hand out to her.

She slapped it and sat down on the bottom bleacher. "Yeah. You too."

I sat down next to her. Too close. Our thighs and knees touched. She looked at our legs but didn't move away. I was breathing kind of heavy from the game and wished I had a Gatorade or something so I'd have something to do with my hands.

I looked over at her. She quickly looked away. We both laughed.

"That was fun," I said, leaning back. My shoulder pressed against hers. "We should do it again."

"And risk pissing off your friends?" she asked.

My face turned hot. "Screw them."

She twisted slightly, leaning her hand into the bench. Which meant that her knee was pushing more solidly against mine. I cleared my throat.

"What the hell did you do to Chloe, anyway?" I asked. I mean, the girl was obviously cool. I couldn't believe she could have done anything that bad. Maybe if I could sort of ease her back into the group, we could hang out. "No one will tell me."

Ally's face grew serious, and she sat up straight. Her leg was no longer touching mine. She looked down at her feet, which she kicked out in front of her. "I skipped out on her sweet sixteen."

"No way." I laughed. "That's the big drama?"

"Yep." She looked away.

"And the punishment for that is a lifetime ban?" I asked.

"The funny thing is, I never even got an invitation," she said. "Chloe claims she sent it, but if she did, I didn't get it. So technically, there's no reason for them to be mad."

"Girls," I said—then hoped she wouldn't take it to mean her.

"Tell me about it," she joked. "It's more what my dad did, I think," she said, swinging her legs back and forth. "When they look at me . . . all they see is him. He really did eff up. They have a right to be pissed at him. We all do."

I swallowed hard. We were getting into heavy territory. I'd never been good at heavy.

Ally sighed and looked down at her hands, fidgeting with her fingers. "I guess we all just need to move on."

Then the weirdest thing happened. I had this sudden itch to hold her hand. My fingers actually twitched toward hers, but I held back. That would definitely be too weird. And definitely be sending a signal I did not want to send. So instead, I pressed my palm into my thigh and sighed. I waited. The rain got harder and louder for a second, and then, all of a sudden, stopped. Ally was done talking. Rain dripped from our hair and clothes. I had to clench my teeth to keep from shaking. Now that we'd stopped moving, I was getting cold.

"So whose idea was it?" she asked suddenly.

"What?"

"The lawn jockey."

I froze. Like I was really going to rat out Shannen. "Why do you want to know?"

She stared at me for a long moment. "It was Shannen's, wasn't it? You can tell me. It's not like I'm going to go fight her or something."

I didn't answer, but my face must have said it all.

"I knew it." She pulled the fabric of her T-shirt away from her stomach and wrung it out. Skin. She was showing skin. And her stomach was seriously ripped. "It's so insane. We used to be best friends." She shook her head and looked out across the court with this sad look on her face. "I knew they were going to be pissed, but I never thought . . . I mean, I thought we'd all get over it."

I swallowed hard. "Sucks."

She nodded. "Yeah. Whatever. It doesn't matter. I guess we're really just not going to be friends anymore. I just have to deal with it."

Ally let the hem of her shirt drop over her abs again and glanced up at me. I tore my eyes from her stomach, and she blushed. Crap. Suddenly I was finding it hard to swallow. And now I was staring at her lips.

"So, then . . . what should we do?" I asked. I mean, she was here. She'd come here in the middle of a downpour to hang out with me. Even though last night she'd been kissing David Drake at the Harvest Ball. That had to mean something, right?

She smiled slightly. "Play another game?"

My heart dropped. Or maybe she was just using me for her basketball court. I stood up, relieved to put some space between the two of us. Relieved to have something to do other than think about kissing her. I grabbed the ball from the ground where we'd left it.

"You're on."

Did you hear? Ally Ryan's going out with David Drake.

Please. Everyone knows that. My mother knows that.

Oh. Well, I didn't. I kind of thought she had a crush on Jake Graydon.

Why did you think that?

I don't know. She's always, like, staring at him.

So is half the female population of Orchard Hill. And some of the male.

Whatever. There's just this vibe whenever they're in a room together.

Okay, Dr. Phil. Whatever you say. But Ally and Jake? That could never happen.

Why not? I think they'd be kind of cute together.

First of all, he's a Crestie and she's a Norm. It's just not done. And second of all . . .

Second of all what?

Second of all, Shannen Moore would scratch her eyes right out.

Why? Do you think Shannen likes Jake?

Isn't it obvious? She's just waiting for him to wake up and smell the soul mate.

Whoa. So, why doesn't Jake ask her out already?

Because. He's a guy.

Which means?

Which means he is, by definition, oblivious.

ally

I dropped my old Orchard Hill High duffel bag on the bottom bleacher in the gym and sat down to retie my sneakers. It was the second week of November and the first day of basketball practice. By Friday Coach Prescott would have to cut the thirty-one hopeful players down to a final roster of fifteen. As I casually checked out the competition, I saw a lot of familiar faces—girls I had played with on JV freshman year. I could imagine that the lineup would be similar to that one, and as long as none of them had developed crazy skills since I'd been gone, I had a pretty good shot of making the team.

"Hey, Ally! Come shoot around with us," Jessica Landry shouted, waving me over.

Jessica was a Norm senior who I'd always thought was the coolest girl on the team. She was one of those girls who wore sweats practically every day but always looked good anyway. Plus, she had a smile for everyone all the time. Not once in my life had I ever felt uncomfortable around her. I jogged over to join her and her friends, slapping a few hands and feeling lighthearted and ready for a workout.

I had just hit a sweet three from the corner when Shannen walked into the gym. My gut twisted with nerves, which just annoyed me. I was not going to let Shannen Moore make me nervous. She had no power over me. If anything, I should be pissed off at her.

Coach gave one bleat on her whistle and shouted at us to grab some water before we got started. I'd just dropped down on the bottom bleacher and was fishing in my bag for my water bottle when the toes of Shannen's sneakers suddenly lined up with mine. My stomach hollowed out.

"Hey," she said. Her foot twisted so that the side was to the floor for a second, then righted itself. She wore an Orchard Hill basketball T-shirt and held a ball loosely between her crossed wrists and her stomach. Her dark hair was back in a sloppy ponytail, those long bangs half-hiding her eyes. How she expected to play ball with her hair in her face all the time, I had no idea.

"What do you want?" I asked, standing.

We were exactly the same height. Always had been. It was like God had put us on the same growth schedule when we were born, and in seventh grade we'd both shot up and started towering over all the boys in our class. By the time I left in freshman year, most of them still hadn't caught up. Even now, we were taller than a lot of them.

"Whoa." She held her hands up and backed up a step. "What's with the angst?"

I rolled my eyes, laughed bitterly, and slammed her shoulder with mine as I walked by.

"Do you have a problem with me?" Shannen asked.

I whirled around on her. "What do you *want*, Shannen?"

She blinked a few times, appearing legitimately surprised. Had she woken up with amnesia this morning? Did she have zero memory of the past two months?

"I just thought since we're going to be on the same team together it might be time to call a truce, that's all."

"A truce," I repeated acerbically.

"Yeah. I mean—"

I took a few steps toward her. "Okay, you want a truce? How about you start by apologizing for the lawn jockey?"

"What?" she said.

"I know it was you," I told her. "That prank had Shannen Moore written all over it. Do you even realize what that did to my mom? You want to screw with me, fine. Whatever. But she doesn't deserve it."

"Wow. Look who suddenly grew a spine," Shannen joked.

I rolled my eyes and turned away from her.

"All right, fine. I'm sorry. The lawn jockey thing was stupid," she said.

I paused, looking down at the floor. At least we were getting somewhere. She dribbled the ball over and held it out to me on her palm. "Are we cool now?"

She had to be joking. Like one apology was going to make up for everything. For freezing me out, for insulting me over and over again, for ostracizing me for something over which I had zero control. I took a deep breath and held it, clutching onto every bit of courage in me.

"No," I said. "I want to know why. Why have you been so awful to me since I've been back?"

Shannen laughed contemptuously and shook her head, dribbling the ball from left to right.

"Don't laugh. I'm serious." I stole the ball with a resounding slap and held it against my chest. "What the hell did I ever do to you?"

She looked up at me, pushed her bangs out of her eyes, and clicked her teeth together twice before she answered. "I know what you and Hammond did the night you moved away. I was there."

The edges of the room blurred, and the laughter and shouts seemed to echo between my ears.

"What?"

She crossed her arms over her chest and cocked one knee, looking off toward the scoreboard. "My parents were arguing, as usual, and I heard my mom say something about how you guys were leaving that night. I tried to call you, but it went right to voice mail, so I snuck out and rode my bike over to your house. I couldn't let you leave without saying good-bye."

She stared at me then, an accusation in her eyes. My heart thumped with guilt. I'd really hurt her by not calling.

"I opened the front door—your parents were fighting too, so they didn't hear me—and when I got to your room there you two were, writhing on top of each other on your bed."

Her lips screwed up in disgust as she looked me up and down. I felt nauseous as the memory of that night swirled through me. I'd been avoiding thinking about it since I'd been back, but now here it was, in vivid HD. Hammond's breath on my face, his hand on my cheek, the scent of the rain on his clothes. He'd asked me to go out with him just a month earlier, and I'd said no. I'd said I thought of him as a friend. And two weeks later he and Chloe had gotten together and were all lovey-dovey and inseparable. Chloe had been in love with him forever—had always thought they were destined to be together—so everyone was happy for them, but I had felt a little . . . jealous. I mean, one minute he was saying he liked me, and the next second he was all in love with her. But even so, I never would have done anything about it. Even then I knew that my feelings were stupid—that I was just wanting what I couldn't have. But then, everything fell apart.

"How could you do that to Chloe?" Shannen asked. "How do you even live with yourself after you stab someone in the back like that?"

"Shannen, I know how it looked, but honestly, it was just a kiss—"

"A very long, very horizontal kiss," she said, snatching the ball back again.

"I know, but it was the worst night of my life," I said. "I didn't even know what was going on. My parents were screaming at each other, and my dad was yelling at me to pack and I didn't even know where we were going or why. All I knew was that my dad had fucked up and he'd lost our house and everyone was mad at us and we were never coming back. That was it. And then Hammond took the shortcut over and climbed up to my room, and he was all upset and saying all this stuff about how he was going to miss me and he wished I'd said yes when he'd asked me out and all this crap, and we just . . . kissed."

Shannen stared at me as if she was letting this sink in. As if she was trying to decide whether or not to believe it.

"It's the truth, Shannen," I said. "I would never do anything to hurt any of you guys. You know that. I was just . . . I wasn't me."

She opened her mouth to say something, but the whistle blew.

"Line it up! Let's do some warm-ups, people! Come on!" Coach clapped her hands a few times. I felt like the real world with all its lights and sounds and colors was suddenly flooding in on me. It made me temporarily dizzy, and I had to shut my eyes. As the rest of the players lined up for drills, Shannen and I didn't move. We stood in the middle of the court, facing off.

"Why haven't you told her?" I asked. "Why have you kept it a secret all this time?"

"Because it would kill her," Shannen answered. "I have a little thing called a conscience. That's why I didn't mail your invitation to her sweet sixteen with all the others. I didn't want you and Hammond hooking up in the coat room or something on the biggest night of her life."

So that explained it. The sweet sixteen confusion. Shannen had taken matters into her own hands.

"We would never have done that," I said, my voice a croak.

"So you say." She looked down, bounced the ball once, then caught it in both hands. "Anyway, I also figured that keeping your secret kind of made us even."

"Even? For what?"

"You've kept my secret, and I've kept yours," she said.

Right. Her secret. I was the only person in the world who knew what had really happened the night her brother, Charlie, ran away. I knew that Shannen's father came home drunk and went nuts when he found out Charlie had crashed his mom's car. And I knew that whatever threats he was making had scared Shannen enough to run to my house and call the police. Her dad had been arrested and thrown in jail for the night to sober up, and her brother was gone by the time their dad got home. Shannen's father had gotten probation and community service for disturbing the peace, since Charlie was eighteen and not around to bring charges, but after that Shannen's father just got mean. And he started drinking even more than he already did—always saying that if he ever found out who called the police on him that night, he'd kill them. I could still see Shannen trembling with fear that night in my dad's home office. Could still see the look of terror in her eyes the night of her dad's court date, when she made me swear I'd never tell anyone. She blamed herself for her dad's humiliation and her brother's leaving. I tried to tell her that it was her dad's fault, not hers, but she didn't think her parents would see it that way.

"Do you . . . did Charlie ever . . . ?"

"Come home?" Shannen said. "No. He e-mails me every once in a while, but that's it. And he made me promise not to tell my parents."

So that made two secrets I now knew.

"Where is he?" I asked.

"Arizona. Eric Toricelli went to school out there, so he's crashing with him, taking classes and working," Shannen said. Then she eyed me up and down. "And if you tell your mother this, I'll hunt you down and kill you."

"I know," I said. "I know how to keep a secret, Shannen. I think I've shown that. So I guess that means I'm not the worst person in the world."

Shannen exhaled through her nose, then cracked a small smile. "Maybe not the worst."

"Ladies! Are you waiting for an engraved invitation?" Coach shouted at us. "Let's go!"

We turned together and walked toward the opposite end of the gym. For the first time since I'd been back, I felt comfortable being in the same room with Shannen. It was a tentative feeling, but it was there. So that was our truce. We each knew something about the other that we didn't want anyone else to know.

It wasn't much, but I would take it.

jake

I used to think there was nothing worse than having my mom's voice pop into my head when I was hooking up with a girl. But I was wrong. There is something worse. It's when I'm hooking up with a girl and my mom's voice *and* Ally's voice *and* the voice of my stupid fucking SAT tutor *all* pop into my head at the same time.

"Jake? What's wrong?" Lisa Freckles asked as I pulled away for the fifth time. Her name wasn't really Lisa Freckles. It was just that I couldn't ever remember her last name, and she had lots of freckles on her shoulders.

"Nothing," I said.

"Good." She smiled. She had a nice smile, especially now that she'd gotten her braces off. "Then come back."

She pulled me to her and kissed me. All around us my friends were partying like the rock stars they thought they were. It was Chloe's seventeenth birthday, and her parents had rented out the entire Houston Hotel in New York. We all had rooms to go back to after the party so we could drink as much as we wanted and they wouldn't have to worry about us getting home.

Yeah. That was Chloe's dad for you. If he'd lost some of his money with Ally's father like everyone else had, he probably still would have found a way to throw this party. Chloe was the center of his universe, or so he was always telling her. It was just too bad that Chloe was freezing Ally out even though her family hadn't been affected. Because otherwise Ally would be here and maybe I could be making out with her instead of Lisa Freckles. Except that Ally would be making out with David Drake. Was that what they were doing right now? Hooking up at some party? Dorkus Drake got to kiss Ally Ryan whenever he wanted. In what universe was that okay?

And now I was thinking about her again. Sonafabitch. I pressed Lisa Freckles back into the couch, trying to concentrate on her and only her. She was a cool girl. We'd gone to a concert together last summer and actually had fun. She deserved some concentration.

Conflagration is to fire as tsunami is to what? my SAT tutor said in my ear.

I kissed her harder, trying to shut out the voice. Lisa moaned a little.

Kissing Lisa Freckles is to kissing Ally Ryan as what is to what? Ally's voice teased.

I shoved my fingers into Lisa's hair.

You have to break thirteen hundred this time, Jake. Fordham does not accept scores beneath thirteen hundred, my mom snapped.

I pulled away again, faked a cough, and grabbed my drink, downing half of it in one gulp. It didn't stop the voices. And Lisa was tugging on my shirt. I took a deep breath and sighed. This was going to be a very long night.

A peal of familiar laughter caught my attention, and Shannen, Faith, and Chloe all semistumbled into the room, clearly drunk. They were cracking up uncontrollably as they teetered over and dropped down onto the couch. Chloe was so out of it, she half sat on my lap, then slid off to the side.

"This is the best birthday ever!" she cheered, throwing her arms up. Champagne sloshed over the rim of her glass onto my leg. There's a reason Chloe hardly ever drinks. She gets sloppy and loud.

"You know it!" Shannen said, finishing off her own champagne.

"Oh, but I wish Ally was here." Chloe stuck out her bottom lip and leaned her head on my shoulder. My heart skipped at the mention of Ally. I shot Lisa a look of apology for the interruption. She sat up straighter and smoothed her hair.

"You so do *not!*" Faith countered, shoving Chloe's knee. "We hate Ally."

"Exactly," Shannen said with a nod.

"Yeah, but . . . don't you feel kinda bad for her?" Chloe said, blinking rapidly. "I mean, she lives in a condo, her mom's all depressed, and her dad's, like, a waiter . . . " She sipped her champagne. "It's just sad."

Shannen and Faith looked at one another as if they'd just been told they won a lifetime supply of nail polish.

"Wait. What?" Shannen blurted.

"Her dad's a what?" Faith added.

Chloe's hand flew to her mouth. She looked at me, wide-eyed.

"I thought no one knew where her dad was," Shannen said, sitting forward.

"I don't. I mean, they don't. No one does." Chloe got up, steadied herself on her high heels, and looked around. "Where's my cake? I want my cake now. Mom!?" She waved her hands over her head, trying to get her mother's attention from across the room. Her mother looked over disapprovingly.

Shannen got up and grabbed Chloe's arm. "You know where Ally's dad is?"

"No." Chloe shook her head.

"Yes, you do. You said he's a waiter," Shannen said hungrily. "Is he working for your dad or something? At one of his restaurants?"

Chloe hesitated. "I can't talk about this."

"Chloe—"

"No. It's my birthday, and I don't have to talk about this if I don't want to."

At that moment, Chloe's parents arrived. Chloe looked up at her tall, broad, seriously intimidating father.

"Can we do the cake now?" she pleaded.

"Of course! You're the birthday girl!" he said in a booming voice.

As her parents whisked her away, Shannen tried to go after them.

"Shannen, leave it," I said, standing.

"What?" Her eyes flashed angrily. "No, Jake, you don't understand. This is huge."

I'll bet. And I had a feeling that whatever Shannen's reasons were for wanting to know where Ally's dad was, she didn't have Ally's feelings in mind.

"But it's Chloe's birthday, and she doesn't want to talk about it. Just leave her alone."

Shannen hesitated. She looked over her shoulder at the front of the room, where two hotel workers were rolling out a huge pink cake.

"Whatever. Since when are you all on Chloe's side?" she groused.

This wasn't about Chloe. It was about Ally. But I wasn't going to tell her that. "Just relax, all right? It's a party."

"Everyone! Let's gather around to sing happy birthday!" Mrs. Appleby called out, holding Chloe around the waist tightly as if trying to keep her upright.

We all moved to the front of the room, Lisa wrapping her arm around me. I held my breath while everyone else sang happy birthday, and I watched Faith and Shannen whisper in a way that could not be good. Not for Ally. Not for Chloe. Not for anyone.

ally

"Anyone want anything else?" my mother asked, placing her fork down on her empty plate.

"No, thank you. I'm stuffed," Gray Nathanson said, leaning back in his chair with a satisfied smile.

"I'm fine, thanks." Gray's daughter, Quinn, folded her hands primly in her lap. She had straight blond hair, a smattering of freckles, and the most perfect posture I'd ever seen outside of Chloe's. I suspected she wasn't overly happy to be there, since she hadn't cracked a smile all night and hadn't said more than three words at a time, but she'd been very polite. "Everything was delicious."

"Seriously, Ms. Ryan. I may never eat at home again," David said.

And suddenly everyone was looking at me.

"Yeah. It was great," I said halfheartedly.

Really I just wanted to get this dinner over with as quickly as humanly possible. It was the day after Thanksgiving, and Mom had decided to invite over her new boyfriend and his perfectly gorgeous daughter for dinner. Of course, she hadn't felt the need to share this plan with me until four this afternoon. Until then I hadn't known about either the dinner or the fact that she considered him her boyfriend. As soon as I heard the word come out of her mouth, I was on the phone with David begging him to join us. Which he had. Because he was the best boyfriend ever.

"Did you like your stuffed pepper, Ally?" Gray asked me.

My mother placed her hand on Gray's arm, which was

119

resting on the table, elbows off, of course. He looked down at her fingers and smiled. Ick. Did people their age really think that the rest of us wanted to be subjected to their PDA?

"Ally? Gray asked you a question," my mother said.

"Oh, yeah," I replied, pushing my fork into the grayish mush at the center of the hollowed-out green pepper on my plate—the one thing Gray had contributed to the meal and the only thing I hadn't eaten. "It's great."

"You haven't even tasted it," Quinn said snidely.

Okay. So much for polite.

But, then, Quinn was fourteen, a freshman, and a Crestie. I was sure she'd been programmed to hate me by the behavior of, the gossip from, and the general vibe coming off my former friends—older, influential Cresties whom she no doubt worshipped. Also, I had to cut her some slack. She'd lost her mom to cancer a few years ago, while mine was alive and well and awesome.

"No, I did. I liked it," I protested. I took a bite and almost gagged. Way too much garlic. Somehow I managed to swallow, then took a huge gulp of soda.

"She did. I saw her," David chimed in. "Didn't you guys hear all the *yums* and *mmms*?"

I shot him a silencing look. That was a little much.

"It's okay," Gray said, smiling at me. "They're not for everyone."

I swear I saw my reflection in those teeth. I forced myself to smile back, remembering that I wanted my mother to be happy and that this doctor man seemed to make her just that. Even if he did have floppy hair that was about twenty years too young for him and was wearing a trendy V-necked T-shirt that exposed his curly gray-and-black chest hair. I mean, really, what did the two of them have in common? Other than the crest, I mean. Was it possible that my mother was dating him solely because he lived up there? Because she thought it would help her get back in with her so-called friends?

I liked to think my mother was better than that, but reclaiming her old life—however much of it she could reclaim—was still so important to her, just like it had been to me when we'd first moved back here. I guess it was possible that she was unconsciously using this guy to get what she wanted. It would definitely explain her spending so much time with a person who was the polar opposite of my father. It was kind of depressing, actually. Back when my parents were together, I had always been so proud of her independence. She was the only Crestie mother who worked—she was the librarian at the middle school—and she was always doing her own thing. Able to go to parties without my dad when he had to work late and not be all self-conscious about it. Always telling my friends how fulfilling it was to have her own career, knowing their moms expected them to be ladies who lunched and spa-dayed, just like them. But now she was looking at Gray with an almost imperceptible desperation in her eyes. Like he was somehow going to save her. From what? I knew we weren't rich anymore, but she had a new and awesome job, and we were doing okay. So, what did we need him for?

"So, Ally, I hear you're a basketball superstar," Gray said, sitting back in his chair and taking a sip of his white wine.

My heart skipped, and I glanced automatically at my mom. So, they'd been talking about me? She shrugged, like, what do you expect? I felt suddenly hot and glanced at the door.

"I used to play a bit myself," Gray continued. "Could never get Quinn here interested in it, though."

I felt like I was supposed to say something, but I couldn't think of what.

"I like basketball," Quinn said. "I cheer for basketball, don't I?"

"That you do," her father said, giving her a fond smile.

A cheerleader. Shocker.

"Were you on the team back in Baltimore, Ally?" Gray asked me.

"Yep," I replied.

There was an odd, uncomfortable feeling rising up inside my chest, and it wasn't from that one bite of stuffed pepper.

"They won the regional championship," my mother put in proudly. "Ally scored twenty points."

"Wow. I didn't know that," David said, his mouth still full of his second helping. "That's awesome."

"Absolutely awesome," Gray added. He was trying too hard. Which made me like him even less. "We should shoot around sometime."

My heart was pounding like I'd just run a five-minute mile. For some reason, the room was swimming. I really didn't want to talk about this anymore. And I really didn't want to shoot around with him.

"So, are you a forward?"

"Yep," I said. I pushed back from the table. "Who wants dessert?"

"There's apple pie in the fridge," my mother said. "But we should clear the table first. . . ."

"I got it." I stood up and gathered as many plates as I could, clanging them together noisily and dropping a fork on the floor, where it bounced under the table.

"I'll help," David offered.

Even though there was still food on his plate, he grabbed a few glasses and followed me over to the open kitchen area. I set the plates down with a crash and took a deep breath. David turned the water on in the sink full blast and whispered over it.

"Are you okay?" he asked.

"M'fine." I rinsed off a plate, my hands still shaking.

"No, you're not. You're step-freaked," David said.

"Step-freaked?" I repeated.

"It's the particular brand of freaked you get when encountering a potential stepdad," he whispered, wiping off a dish with a purple sponge.

"Gray is not a potential stepdad," I said through my teeth.

"Every dude they bring home is a potential stepdad. That's why you get so step-freaked. Believe me, I know. My mom one time brought home this guy from Chadwick's Pub with forearms wider than my head. I looked exactly like you do right now."

"Your parents are divorced?" I asked. Even though we'd been hanging out for the past few months, we did it mostly at school or at Annie's house, and I realized now that David didn't talk much about his family. Maybe this was why.

He nodded as he scraped the contents of a dish into the garbage. "Yeah. They were high school sweethearts, so my mom never dated anyone else. She's spent the past two years making up for lost time."

"Wow. That sucks. I'm sorry," I said.

David shrugged and straightened up. "It's no big deal."

But it was. It was a big deal. As David kept cleaning up, I felt as if the walls were crowding in around me. He clearly had it much worse than I did, and he talked about it like it was nothing. Like it was a normal part of life. Was that how I was going to be talking about my mom's men in a couple of years? The thought made my stomach turn.

"So? What do you think of Gray?" my mother asked, coming up behind me and placing her hands on my shoulders. "He's nice, isn't he?"

I couldn't respond. Couldn't talk at all. The lump in my throat was too large.

"He's great. Not to mention a culinary genius," David replied brightly, coming to my rescue. He tugged on a pair of pink dish-washing gloves and snapped the cuffs. My mother and I both stared at him. David paled slightly. "In fact, I think I'll go ask him for that pepper recipe," he said, getting the hint and moseying off.

"You like him, right?" my mother whispered. "I hope you do, because I think we're going to be seeing a lot more of him. He even invited us to the holiday Sunday dinner next month."

My eyes instantly prickled over with memories. Sunday dinners. They were an old tradition that normally included just the six families—us, the Applebys, the Moores, the Kirkpatricks, the Rosses, and the Steins. But at Christmas, the dinner was usually held at Chloe's house, and the rest of the crest families were invited. Finding an in to this particular soiree must have been a dream come true for my mom—a chance to finally get back in with her friends. Didn't she realize that if they hadn't tried to hang out with her by now, there must have been a reason? If my friends couldn't be around me because of what my dad had done, their parents were probably ten times as pissed off.

"Are you sure you want to go?" I asked, trying to keep my voice neutral. "I mean, we barely know those people anymore."

A flash of uncertainty passed through her eyes, but it was gone as quickly as it came. "Oh, hon, they're my lifelong friends," she said, giving me a squeeze. "They may be angry now, but they know I didn't have anything to do with what happened. Once we're all together again, they'll realize how silly they've been."

Yeah, right. Just like my friends have.

"Okay," I said, my voice thick.

"Besides, Gray invited me, and I don't want to let him down," she said, smiling across the room at him. "I really like him, Ally."

I took a deep breath and silently recited as many NBA basketball teams as I could think of to calm my racing thoughts. My insides felt all hot and gooey. Between thinking about my dad, about Gray, about my possible future as the daughter of either a serial dater or of Gray's second wife, and about Sunday dinner— which Jake Graydon would most definitely be attending—I was completely overwhelmed.

"That's great, Mom," I said finally. "I'm really happy for you."

I just wished that I meant it.

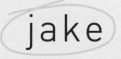

jake

"Dude, so what are we *doing* tonight?" Todd asked, turning the sugar canister upside down over his large coffee at Jump, Java, and Wail! on Friday night.

"I thought we were going into the city," I said, reaching past him for a napkin.

"Yeah, but what're we gonna *do* in the city?" Trevor asked.

"I say we hit Rock Center and trip as many people on the ice as we can," Todd said.

"The line to get on the ice is, like, three hours," Hammond said, leaning back against the wall and taking a sip of his drink. "Your balls'll freeze right off."

Trevor covered his balls with both hands and pulled a face. "All right. Not doing that."

"Dude. Ally Ryan." Todd nodded toward the front of the shop.

My stomach dropped and we all turned to look out the plate glass window. Ally was across the street, outside Scoops Ice Cream, with David Drake. He was trying to attack her with his ice cream cone. She screeched and ran.

"Dork," Hammond said, earning a laugh from the Idiot Twins.

Slowly, not taking our eyes off them, we all walked over to the counter at the window. In the corner, some dude with a beard played acoustic tunes on his guitar. A couple of older people sat in chairs nearby, swaying to the music.

"Dude, is it just me, or did Ally Ryan get hot?" Trevor asked.

"She was always hot," Hammond replied, taking a sip of his coffee as he stared.

I glanced at him, but he didn't follow with an insult. Which he totally would have done if Chloe, Shannen, or Faith had been there. I wondered if Chloe really did know where Ally's father was. And would Ally want to know, if she could?

"What do you think *they're* doing tonight?" Trevor asked, taking a long swig of hot chocolate.

"Looks like they're having ice cream," I said. David went in for a kiss. I looked away.

"Yeah, but after," Todd said as he took a seat on one of the stools. "Like, what do Norms *do* on weekends?"

Hammond and I exchanged a glance.

"They have parties and shit, right?" Hammond said.

"Of course. It's not like they're aliens or something," I said.

"I wonder what a Norm party's like," Trevor said, narrowing his eyes and sticking his chin out. "You think they have chips and dips?"

"Dude. We should totally crash one," Todd said.

"Tonight?" Hammond asked.

"No. Not tonight. Tonight we are city-bound!" Trevor announced. He and Todd slapped hands above their heads, dumping out half their drinks in the process.

As we got up to walk out, I glanced back at Ally and David again. They were sitting on a bench in the freezing cold, cuddled against each other, eating their ice cream. I felt a surge of jealousy and suddenly wanted to go over there and pummel Dorkus Drake to within an inch of his life. And just like that, I didn't want to go into the city. I wanted to crash a Norm party instead. If I could just guarantee that Ally would be there. And that David Drake wouldn't.

ally

"Yes! That's game!"

I threw my arms above my head, holding the air hockey paddle aloft. The crowd cheered and lifted their plastic cups.

Across the table, David hung his head, shaking it in what could only be wonder at my air hockey prowess.

"Two out of three?" he asked.

I laughed and twirled the paddle in my palm. "I don't know. Are you sure you can take it?"

David blushed but laughed. One of the best things about him was his ability to take a joke. I loved that I didn't have to walk on eggshells with him. A lot of people wouldn't have enjoyed being trash-talked by their girlfriends in front of a party full of people. But David had a sense of humor.

"Come on, Ryan. You've gotta give the kid a chance to redeem himself," Marshall Moss said, sliding out of the crowd and slinging one of his long, lanky arms around my shoulder. Marshall was the center of the boys' basketball team and one of the nicer guys I'd re-met since coming back to Orchard Hill. Not to mention cute with his warm brown eyes, dark skin, and lopsided smile. He lived on the Norm side of town, but in one of the bigger houses near the library.

"Well, it is your party," I said, pushing him lightly away with my elbow. "Guess I have to do as you say." I looked across at David. "Wanna take the first shot?"

"I think I have that right as the loser," he replied. He yanked the puck out of the slot and placed it on the table as I clicked my scorekeeper down to zero-zero. "Here we go."

I held my paddle on the table, feeling the tickle of the air under my arm. I was totally on my game tonight. David was going down. Poor dude had no idea.

Behind him I saw a couple of pairs of legs coming down the basement stairs. The second David hit the puck, the first person arrived in the doorway. It was Jake Graydon. What. The eff. Was he doing here?

"Yes! One nothing!" David shouted.

Half the crowd cheered. As David turned to high-five with a couple of the guys, I tore my eyes away from Jake. Sure enough, the red puck was sitting in the slot right in front of me. Jake smirked at me. I narrowed my eyes. Thanks a lot, buddy.

Did he not know that this was a Norm party? Didn't he have somewhere more Crestie to be? Somewhere fabulous and expensive where he could be surrounded by a hundred drunk hotties to choose from?

We hadn't spoken once since our basketball game in the rain, and part of me had started to feel that the Jake chapter of my life—short as it was—was officially over. That I'd only be seeing him from afar for the rest of my life. And I was fine with that. I was. Because I had David. And in the past few weeks we'd been hanging out together a lot. And kissing a lot. And I was even getting used to it. It was . . . nice.

But now here Jake was, and instantly the Jakesession was back full force. The entire atmosphere of the party changed with him in the room. The air actually thickened and sizzled. No one could tear their eyes from him.

Or maybe that was just me.

I took the puck out of the slot and placed it on the table. "Lucky shot."

"Yeah, yeah. More like the beginning of your downward spiral." David flicked his fingers at me. "Bring it."

Slowly, Jake slid behind David over to the wall at the side of the table. I wished he would just go away. Go find some freshman to scam on or get himself a beer and a spot on the couch.

But he didn't. A couple of the guys made room for him, and he leaned back against the wall to watch. He was wearing a black sweater with a half-zip and a high collar that just about grazed his perfect cheekbones. And he was staring at me with those light blue eyes. I felt as if my blood were thinning out. No air was getting to my brain.

"What're you, scared?" David taunted, oblivious.

I looked at him. My boyfriend. David Drake, my boyfriend. Adorable David in his Adidas hoodie who had just last night selflessly saved me from alone time with my potential step-family. What was wrong with me?

Taking a deep breath, I leaned into the table.

Jake is not here. Jake is *not* here.

"Go, Ally!" Jake cheered.

I slammed the puck. It ricocheted right off the far wall and zoomed into my goal without David ever touching it. Laughter and cheers filled the room. My face burned. This was going to be a very short game.

When I made my first goal, Jake slow-clapped for me. When David scored three in a row, he put his fingertips at the corners of his mouth and made a little sad-clown face. When I was down three to fourteen and about to lose, he simply stood there, smiling and shaking his head.

And as annoyed as I was, the entire time I was *this close* to breaking out in a grin. Because he was flirting with me. No one but he and I knew that he was, but he definitely was. Why? Why was he here? Why was he wasting his time watching me play air hockey?

"Game point," David announced.

I decided at that moment to do something I'd never done before in my life: let someone win. Considering I'd spent the past fifteen minutes obsessing not about him but about the guy silently mocking me from the sidelines, I figured he deserved it. Besides, chances were he was going to win anyway. I was just putting myself out of my misery.

He hit the puck. It went wide. I sent it back, right to him. He slammed it off the sidewall, and it sailed into my goal.

"Yes! That's game!" David said, double high-fiving anyone who'd reciprocate. "All right. One more."

I didn't think I could take one more game. I dropped my paddle onto the table. "How about we just call it a tie?" I said.

"Oh, come on! You're just scared I'll beat you," David replied.

"No. I'm just scared I'll beat you and your fragile male ego will never recover," I replied.

A bunch of people responded to that one, but David placed his paddle down and raised his hands in surrender.

"All right, all right. I'll take the tie."

We walked around the table and met in the middle, about two feet from where Jake was standing.

"Good game," David said, putting his arms around me.

I felt hot and conspicuous all of a sudden. Jake's gaze burned a complete hole in my cheek. "Good game," I replied.

Then David leaned in to kiss me, and everyone *awwwed* and jeered.

"Get a room!" someone shouted, earning a round of laughter.

When I pulled away, David gave me a hug and I rested my chin on his shoulder. Jake was right there, staring into my eyes. My heart tap-danced like mad. He smiled at me, shaking his head. I wasn't even sure what the joke was, but I finally let myself smile back.

Kissing and hugging one boy, smiling behind his back at another.

This was very not me.

Ally Ryan is coming to Sunday dinner.

No.

I swear. I was at Song's getting my mani-pedi, and Faith and Chloe were there and they could not stop talking about it.

But how? Norms never get invited to Sunday dinner.

I heard her mom is dating Dr. Nathanson.

Quinn's dad? Shut. Up.

Wow. Looks like Mrs. Ryan is trying to claw her way back up the social ladder.

Like mother like daughter.

What do you mean?

I heard Ally Ryan was totally flirting with Jake Graydon at some Norm party over Thanksgiving.

No way. Isn't she going out with that David Drake person?

Yeah, but why drink the milk when you can get the crème de la crème?

There is no way those girls are going to let that happen.

I don't know. She is Ally Ryan.

What does that mean?

Somehow that girl always gets what she wants.

ally

It was weird, being back in Chloe's house. Aside from the fact that pretty much everyone in the library was staring at me or whispering about me, not one detail had changed. The antique velvet chaise we used to get yelled at for climbing on still sat in the corner beneath the green glass reading lamp. There were fresh flowers on every table—red and white poinsettias, just like every other December. The leather couches at the center of the room still looked like they'd just been reupholstered, and the same five coffee table books were displayed on the table between them: *Victorian Homes of San Francisco*, *The Art of Georgia O'Keeffe*, *Covered Bridges of Massachusetts*, *The Life of Paul Newman*, and *The True Story of the* Titanic. I could still remember the day we'd flipped through that last one fifty times, page by page, looking for a photo of Kate Winslet and being thoroughly baffled when there wasn't one.

On the other side of the room, next to the twin study desks, Jake was talking to Hammond, both of them keeping their eyes on the crowd. Suddenly I caught his eye, and he tilted his head in an almost imperceptible nod. My body temperature skyrocketed to nuclear levels. I turned around and studied the spines of the books, pretending not to notice him. My phone beeped, and I fished it out of my clutch purse. It was a text from Annie.

Still alive?

I laughed under my breath and texted back.

So far.

Good. Take notes!!! & come over after. We can
detox you! :p

"So. Having fun?"

I tucked the phone away as Shannen sidled up to me and
offered a cup of cider. She was wearing a black silk dress with
a high, ruffled neck and no sleeves. Her heels gave her a good
three inches on me. She leaned back against the floor-to-
ceiling bookshelf behind me and surveyed the room. I put my
clutch down and took the cup.

"Couldn't you get excommunicated for talking to me?"
I said, feeling grateful nonetheless. She was the first person
who'd spoken to me all night. I took a sip of my drink. It tasted
like the apples had already turned. Weird. Mrs. Appleby was
nothing if not a perfectionist.

"Yes, but I have my excuses all lined up," she replied, talking out of the side of her mouth. "First, it's the holidays, and
talking to you is a form of charity."

"Gee, thanks," I said.

"And second, I'm drunk," Shannen added, lifting her cup
in a toast.

My lips pursed. "Is that what I taste? Did you spike this?"

Shannen shrugged. "What's Sunday dinner without a little
smuggled alcohol?"

I bit my tongue to keep from rattling off the ten things
wrong with her logic, not wanting to browbeat the one person
who had acknowledged my existence. Other than Jake and his
nod.

"You should have some. Drown your sorrows," she said.

"What sorrows?" I asked.

She took a deep breath and turned toward me, resting her

shoulder against the shelves now. "You know, it's the holidays . . . your dad is MIA. . . ."

My throat completely closed off.

"I mean, don't get me wrong, sometimes I wish *my* father would disappear," she joked. "But do you ever wonder where he is . . . where he's living . . . whether he's working?"

"Of course I do," I said, telling myself she was just making conversation. That she wasn't trying to be mean. She couldn't know what it actually felt like, the not knowing. How whenever someone brought it up, it was like they'd attached a vacuum hose to my heart and hit the "maximum suckage" button.

"Did your dad ever work in a service job? Like as a waiter or anything?" she asked, narrowing her eyes.

"What? I don't know. Why?" I asked, my pulse racing.

She shrugged and turned to face the room again. "No reason. I just sometimes wonder where a person like that ends up."

I took a shaky breath and sipped my cider, then spit it back into the cup when I remembered there was alcohol in it. What the hell was this line of questioning about? I felt an intense need to change the subject but couldn't think of a single thing to talk about, what with all the emotional trauma. My gaze immediately traveled to Jake, the one remotely friendly face in the room.

"So, what do you think of our Jake?" Shannen asked, as if reading my mind.

I started. The girl was seriously fraying my nerves. "Why? Did he say something about me?"

Shannen frowned thoughtfully. "No. I just thought you might have formed an opinion about the guy who now lives in your room. Why? Should he have said something about you?"

Out of the corner of my eye I noticed Faith slipping through the side door that led to the conservatory. I took it as a good excuse to bail.

"I'll be right back," I told Shannen.

I set my drink on the bookshelf and took off after Faith, knowing Shannen would think I was rude, but not caring. The conservatory was cool and quiet, the glass walls surrounding the grand piano looking out over Mrs. Appleby's prize rose garden. Faith stood in the center of the room, fiddling with her cell.

"Faith," I whispered.

Her hand flew to her throat. When she saw it was me she grimaced. "God! You scared the hell out of me," she said in full voice. Then she looked me up and down. "Where'd you get that outfit? Walmart?"

I chose to let the comment roll off my back. "Can we talk?"

Faith crossed her arms over her chest. Her long blond hair was back in a sleek ponytail, and she wore a pink party dress with cap sleeves and a black sash around the waist.

"Why? So you can call me a bitch again?" she asked.

"No. I'm sorry about that," I said. I ran my fingertip along the music stand where Chloe used to practice her flute. "I just . . . you're so different," I said, trying to sound diplomatic. "I guess I was just shocked."

"Different how?" she asked, her eyes like slits. "Oh, you mean because I have a life? Because I'm not just following you around like some puppy dog?"

I blinked in surprise. "You never followed me around like a puppy dog."

"Whatever. You loved the fact that you were more popular

than me. That you got to bring me along to parties I wasn't exactly invited to, like I was some orphan you were helping out. That you and Chloe and Shannen were like a little threesome," she said, lifting a hand. "Well, guess what? There's a new threesome now. And we don't need a fourth."

I swallowed hard. "I don't understand why you have to be so mean," I said. "I thought we were friends."

She pulled her head back, and for a second, I saw her. The old Faith. My friend who was sweet and kind and cared about other people's feelings.

"Yeah, well, friends don't just disappear in the middle of the night and never call," she said. "Friends don't desert each other."

"But it wasn't my fault. And I'm sorry I didn't call. I—"

Faith took a step toward me. "It doesn't matter. Your father stole from us. He broke up my family."

"Wait, what? Your parents are—"

"Getting divorced? Yeah. Thanks to you," Faith spat. "That's what happens when *your* dad loses all *my* dad's money. But instead of blaming your father, my mother blamed mine, so here we are. One more statistic. Do you know what it's like having to explain to my brothers why my dad's moving out? To listen to my mom crying in the middle of the night? I wish you'd never existed. You and your entire family. I wish you'd never come back here."

My hands shook. Okay. Apparently coming in here after her was a bad idea. I had no idea her parents were splitting up. Here I'd thought I'd be able to make up for everything with a simple apology, but I'd had no clue how much she'd been hurting. "I'm . . . I'm sorry. I—"

"What's going on in here?"

We both turned around to find Chloe and her mother framed in the doorway. Chloe wore a dark green velvet dress and pearls, while her mother looked very First Lady in a crisp white blouse with puffed sleeves and a slim black skirt.

"Allyson. How nice to see you," she greeted me politely. "Faith. You both know, however, that we aren't allowed in the conservatory unattended."

I glanced at Faith, and for a split second she forgot to be a bitch and started to smile. We'd never been allowed anywhere in this house unattended, but that's what we always were. It was a long-standing joke. But just as quickly as it had come, the smile was gone.

"Sorry, Mrs. Appleby," Faith said, tucking her phone away. She slipped past Chloe and her mom back into the library.

"Allyson?" Mrs. Appleby said.

I ducked my head and followed Faith. Chloe didn't bother to move out of my way, so her mother had to turn sideways for me to get by. Unbelievable. No matter how hard I tried with these people, they were never going to give me an inch.

jake

"Dude, Ally Ryan looks hot *again* tonight," Trevor said as we walked into the dining room. There was one huge table running the length of the vast room, with at least fifty place settings.

"Yeah, too bad I never got a chance to tap that," Todd added.

They laughed and slapped hands. I swallowed my disgust.

"Don't be a jackass," Hammond said, buttoning his jacket as he came up behind us.

We all looked at him, confused. Hammond had never scolded anyone for anything, especially not sex talk.

"What?" he said, pausing. "There are parents all over the place. Get a life."

He moved off to join Chloe and her family near the huge Christmas tree at the head of the table, where a professional photographer was going to snap a family photo. Keeping one eye on Ally, who was slowly making her way along the opposite side of the table, I glanced at the place cards. Mrs. Appleby liked to mix kids and adults. She put everyone near people they wouldn't ever talk to, like her parties were some kind of experiment.

Who was I going to spend the night making tortured small talk with?

Finally I spotted my name. I was between Mrs. Moore and Mr. Shale. Great. Mrs. Depressed and Mr. Loud. I glanced around and saw Ally's name on the next card. Instant excitement. I looked over my shoulder at Mrs. Appleby, made sure no one else was watching, then quickly switched Ally's card with Mr. Shale's. Then I shoved my shaking hands into my pockets. I had just broken a major Crestie rule. No one messed with Mrs. Appleby's order of things.

"If everyone would please take their seats!" Mrs. Appleby announced, ringing her obnoxious little dinner bell.

I sat, watching out of the corner of my eye as Ally came around the end of the table, still searching for her place. When she found it, she looked at me and blushed. As she slipped into her seat, her arm grazed mine. She was wearing this dark purple blouse with a wide neck that exposed her collar bone. All I wanted to do was kiss that collar bone. Trevor was right. She did look hot.

"Hey," I said.

"Hey."

I felt like every inch of my skin was on fire.

"A toast," Chloe's mother announced. She lifted her champagne glass, and we all followed. Even the eighth graders at the table had champagne. Cristal was not considered alcohol on the crest. "To a happy holiday season!" Mrs. Appleby announced. "And to us!"

"To us!" everyone chorused. We always toasted us. Just to remind ourselves that there were people out there who weren't part of us.

"Having fun?" I asked as a waiter in a tuxedo placed a dish of risotto in front of me. My stomach grumbled. There was always one good thing about Sunday dinners: The food kicked ass. Everyone started to eat, and the room got loud.

"Oh, so much," Ally answered sarcastically. "You?"

"Totally." I chewed and swallowed. "So. Where's your boyfriend tonight?"

Her cheeks turned crimson.

"He has a gig."

"A gig?" I laughed. "He's in a band?"

"Yeah. And they're pretty good, actually. Why do you care?"

"I don't. Just making small talk," I said with a smile.

She smiled back. This was going well.

"So, I'm thinking . . . after this we should go somewhere," I whispered.

She ducked her head. The blush deepened. "Go somewhere?"

"Yeah. You and me."

"Are you forgetting about the previously mentioned boyfriend?" she asked.

I grinned. "No. What does he have to do with anything? All I want to do is talk."

She scoffed and tore off a piece of her roll. "Yeah, right."

I sat back, faking offense. So innocent. "Why? What do you think I want to do?"

She looked at me and rolled her eyes. "Shut up."

"No, really. Tell me. Is there something you want to do other than talk?"

Ally shoved a huge piece of bread in her mouth. I'd been right about one thing. Sunday dinners were way more fun with her there. I took another bite of my risotto and looked across the table for the first time. Shannen was glaring right at me as if I'd just stomped on her foot.

Crap. I glanced quickly away.

"So, Gray, how are things at the hospital?" Mrs. Kirkpatrick asked.

"They're fantastic, actually," Dr. Nathanson replied. "We've just been given the go-ahead on the new cancer wing."

"That's fabulous news!" Mrs. Appleby remarked. "I'm so glad my little fund-raiser this fall was a success."

"It certainly was," Dr. Nathanson replied, tipping his glass toward her. "Thank you again for sponsoring it. And thank you for inviting us tonight. It's an honor."

"It's our honor to have you," Mrs. Appleby replied. "And I'm so glad you brought along our old friend." She smiled at Ally's mother. "I would have invited you myself, Melanie, but I wasn't sure you'd be interested."

I felt Ally tense up next to me, but her mother beamed. "Oh, please, Clarice. Of course I'm interested. You have no idea how much I've missed you girls."

She grinned at Mrs. Moore, who gave her what I thought was an encouraging look, and at Faith and Hammond's moms, too. My mother looked kind of pale as she touched her napkin to her mouth and cleared her throat.

"Yes, Melanie, they've missed you, too," she said. "I can't tell you how often they talk about you. It's always Melanie this and Melanie that."

Ally's mom seriously looked as if she was going to shit with happiness.

"It's true," Mrs. Kirkpatrick said. "We've especially missed your seven-layer chocolate cake."

Ally smiled as her mom beamed. "That was always a crowd-pleaser," Mrs. Ryan said.

"Very much so," Mrs. Appleby said. "You should think about making this a weekly thing again."

My skin tingled. Ally at every Sunday dinner? That would be the greatest thing ever. And if she were here every week, my friends would have to get used to her again. And then, who knew?

"Clarice, I would love that," Mrs. Ryan said happily.

"Good." Then Mrs. Appleby sat back in her chair, and something in her eyes shifted. "In fact, perhaps you should host next month."

Ally's smile faded.

"Oh, what a fabulous idea!" my mother trilled, catching on to the joke. "But don't you live in the Orchard View? Would you even be able to squeeze us all into that tiny place?"

Ally's mother went ashen. I wanted to launch myself over the table and wring my mom's neck. How could she say that? What the hell did she have against Ally's mother? They didn't even know each other. Suddenly she seemed no better to me than Faith and Shannen when they were shredding Ally for no reason. Just for fun. Just to win each other's approving laughs. I hated her in that moment. Her and all her fakeness.

"Ladies," Shannen's mother scolded. Across the way, Shannen's dad let out a loud burp.

"Excuse me," he said loudly.

"Nonsense, Brendan," Mrs. Appleby said, barely stifling a laugh. "It's the highest form of flattery."

A few people laughed under their breath. There was a long silence as Mrs. Moore blushed purple. Ally's mother leaned behind Todd's back to whisper something to Dr. Nathanson. He nodded and pushed his chair away from the table.

"Thank you for having us, Clarice, but I think we should be going," he said, standing.

"Oh, Gray, please," Mrs. Appleby said, standing as well. "Is that really necessary?"

"Yes, I believe it is," he replied.

Good for him.

He took Ally's mother's hand as she got up as well. She turned away from the table, her head down.

"Ally? Quinn?" Dr. Nathanson said.

Quinn's face was on fire. She looked like she was about to cry, probably out of embarrassment, but she got up. Ally didn't move. I looked at her. The mortification was written all over her face. So blatant I felt it in my gut. Suddenly I didn't care about Shannen's glare or the fact that Chloe and Hammond and Faith were watching. Or my parents. I leaned toward her ear.

"Don't listen to them," I said. "They're just a bunch of sad old bitches with nothing better to do."

Ally looked at me, her eyes shining. I wanted to kill every person in the room who'd ever made her feel bad. But then she pressed her lips together and shoved herself up from the table. As she followed her mom toward the door, the room was dead silent.

"Thanks for coming," Faith said sarcastically under her breath. Some of the kids giggled. Chloe shot her a scornful look, but Faith just rolled her eyes.

Ally paused, turned around, and faced the table. Dozens of unsympathetic faces stared back at her.

"No, thank you . . . all of you, really, for a *lovely* evening," she said pointedly.

And then she was gone.

ally

After spending the night listening to my mother crying into her pillow, the last thing I was up for on Monday morning was a full day of school. But if she was going to rally and go, I was going to rally and go. I just hoped none of those Crestie bitches said a word to me in the hall. Otherwise, there was going to be blood.

"I can't believe it," I ranted to David and Annie as we walked down the main hallway. "I can't believe I ever cared about being their friend again. Clearly everyone on the crest is pure evil."

"I don't know. Gray's pretty cool," David said, shedding his jacket. "And Quinn seemed nice at dinner that night—"

Annie and I turned, and we both gave him a look that could have stopped a charging bull in its tracks. He lifted his hands in surrender.

"Sorry. You're right. Pure evil."

"Thank you."

Not that I didn't think Gray was cool. Especially after he'd been so chivalrous at the Applebys' party, going against the Crestie pack and getting my mom out of there after she was attacked. I just didn't feel like being contradicted in all my fury.

We kept walking. "All I know is, after the obnoxious presentation their moms put on last night, I never want to be friends with them again."

At that moment, we came around the corner and stopped, bumping into each other one by one like an overdone comedy routine. Shannen, Chloe, and Faith were all standing right next to my locker.

"Uh-oh. This is not going to be pretty," Annie said under her breath. She whipped out her camera phone and hit record.

"Unbelievable," I said through my teeth.

I shouldered Shannen out of the way and spun the lock on my locker door. Annie and David hung back on the other side of the hallway, Annie moving back and forth as she tried to get the best angle on Shannen's face.

"Well, good morning to you, too," Shannen said.

I ignored her. My shoulder muscles were so coiled that if they sprang apart they'd take out the entire hallway full of students like a whip.

"Ally, we wanted to say we're sorry about last night," Chloe said.

From the corner of my eye I saw Jake, Hammond, and the Idiot Twins enter the hallway. Jake paused at his locker a few doors down, but I could tell he was listening in. The other guys gathered around the girls.

"Yeah. That's not even going to come close to cutting it,"

I said, jamming up on the locker handle and letting the door slam open against the wall.

"Oh, that's fair," Faith said sarcastically, shifting her weight from one tiny hip to the other.

I laughed and whirled on her. "I'm not being fair? Were you even there? All my mom wanted to do was please you people, and she got torn to shreds."

"Well, if you don't want us to hold what your dad did against you, then you can't hold what happened last night against us," Faith said, arching her eyebrows. "We didn't do anything."

My spirits fell slightly. Okay. She had a point there. Except—

"Right. So, what was that little parting comment you made on my way out?"

Faith blushed and looked away.

"She's sorry for that. Right, Faith?" Chloe said, staring her down.

"Yeah. Sorry. It was a knee-jerk thing," she replied, not looking me in the eye.

"Look, after last night we all got together and talked about it, and we realized you're right," Chloe said, tossing her perfectly coiffed hair over her shoulder. "Your dad was the one who messed up. Not you."

I automatically glanced at Hammond. He cleared his throat and looked away. Little did Chloe know that I had messed up too. Big time.

"So listen, we're having our annual going away party next Sunday night," Shannen said. "We're all going to meet at the new pool annex at nine o'clock. You in?"

"We're breaking into the pool?" Trevor said excitedly.

"Skinny-dipping! Sweet!" Todd added.

They slapped hands over their heads.

I couldn't contain the rush of excitement, even as I hated myself for having it. They were actually inviting me to something. One of our old traditions. Every year we all went away for a few days over Christmas, and every year we said good-bye to each other by throwing a private party in some forbidden location. Of course, I wasn't hopping a flight out of Newark this year, but that didn't mean I couldn't go to the going away party.

Annie trained her camera phone on me. Right. Hadn't I just sworn to her and David that I never wanted to be friends with these people again? But that was before this. Before they'd blindsided me with a white flag. Jake quietly closed the door of his locker and wandered over, standing behind Shannen's left shoulder. I didn't dare look at him, but I could feel the warmth of his gaze all over my skin.

"It'll be just like old times," Chloe said with a smile.

My heart fluttered. Just like old times. They were offering a truce. A real one. Wouldn't it be kind of jerky to throw it back in their faces?

"So? What do you say, Ally?" Shannen asked.

I glanced at the camera apologetically. "Okay. I'm in."

"Cool," Shannen said with a smile. "We'll see you there."

After the Cresties had walked away and Annie, David, and I were left alone, none of us said anything for a solid minute. With Jake gone, I finally started to cool down—to think clearly again.

"Come on, you guys, it's just one party," I said.

David pushed himself away from the wall. "Yeah. A party with evil."

"But you heard what they said, right?" I asked, tugging a few books out of my locker.

"Got it all on film," Annie said, pocketing her phone.

"And it sounded real, right? They really felt bad."

David and Annie looked at each other. "Sure. If you trust the face of *evil*," Annie said.

"You can't play both sides, Ally," David said. "You can't be both a Crestie and a Norm."

A tingle of apprehension went through my chest. "Why not?"

"Because . . . it's just wrong," David said, lifting both shoulders. "Like, on a primordial level."

"He's right. Your head might actually, literally explode from the pressure," Annie said. She looked at David. "We are so going to lose her."

I sighed and slammed my locker door. "Okay, Melodrama Girl. You're not going to lose me. It's just one party."

David took my hand and looked into my eyes, his expression all mock-serious. "Just promise me you'll come back."

He was kidding around, but a hard stone of guilt formed in my gut. Because one of the reasons I had said yes, one of the reasons I was already looking forward to this, was that Jake was going to be there.

"I promise," I said. "I'll come back."

jake

I paused my Xbox and glanced at my watch. It was nine fifteen. The going away party started at nine. Was Ally there yet? Were they actually being nice to her? My whole body itched, and I leaned back against my bed, my legs splayed out on the floor. I wanted to get the hell out of here, but I couldn't leave. Not yet. Because I was grounded. I hadn't talked to my mother since

Sunday night dinner. By Tuesday my parents had decided that I couldn't go out with my friends until I started acting like a grown-up. As if that was how they were acting.

"Jake, aren't you supposed to be taking a practice test?" my mother asked, appearing in my doorway. She was all dressed up in a fancy black dress, diamonds dangling from her ears.

I felt hot all over. Just like I did every time I was forced to ignore her.

My father joined her. "Jake. Your mother is talking to you."

"Have a good time, Dad," I said.

My mother heaved a sigh and walked away. My father straightened his tie as he entered my room. "Jake, I've had just about enough of this behavior."

"Yeah, well, I've had just about enough of hers."

"That's it!" my father shouted. My heart stopped. He never shouted. Ever. "I want you to go downstairs and apologize to your mother right now."

I stood up from the floor and faced him. I felt shaky inside but wasn't about to cave. "Is she going to apologize for what she did?"

"And what offense, exactly, do you imagine your mother has committed?" my dad asked.

"You were there. You saw what she did to Ally Ryan's mom."

"And why do we care so much about Ally Ryan or her mother?" he asked.

"What does it even matter? She was awful to her and she doesn't even know her," I shot back. "I'm supposed to be okay with that?"

My father sighed and looked at the floor. "Son, these women . . . these dinners . . . they're very important to your mother."

150

"I know." It had taken just over a year of ass-kissing and designer-clothes hoarding for my mother to get us our invite into the Sunday dinner crowd. When it had finally happened she'd actually cried from happiness. I'd never remotely understood why, but I knew it was important to her.

"So, you have to understand, son, this Melanie Ryan woman . . . she's known your mother's new friends for years," my father said. "They grew up together, went to school together, vacationed together. And now that she's back—"

The truth hit me like a lacrosse stick to the head. "She's scared. She thinks they're gonna dump her."

"Well, yes," my father said matter-of-factly.

Unbelievable. My mother had the exact same mentality as my friends. When in doubt, be a bitch. What little respect I had left for her started to crumble.

"Try not to be so hard on her, Jake," my dad said, putting his hand on my shoulder. "Everyone makes mistakes."

"Yeah," I said, looking at the floor. I wanted out of this conversation. "Okay."

He patted my cheek twice and walked out, off to dinner at Ruocco's, where they were meeting up with all the other parents. I watched them from my window, the same one I'd been looking through when I'd first seen Ally, as they got into my mom's Mercedes and pulled out. I waited until the lights had disappeared at the bottom of Vista View Lane before I went down to the garage to get my bike.

Not the ideal mode of transportation, but unlike Shannen I wasn't into stealing my parents' cars without a license. I had just hit the automatic garage door opener when my cell phone rang. Shannen stuck her tongue out at me from the screen.

"Hello?" I said.

"Jake! Where are you!? The Idiot Twins brought this mini Ping-Pong table, and we're playing beer Pong! Chloe's already losing, and guess what? She finally cracked and told us where Ally's dad is."

Shit. My mouth went dry. "She did?"

"Yeah. He's working at one of Mr. Appleby's delis in the city. He's not even a waiter. He's a counter dude, like, slicing bologna for a living!"

I heard Faith crack up in the background and Chloe begging Shannen to shut up. Babbling that she shouldn't have spilled. Couldn't have agreed more.

"No way," I said flatly. Because I had to say something.

"It's so hilarious, you know? Ally was always showing off about how perfect her father was, and now it turns out he's a cheat, an abandoner, *and* a minimum-wage earner."

I had to bite my tongue to keep from snapping. I guess the fact that they were talking about this meant Ally wasn't there yet.

"Anyway, get your butt over here," Shannen said.

"I'll be there in two minutes."

"Oooh! Are you taking the Jag? You have to give me a ride when you get here."

"No. I'm taking my bike."

I was about to hang up when she cackled, "You can't ride your bike all the way to the club!"

I froze, my fingers curled around the handlebar. "I thought we were going to the pool annex."

The cackling got louder. "No! That's just what we told Ally! We're at the boathouse."

"What?" I said through my teeth.

"Yeah. We already called the cops to tell them someone was breaking in at school," Shannen said with a laugh. "They should be there in . . . well, now."

More laughter. WTF was wrong with them? Ally could get in serious trouble. She could get arrested. Why the hell would they do this to her?

"Sorry. I thought you knew. Now get your ass in the Jag and get over here!" Shannen said, still laughing.

I wanted to tell her off. Tell her what a total bitch she was being. Ask her how she could possibly be so cool one second and such a psycho the next. But I bit down on my tongue and said nothing. It wouldn't have mattered anyway. And I was losing time. I turned my phone off and tore out of the driveway as fast as I could pedal.

ally

I told my mother I was going to visit David at Dunkin' Donuts, where he worked a few nights a week. After the Sunday dinner debacle, she hadn't mentioned my old friends or prodded me about hanging out with them. Not once. Ironic that I was finally going to a party with them now that she was no longer interested. I felt bad about lying to her, but it was just a little white lie. I was going to be right across the street, and it wasn't like I was going to do anything she wouldn't approve of. Other than breaking into the school.

Tugging my coat close to my body against the frigid December air, I jogged over to the school parking lot and walked up the hill to the new annex, my shoes crunching on the leftover salt from the last ice storm. My heart pounded with excitement, and I told myself it was because I was doing something border-line bad. It had nothing to do with Jake Graydon. Nothing at all.

Maybe, after the party, I actually should go visit David.

There were no cars in the parking lot, but I wasn't surprised. Chloe was the only one with a license and a car, and they'd probably parked on a side street to avoid suspicion. I walked up to the double metal doors and pulled on the handles. Nothing. They must have found another way in. All the top windows of the annex were open. I crept slowly around the side of the building, looking for some clue as to how to get inside. There, pasted to a new green Dumpster, was a big red arrow pointing up. There was another taped to the top, and a third pointing up at the window above.

I paused, my pulse skipping around in trepidation. Chloe and Faith had scaled a Dumpster and climbed through a win-dow two inches from the ceiling? Somehow, I didn't see it. But then, Hammond had probably let Chloe climb up his back and step on his head to get through.

I laughed at the visual. Well, it was either go up or go home. I'd never been one to back down from a dare, so I decided to risk it. I grabbed the hinge on the lid of the Dumpster and scrambled on top. The noise reverberated for miles, scaring the crap out of me. I caught my breath, looked up at the window over my head, said a quick prayer, and jumped. My hands grasped the cold, sharp and unforgiving window ledge. I grit-ted my teeth and pulled myself up. My blood rushed in my ears, and I strained with all my strength.

Worth it. This was all going to be totally worth it.

I hoisted myself up and twisted sideways to get through the window. On the other side were the bleachers. I eased myself onto the top row and lay there for a moment, breathing in the thick scent of chlorine. I'd made it. I was okay. When my breathing finally started to slow, though, I realized something was very wrong. The place was dead silent.

I sat up. The pool was open but dark, its clear water so still I could read the depth measurements painted on the wall on the far side. The only light in the place came from the glowing, red emergency exit signs over the doors, and through the windows from the parking lot lights. It was freezing. Even colder than it was outside.

"Hello?"

My voice echoed throughout the room. No response.

Fear tickled my veins. They were screwing with me. Any second they were all going to come bursting out from under the bleachers and frighten me. Great. Was this going to be our new relationship? They'd let me back in but make me the butt of every joke for the rest of my life, just to remind me of my place?

"Ha ha. Very funny, you guys." I stood up and walked down the bleachers, looking around carefully. "Come out, come out, wherever you are!"

There was a scraping noise behind me. I whirled around, my heart in my throat, and saw Jake Graydon fumbling through the window.

"Omigod. You scared me," I said.

He dropped onto all fours on the bleachers and sprang up as if singed. His face was sweaty and red, and his eyes darted around the room fretfully.

"Come on," he said, his steps heavy on the bleachers. "We have to get out of here."

He grabbed my hand as he passed me by, but I didn't move.

"What do you mean? Where is everybody?" I asked.

Jake sighed. "They're not coming. Let's go!"

He tugged on my hand. A cold trickle of dread sliced down my spine. "What do you mean, they're not coming?"

"We don't have time for this," Jake said tersely. "I swear I'll explain everything once we—"

Suddenly the door swung open, and a flashlight beam hit me dead in the face.

"What the hell do you two kids think you're doing in here?"

Two cops stood in the doorway, along with our principal, Mr. Lawrence, who was holding a jam-packed key ring. At that moment, three things occurred to me. First, I was in serious trouble. Second, the Cresties had set me up. And third, Jake was still holding my hand.

jake

"I thought this was supposed to be my day off," Principal Lawrence joked.

It was the first day of winter break. Orchard Hill High was deserted, except for the janitors. They already had the entire place reeking of ammonia. The principal lowered himself into his huge leather chair and laced his fingers together on the desk. I glanced at my mother's foot. It was bouncing up and down like crazy. My dad sat next to her in a button-down, tie, and houndstooth jacket—his casual weekend gear. I couldn't even look at Ally, even though she was sitting right next to me. She was probably so pissed she could kill me with one glance.

"Mr. Lawrence, Ally has something she'd like to say," Mrs. Ryan stated.

Ally shifted in her chair. "I'm very sorry for breaking into the pool. I know it was stupid and dangerous, and I'll accept whatever punishment you think is right."

"Thank you, Miss Ryan," Principal Lawrence said. He looked at me. "And Mr. Graydon? Do you have anything to add?"

I looked at my parents. They had told me not to say anything. I couldn't have anyway. My guilt was lodged in my throat like I'd swallowed Shaquille O'Neal's shoe. My dad nodded at me. What was that supposed to mean? "Um . . . I'm sorry, too?"

Ally's mother snorted. My face burned. Was that wrong? I hated this. Every minute of it. Hated not knowing what I was supposed to do.

"Mr. Lawrence, it's Christmas vacation," my dad said, leaning forward. "None of us wants to be here right now. These are two good kids who didn't damage any school property and who have wholeheartedly apologized. Don't you think we can just end this with a warning and move on with our lives?"

Sounded good to me.

"I'm sure we could make it worth your while," my mom added. "A donation to the library, perhaps." She slid a glance at Mrs. Ryan, and I knew exactly what she was thinking—don't worry, poor person, we'll take care of this with our big, fat checkbook. Maybe not in those words, but that was the idea. My face burned brighter.

Mr. Lawrence's eyebrows rose with interest. He took a

breath. I could tell he was going to take the money and run. This was it. We were out of there.

"No," Mrs. Ryan snapped.

"What?" my mother said.

"What?" Ally repeated.

"No," Mrs. Ryan said, even more firmly this time. "If there's one thing I've always taught my daughter, it's that actions have consequences. Unlike some parents, I'd like her to grow up with some sense of responsibility for her own conduct."

Oh, just kill me. Kill me now.

"So, Mr. Lawrence, I would appreciate it if you would not grant her any special treatment," Mrs. Ryan continued. "Whatever the normal punishment is for breaking into school property after hours, that's what I'd like her to receive."

Mr. Lawrence frowned. I think he was impressed.

"Fine. Two weeks of school beautification duty," he said. "The work will commence when school reopens. You'll be responsible for two hours a day, which can be served directly before or after school."

"Both of them?" my mother blurted.

As if Ally deserved to be punished and I didn't. It wasn't her fault. It was mine. My stupid friends had tricked her into it, and I'd been too dense to realize what they were doing. I felt hot all around the collar of my sweater and under my arms.

My father scoffed. "But, Mr. Lawrence, surely you don't expect Jake to miss swim practice."

My fingers curled into fists on the chair's armrests.

"He can't—"

"I'll do it," I blurted.

"What?" my parents said in unison. Everyone was staring at me. Including Ally.

"You said I can do it before school, right?" I asked. "So I don't miss swim?"

"But, Jake, that would mean getting here at . . . five thirty every day!" my mother said.

"I can do the math," I said to her through my teeth. Her mouth snapped closed. I was in trouble for that one, but I didn't care. I'd already been grounded twice. A third time couldn't hurt that much. Especially since I was too pissed at my friends to care about not being able to hang out with them. I looked at the principal. "So. Can I? Can we? Ally has basketball, too."

"Well . . . yes, Jake. I think that would be just fine," Mr. Lawrence said. He smiled at me, looking almost proud. "Does that work for you, Ally?"

"Yes, sir," Ally said.

"All right, then. We have a deal," Mr. Lawrence said, standing. "Now, as you mentioned, none of us really wants to be here, so unless anyone has any further questions . . ." He offered my dad his hand, but Dad ignored it. Dad buttoned his jacket and grabbed his trench coat from the hook by the door.

"Jake. Let's go," he snapped.

I got up to follow him, letting my mother walk out ahead of me. As I slipped sideways through the door I glanced over my shoulder at Ally. I couldn't help myself. I had to know if she was mad at me for letting her get set up. But she was barely containing a smile. Stunned, I automatically smiled back.

"Jake! Now!" my father snapped from the hallway.

I yanked my varsity jacket on and let the door swing closed

behind me. It wasn't until we were in the car, my parents giving me the silent treatment, that I realized that I maybe knew why Ally was smiling. We had just been sentenced to twenty hours of school service. The two of us. Together. Alone. For twenty hours.

Sweet.

january

Did you hear? Jake Graydon got busted for breaking into the pool annex over break.

Yeah. But did you hear who he was with?

Who?

Ally Ryan.

No way. What the hell were they doing together?

Apparently our playboy has a new girl to play with.

Isn't she with David Drake?

Like that matters.

Oh, please. Jake and Ally? No way. The Cresties would freak.

Yeah. Those two cannot get together.

Nothing around here would ever be the same.

jake

"You got arrested!?"

Shannen stomped into my room, leaving wet boot prints in the thick carpet, and flung herself onto my bed facedown, arms splayed. There was snow in her hair and on the shoulders of her black pea coat. I paused my game of NBA 2K10, which I'd been playing a lot more often since Ally had whipped my ass in the driveway back in October. Like I could really learn new moves from a video game.

"Who let you in?" I asked.

It sounded more pissed than I intended. But then, I was pissed. I hadn't talked to any of my friends since the night of the going away party. Hammond had called twice. Shannen, every day. Plus texts. But I hadn't wanted to talk to any of them after what they'd pulled. My family had stayed local for the holidays while everyone else had flown somewhere. Kinda sucked, but made it easier to avoid them.

She lifted her head and blew her bangs out of her face. She'd gotten tan in Florida. "Like anyone lets me in. Your door is always unlocked."

She was right, of course. Shannen was always just walking into my house without ringing the bell. She practically lived here. And at Chloe's and Faith's. Even Hammond's and the twins'. Anywhere to get away from her father. I guess I just figured, considering I was still grounded, someone might have intercepted her.

I went back to my game, leaning against the foot of my bed.

"What's the matter? Are you pissed at me or something?"

she asked. She came to the end of the bed, swinging her legs around so they were next to my right cheek.

"Why would I be mad? You almost got me thrown in jail, but no, I'm not mad."

"Oh, come on. Like it's somehow my fault." She shoved my shoulder. I ignored her and kept playing. "What were you thinking? Why did you have to go all Batman on us?"

"Batman?"

She slid down to sit on the floor next to me and rolled her eyes. "You know . . . running off to save the damsel in distress?"

"I wouldn't've had to if you guys hadn't pulled that stupid-ass prank," I replied. I paused the game again and flung the controller down. "What were *you* thinking?"

Shannen shrugged. She tossed her bangs out of her face again, but they fell right back into place. "I don't know. I thought it would be funny."

"Funny?" I blurted. "Shannen, I could have gotten a record!"

"But you weren't supposed to be there!" she said, leaning back on her hands.

"That's not the point. Why did you do that to Ally? I thought you guys were, like, getting along at basketball and stuff. Did you really want her to get in that much trouble?" I asked.

"Whatever. I heard they dismissed the charges," she said, looking at the TV.

I pushed myself to my feet and stood over her, so angry that I had to move to keep from exploding. "They did, but you didn't know that was going to happen. Why would you do that to her?"

"Okay, first of all? It wasn't my idea, it was Faith's," she said, shoving herself to her feet as well. "And second of all, why do you care so effing much what happens to Ally Ryan?"

"I . . . I don't," I said. "I just . . . I don't get what she did that was so fucking awful that you guys need to keep screwing with her. What's the point?"

Shannen rolled her eyes, sat down on the bed, and held her head in her hands. "I don't believe this," she said to the floor.

"What? Just tell me. What the hell is going on?" I asked.

Shannen glared up at me, her eyes on fire. "Fine, you want to know what Ally did that was so bad? She fooled around with Hammond. While he was going out with Chloe."

My stomach turned, and bile rose up in my throat. Ally and Hammond? Hammond had fooled around with Ally?

"What does that mean, exactly, 'fooled around'?" I asked.

"I don't know. I never asked for the details," she spat. "Does it matter? The girl's a backstabbing whore."

My knees were too weak to stand. I couldn't believe that Hammond had been with Ally. A million flesh-heavy visuals shot through my mind rapid-fire, and I closed my eyes. Hammond and Ally. Hammond and Ally. I was starting to sweat.

"Does Chloe know?" I asked, because it seemed like the right thing to ask.

"No. I've never told her. No one knows that I know."

"Not even Ally?" I asked.

She looked me in the eye. "Not even Ally." She blew out a sigh and turned away. "The thing is, I think Hammond still likes her," Shannen said, lacing her fingers together and kneading her knuckles.

"Hammond? No, he—" But then, the day after I met her hadn't he grilled me about how she looked? Hadn't he been the one telling me to stay away from her all along? He'd told the Idiot Twins to shut up about her at Sunday dinner, and the night of the lawn jockey incident, he'd hesitated, too. He hadn't wanted to be there any more than I had. Was it for the same *reason* as me? Because he liked her?

"He always liked her. Since, like, fourth grade. And Chloe always liked him. It was like our very own *Degrassi*-style love triangle," Shannen said, lifting a hand and letting it fall at her side. "Finally in ninth, Hammond asked out Ally and she turned him down cold, so he asked out Chloe. They've been together ever since."

"So you think that all this time, Hammond never stopped liking Ally?" I said.

"I don't know. I mean, I know he cares about Chloe, but . . ." She paused and shook her head. "All I know for sure is, we cannot let that girl back in," she said firmly. "If Hammond cheats on Chloe and she finds out about it, it'll break her heart. And I don't know about you, but I don't think we need someone like her in our group. Someone none of us can trust."

I swallowed back the bile in my throat. I couldn't say what I was thinking. Because she would kill me. The thing was, I didn't think it was that big a deal that Hammond and Ally had hooked up. Everyone hooked up behind their boyfriend's or girlfriend's back. It happened all the time. It wasn't the cheating or the so-called backstabbing that threw me.

It was that Hammond had kissed Ally Ryan. And maybe more. I liked a girl who'd been with one of my best friends. He'd gotten to her first. I took a breath and clenched my jaw.

"So . . . you're not in trouble, right? I mean, with the police?" Shannen asked, chewing on her lip.

"No." I leaned forward with my elbows on my thighs.

"But Principal Lawrence gave us two weeks' janitor duty."

"Janitor duty?"

"Yeah."

I felt a thrill in my heart area every time I thought about it. Me and Ally alone together every morning for two weeks. But then . . . Hammond and Ally. Ugh. Why did she have to tell me this?

"Oh my God! That's classic! Do you have to wear the coveralls and everything? I'm so filming this for YouTube," Shannen said, laughing as she got up and shed her coat. That was Shannen for you, all serious one second, all jokes the next.

"No. I don't know."

"So, just tell me the truth," she said, standing in front of me. "There's nothing between you and Ally Ryan?"

I looked up at her. She was my best friend, but I couldn't tell her. Because there was nothing to tell. And clearly, even if there was something to tell, that something would totally piss her off.

"No. There's nothing between me and Ally Ryan," I confirmed.

"Good," she said, her expression serious. "Because you deserve better."

Whatever that meant. "Thanks."

I switched the TV to one of the movie channels, looking for something familiar for us to watch. Something to distract me from the images of Hammond and Ally half-dressed and sweating that kept flipping through my mind.

"So . . . how was Florida?" I asked as she sat down next to me again.

"It was all right. Waterskiing, lying out, a lot of drunken reminiscing, but luckily everyone managed not to mention

Charlie," she said, fiddling with her hair now. "My dad was actually pretty cool. On Christmas he even smiled."

"That's good."

"But then we got back home, and it was right back to the den and the Jack bottle," she said.

"Sorry." I put my arm around her and gave her shoulder a quick squeeze. "You can hang out here till you think it's safe to go back."

She put her head on my shoulder. "Thanks. You're the best, you know that?"

"I'm aware."

She laughed, and I got back to channel surfing. When I landed on *Forgetting Sarah Marshall*, one of our favorites, Shannen yanked the remote away so I couldn't change it. We settled in on the bed, sitting next to each other against the headrest.

But all I could think about was Hammond and Ally. Hammond and Ally on a bed. Hammond and Ally undressing each other. Hammond and Ally with their tongues in each other's mouths.

And as much as I liked Shannen, I wished she'd never come over.

ally

Five thirty in the morning in January may as well be midnight. It's so freaking dark out that it should be illegal for anyone to be up, let alone working. And it's freezingly, frigidly, bitingly cold. By the time I'd walked up the hill to the school and around to the service entrance—located directly across from the annex of infamy—my nostrils were frozen together.

But as I knocked on the door, I was actually trembling more from excitement than the cold. Excited for ass-crack-of-dawn detention. What was wrong with me?

A rotund man with red hair and a matching moustache opened the door for me. He was wearing perfectly clean, pressed coveralls. Color: paper bag brown.

"Good morning! So. You must be Ally!" he said brightly.

"Yep."

"I'm Barry," he said, offering a meaty hand. "So. Nice to meet you."

"Thanks. You too."

We stepped just inside the door. He stood there for a pro- longed moment and just smiled at me. Jake was clearly not here yet.

"So. Got yourself into some shenanigans, did ya?" he said.

The "so" thing was going to get old really fast. "Apparently," I replied.

"So. Should we wait for your friend, then?" he asked. "Or would you like to just get started?"

"Uh, I guess we should—"

There was a bang on the door. One loud bang. My heart skipped a nervous beat. I hadn't seen Jake since the morning our punishment had been handed down. My mouth went dry as Barry leaned by me to open the door.

"Jake Graydon?" he said.

"Yeah."

His voice sent a shiver down my spine. This was very not good. In a deliciously forbidden way. Jake slipped inside, hands in his jacket pockets. He'd gotten a haircut. It was all buzzed short on the sides. He looked hot. He gave me a quick sideways glance and I started to smile, but he quickly averted his eyes.

Ouch. What was that about? Was I wrong when I thought he'd be looking forward to this, too? Hadn't he smiled at me that morning as he was walking out? I'd thought that had meant something. I'd been counting on it, actually.

Barry introduced himself and they shook hands.

"So. Let's get to it then."

Barry led us down the dimly lit hall, past the science labs, and into one of those rarely visited corners of the school where there were random offices and a bathroom no one ever used. Jake and I fell into step behind him, only about two feet apart, but it felt like there was a wall between us.

Barry shoved open the door of a closet marked CUSTODIAN ONLY and went inside. It wasn't big enough for all of us, so Jake and I waited on either side of the door, facing each other but not talking to each other.

I had no idea what was going on, but I was not going to be the first to speak.

"So. Here you go!"

Barry reemerged and handed us each a putty knife and a plastic bucket. They looked as if they had seen better days.

"What're these for?" Jake asked.

"They're for scraping!" Barry announced happily, walking past us. He was like a Disney World ice cream hawker. On speed. "Come on!"

Scraping. Why did I not like the sound of this? Barry led us down the main hallway, which was quiet as a church on Friday night, and into the cafeteria. The lights were ablaze, and every single table in the place was turned upside down. Instantly, I knew what we were going to be scraping. The tables' undersides were all pimpled with a disgustingly colorful array of gum wads.

"We didn't get a chance to clear away all the gum over break," Barry said, putting his hands on his hips and sticking his gut out as he surveyed the tables with what seemed like pride. "I got 'em all turned over before you got here, so I saved you that." He whipped out two pairs of plastic gloves as if from nowhere and handed them to me. Then he slapped us on our backs. "So. Enjoy!"

The cafeteria door let out a loud squeal as he shut us in together. Jake and I looked at each another. It was almost like he was seeing me for the first time and he didn't like what he saw.

"Is something wrong?" I asked, unable to take the silence any longer.

"No. What could be wrong?" he asked, dropping to the floor next to the first table. His vibe was so cold I was turning into a Popsicle.

"I don't know. You tell me." I sat down next to him, my bucket clunking against the floor. "Are you mad at me? Because it's not like it's my fault we're here."

"I know that," he said through his teeth.

"Then, what?" I asked, my voice small.

Jake looked up at me. He did a sort of double take and rubbed his forehead with his hand. "It's nothing. Sorry. I just . . . I guess I'm not a morning person."

I snorted a laugh, relaxing a little. "Maybe tomorrow I'll bring coffee."

"Yeah. Good idea."

There was a long moment of silence. I fiddled with my putty knife and bit my lip, trying to think of what to say next.

"Listen, I'm sorry about all this," Jake said finally.

I handed him a pair of gloves. "I should have figured out they were setting me up. You were just trying to help."

Jake looked down at the gloves and blushed.

"So, really I should be thanking you," I rambled on, "for, you know, swooping in and trying to save me."

Jake smiled for the first time. "I thought you didn't need a knight in shining armor."

I was pulling on a glove as he said this, and it snapped against my wrist. Ow. But I couldn't believe he'd actually remembered something I said back in September.

"Yeah, well . . . I guess sometimes I do," I said, tugging the other glove over my fingers. "But in the future, try saving me before the cops show."

Jake's laugh filled the cafeteria and melted my insides like s'mores over a flame. He had this deep, uninhibited laugh. I could listen to it all day.

And then I realized that I would be listening to it—to his laugh, his voice—for two hours every day for the next ten school days. Who ever said detention was a bad thing?

ally

"Heads up!"

I looked up just in time to stop the basketball that was hurtling toward my head. I batted it down with my forearm and glared at Shannen as she strolled across the gym toward me.

"Nice reflexes." She picked up the ball and cradled it between her wrist and hip. "Wanna warm up?"

She had to be kidding me. I got up and walked past her, grabbing a ball from the rack near the wall and shooting it over her head. It swished through the hoop, and I grabbed another.

"Oh. So, what? You're not talking to me now?" she teased, tossing her ball from hand to hand.

I glared at her and shot another perfect, arcing shot over her head.

"Come on, Ally. It was just a joke. God, you're as bad as Jake," she said, grabbing my third ball out of my hands.

"A joke?" I blurted. "I thought we called a truce. What the hell, Shannen?" I jogged over to the corner, picked up my ball, and shot a layup, then got out of the way as some of our teammates started to take their warm-up shots.

"Calm down," Shannen said, looking me up and down. "It wasn't even my idea."

"Oh, please. Don't talk to me like I don't know you," I said, unzipping my hoodie and tossing it onto the ground. "You're always the mastermind of these things."

"Not this time! This one was all Faith," Shannen protested.

I looked at her doubtfully. "Okay, fine. Let's say I believe you. That means you had nothing to do with it? What is Faith, the Megatron of the crest or something? She's so freaking unstoppable? You can't talk her out of doing something intensely mean and stupid to people you supposedly like?"

"I didn't know Jake was going to be there," she said.

"Right. So if you did, *then* you would have stopped her," I said, turning away as my face started to burn. "Thanks a lot."

"I didn't mean that," Shannen said, the eye roll obvious in her voice. "Come on, Ally, take a joke." She bounced her ball off the center of my back, right between my shoulder blades.

"It's not a joke," I said through my teeth, turning to face her. "And you can take your truce and choke on it."

"What's that supposed to mean?" she asked.

I stepped up and squared off with her. "It means unless we're on the court, don't talk to me. Don't come near me. Just leave me alone."

Shannen took a step back, shoving her tongue into her cheek. "Fine."

"Fine."

"Are you sure about this?" Shannen said, her tone growing darker.

"Sure about what?"

"About making an enemy of me, knowing what I know?" she said.

My cheeks colored. She was threatening me now? My adrenaline took over, even as fear sliced through my heart. "I'm pretty sure you won't say anything about that, knowing what I know."

She gaped at me, stunned. It was a low blow, considering how much more personal and potentially devastating the secrets were that I held. What she didn't know was, I would never tell anyone about them, even if she called my bluff.

Which was why it was called a bluff.

Then Shannen's eyes flashed with ire, and for a moment I felt uncertain. She looked like she was about to say something— something devastating—and my stomach hollowed out. What? What horribleness was hanging on the tip of her tongue?

Coach blew her whistle to start practice, and I turned around, acting casual. Trying not to let her see that I was shaking. I grabbed a ball off the floor and shot one last three, which bounced off the rim and flew toward the bleachers. As we lined up for drills, I made sure to avoid any and all eye contact with Shannen and tried not to think about what we'd just done. What she'd been about to say. What it might actually mean.

jake

It turned out I didn't care. That was the thing. I didn't care that Hammond and Ally had hooked up. I thought that every time I looked at her I was going to see him, but I didn't. All I saw was her.

And I couldn't stop staring.

"What? Do I have something on my face?" Ally lifted her rubber-gloved hands toward her nose.

Snagged. "No. Sorry. I just zoned out for a second," I said.

It was our third morning of detention, and we were still scraping gum. I never knew the people at my school chewed this much gum.

"Oh. Okay." She got back to scraping. "So, Jake Graydon, tell me about yourself."

My brain went completely blank. I picked up my putty knife and went to work on a wad of pink gum. "Tell you about myself?"

"Yeah. I mean, we're gonna be here every day for the next seven days." She smiled over her shoulder at me. "May as well talk."

We'd talked yesterday. And the day before. About basketball

and soccer and lacrosse and swimming and the shore and the city and Baltimore, where she'd lived before moving back. But I guess we hadn't talked about anything real, really. The way girls seemed to love to do.

"What do you want to know?"

"I don't know. What'd you do for Christmas?" Ally asked. She tossed her ponytail over her shoulder as she bent over the table.

"Visited my grandparents in Philly," I said. "It's the only time all year I get to see all my cousins at the same time, so it was pretty cool."

"Really? How many cousins do you have?" she asked.

"Twenty-three."

Her jaw dropped. "Shut up!'

"Why? How many do you have?" I asked, sitting up straight.

"Um, five," she said. "And they all live in California, so I never see them. Can you, like, name them all?"

"Sure," I said. I recited the list from oldest to youngest. Told her all about how everyone was excited to see my crazy cousin Devon, who'd spent the past year studying art in Italy and then come back and acted so superior we'd all ended up throwing canapés at him until he finally broke and launched a counter-attack. I told her about Leanna, who had sent in applications to be on *The Bachelor* for five years in a row and had finally made the cut, so she refused to consume anything other than celery and water. When I told the story of how the toddlers had tried to use my uncle's old waterbed as a trampoline she laughed so hard coffee came out her nose.

"Omigod!" she said, lifting a paper towel to her face. "I'm so gross!"

That was it. She didn't squeal, scream, run for the bathroom, or leave the school never to return. She sniffled and got back to work, telling me all about her chill Christmas and how her mom had loved her present.

This girl was effing awesome. As I listened to her relate the details of the Christmas tree and the dinner and the presents, I realized I wasn't bored.

"Then, of course, we spent the day after Christmas with the Nathansons," she said, shaking her head. "This is a new tradition, apparently. Day-after dinner with le boyfriend. Except this time it was at their place, so I got the full tour of Quinn's very pink, very huge bedroom suite. Not that she wanted to show it to me."

"What do you mean?"

"Let's just say I'm not so sure Princess Quinn is too psyched about having to hang out with a Crestie reject like me," Ally said, then blushed.

I felt hot all of a sudden, too. Since it was my friends who had made her a reject. I sat back on my butt and fiddled with the putty knife. "Is that weird, your mom dating someone?"

"Everything's weird," she replied, sitting back as well.

"What do you mean?"

She dropped her knife and leaned back on her hands. Her gloves made squishy, squeaky noises on the floor. "I don't know . . . it's like I'm back but I'm not back. I'm here . . . I'm home . . . but nothing's the same. My friends are here but they're not my friends. My house is here but it's not my house."

I looked down at my hands, feeling responsible somehow. I would've given her her room back if I could.

"And my family . . . it's just weird being here without my dad. Everywhere I go it's like I expect to see him there waiting for me. There are all these memories, but he's not here."

Her voice broke, and she stopped. My heart did this weird clenching thing at the mention of her father. But I couldn't tell her what I knew. Because I didn't really know anything for sure. And it also was none of my business. Wouldn't it freak her that someone she barely knew kind of knew where her dad was?

I wished my friends were here listening to this. They'd never be able to blame her for all the crap her dad did if they knew what it was doing to her. And they also wouldn't be able to laugh about where her dad was now. Or about the fact that they all knew and she didn't. Not that there weren't other reasons for them not to like her, but only Shannen and Hammond knew about those.

"You know that box score?" she said suddenly. "The one from the JV championship?"

"Yeah."

"That was the night we left. I wrote that in while my dad was yelling at me to get in the car," I said. "I had this, like, need to record it there before we left. Like it would somehow mean something if it was there. It should have been the best night of my life, but instead it was the worst. I never got to go to the banquet and get my championship ring. I never even got to go over the play by play with Shannen and Hammond like we always did. Instead it was all just over. My life as I knew it was just over."

"Wow. That sucks," I said. "You never even got your ring?"

She cracked a sad smile. "Nope. I figured they'd mail it to me, but . . ." She shrugged and looked down at her hands.

"Sorry. I shouldn't have asked," I said.

"No. It's okay. Maybe we should just change the subject." She quickly reached for her putty knife, but it slipped out of her hand. We both grabbed for it, and my gloved fingers closed over hers. We froze. I stared down at our plastic hands, my heart pounding.

"Well," Ally said. "That's romantic."

And we laughed. Suddenly my palms were sweating under my gloves. I slid my hand away and we got back to work, but I felt as if my whole body was on high alert. There was no getting around it anymore. I was falling for this girl.

Big-time.

ally

"What about this? You'd look hot!" I sang, holding out a brown suede jacket to David in the middle of the men's section at Macy's. "Your groupies would be all over you."

David looked at me dubiously, and I paused, suddenly hot with guilt. Did he realize I was trying too hard? When he'd asked me to come to the mall this afternoon to help him construct a new look for his band, I'd practically pole-vaulted at the chance, feeling like I somehow had to atone for all my Jakesession over the past week of morning detentions. But all I'd been thinking about since arriving at the Garden State Plaza an hour ago was how I had to break up with him. How I liked him too much to do this to him anymore. My stomach was in knots, my heart was in pain, and my brain felt like it was going to explode from trying to make myself appear chipper when I was anything but.

I kept thinking about that moment before Christmas. When

he'd held my hand and jokingly made me promise that if I went to the Crestie going away party, I'd come back. He was so cute and clueless to the fact that I was the most awful girlfriend ever. And now it looked like I was never coming back.

"I don't know. It's kind of seventies," he said. "Besides, do you really want my groupies to be all over me?"

He looped his arms around my waist and gave me a quick kiss on the lips.

I was a horrible person. A horrible, dishonest, nefarious person.

David turned away without waiting for an answer. As he flipped through a rack of plaid cowboy-style shirts, I felt like I was going to cry.

"What about this?" He lifted a distressed waffle-knit T-shirt off a separate rack.

"Jake has that shirt," I said, before I could edit myself.

David's face fell. He turned and jammed the shirt back on the rack. "Never mind."

"Sorry. I just . . ." I followed after him, my underarms prickling. Was it always so damn hot in this place? "Is something wrong?"

"No. Nothing," David said facetiously. "But do you even realize that's, like, the tenth time you've mentioned Jake today?"

He turned to face me between two huge racks of Tommy Hilfiger sweaters, his jacket folded over both hands. This was it. This was my chance. I had to tell him the truth. I had to tell him how I felt about Jake. He'd just given me the perfect opening.

"Ten times?" I said with a gulp. "Come on."

Chicken. Sorry-ass chicken.

"Okay, ten is a stretch, but still. In the Gap that guy behind the counter looked *just* like him, and in the food court? That whole story about how he ate five Egg McMuffins one morning during detention?"

Crap. Was it really that bad?

"Um, that adds up to three," I joked lamely.

"You like him, don't you?" David said.

Okay. It was now or never. I took a deep breath and held it for a moment. This was going to suck. Hard. "David, I'm really sorry—"

"I knew it!" He turned away from me and started speed walking for the aisle. "I am such an idiot. The guy asked you to dance right in the middle of me asking you out. If that's not a sign, what is?"

"David. Come on. Wait up!" I said, hustling after him as best I could with my bulky coat over my arm and my bag slung over my shoulder. "Can we just talk about this?"

We burst out into the aisle, and a woman wielding a perfume bottle squeaked as she sidestepped out of our way. David stopped in front of a Calvin Klein fragrance display and whirled on me. I'd never seen him angry before, and it was not a good look for him. His face was all blotchy, his nostrils flared, his eyes wet. My heart collapsed in on itself. It was my fault he looked like that. All my fault.

"What's to talk about? My girlfriend likes some other guy," he said, looking me dead in the eye. "So I guess she's not my girlfriend anymore."

Ouch. That hurt everywhere. David turned on his heel and stormed away.

"David. Wait!"

I wasn't sure why I was calling after him. What I expected to say. I just didn't want him to leave like that. I didn't want him to leave hating me so much that his entire walk was different.

And just like that, my first relationship ended. With all the Macy's fragrance-spritzing ladies as an audience. I supposed I should have been relieved. I'd known for weeks this was going to happen, and now it was finally over. But I'd hurt David. Just like Annie had predicted I would. And he was definitely one of the top four people I never wanted to see hurt.

God, I hate Valentine's Day. Whose idea was this stupid holiday anyway? Are they dead, or can I still kill them?

Whatever. It's one day.

Says the girl who has the boyfriend.

Well, don't worry. I sent you a flower.

Ugh! The flowers! I forgot about the stupid flowers. I only ever get the white ones. It's so humiliating.

Well, the flower sale is the cheerleaders' thing. Maybe you can just kill them.

Huh. That might make me feel better.

At least you're not a leper like Ally Ryan. Now that Dorkus Drake dumped her I bet she gets nothing.

Oh, sad. But that would make me feel better.

ally

Valentine's Day. The moment Quinn bounced into my home-room wearing a fake cotton diaper over her Seven For All Mankind jeans, carrying a foam bow and arrow and a quiver full of carnations, I knew I should have stayed in bed. It was an annual cheerleading fund-raiser, selling flowers for V-Day. White meant friendship. Pink meant secret admirer. Red, true love. The order forms had been handed out the week before. I'd torn mine up into exactly forty-eight pieces before tossing it into the garbage.

I wasn't with David, who refused to return my texts, my e-mails, and my calls and was now sitting with his bandmates at lunch every day. I wasn't with Jake, who I hadn't spoken to since our detention stint had ended almost a month ago because he'd never approached me in public, which made me feel like I shouldn't approach him—which, after all the fun we'd had together, seriously sucked. And my mom was going away to the Adirondacks with Gray Nathanson for the weekend. Valentine's Day could bite me.

"Flower delivery! Someone loves you!" Quinn announced, bouncing down the aisle distributing flowers. When she stopped next to my desk, I almost dead-legged her. "Hi, Ally! Somebody loves you!"

My heart stopped as she reached into her quiver and extracted a huge bundle of pink carnations tied with a red ribbon. Her grin was wide as she placed them in front of me. Probably she felt happy that I wasn't as big of a loser as she'd thought. I, however, was stunned speechless. Then she took out one lone pink and dropped that in front of me too.

"Who're they from?" Annie asked as Quinn moved on.

I flipped over the white slip on the bouquet. It had been decorated by the cheerleaders with glittering heart stickers, but the message was simple and written in careful letters.

HAPPY VALENTINE'S DAY

—Your secret admirer

Next to the signature was a small drawing of a sword and shield.

My knight in shining armor. I almost laughed out loud. Unbelievable. Jake had sent me Valentine's Day flowers. What did this mean? Did he like me? Was he going to ask me out? Or was he just trying to do something nice for me? Every day since detention ended, I had missed being with him. Maybe this was his way of telling me he missed me, too. That he wanted us to talk or something.

Maybe Valentine's Day wasn't all bad.

"Well?" Annie prodded.

"I don't know," I replied, avoiding eye contact. "Pink is secret admirer, remember?"

The tag on the second flower was blank. I had a feeling I knew who it was from, and I suddenly felt unpleasantly warm. Hammond had sent me a secret admirer flower that last Valentine's Day before I left, even though he and Chloe were already going out. What was wrong with him? Was he just messing with me? Trying to be nostalgic? Or did he actually still like me?

But no. A person who likes you doesn't help his friends prank you and invite you to parties that aren't there. They don't completely avoid talking to you for six months straight and then send you one lame flower. No. He was just messing with me. That had to be it.

Quinn deposited a white flower on Annie's desk. I could see David's handwriting on the slip and felt a momentary pang. If we'd never gone out, if we'd stayed just friends, I'd probably be receiving one from him now too. But I'd royally screwed up that one. Even though I understood why he wasn't speaking to me, it sucked that he wouldn't let me apologize. I missed him, too. Just in a completely different way than I missed Jake.

"Oh my God," Annie said, staring at the flower.

"What?"

"Logan didn't send me a flower," she said, glancing at Quinn's retreating back. "For the first time in three years, Logan Pincus did not send me a red flower."

"But that's a good thing, right?" I asked.

She slumped back in her chair. "I don't know."

I laughed. "Girl, you have some issues. Here. Want this one, too?" I said, tossing the extra pink at her.

"Oh, you have so many that you can give a few away to the pathetic masses?" she joked.

"Fine. Give it back," I said lightly.

She held the flower to her chest with a pout. "No! It makes me feel loved."

I laughed as the bell rang and everyone scrambled to their feet. I tried to shove my bouquet into my messenger bag, but there were too many. Instead I was forced to carry them in the crook of my arm like some pageant contestant.

"Well, obviously they're from Jake," Annie whispered as we hit the crowded corridor. All around us, people squealed over one another's flowers, thanking one another and debating who their secret admirers were.

"Uh, no," I said, even as I blushed.

"Why not? How many other guys have you besotted since you've been here?" Annie demanded, sidestepping another quiver-wielding cheerleader.

"Jake is not besotted by me," I said through my teeth, looking around to make sure neither he nor any of his friends was in earshot. What was I going to do when I saw him? What was he going to do?

"Please. I have the evidence right here in my notes," Annie said, whipping her sticker-covered notebook out of her bag. "He asks you to dance in front of all his anti-Ally friends, he takes back bad Shannen Moore pranks, he gets arrested for you and lands in detention. Look up *besotted* in the dictionary, my friend, because there will be a droopy-eyed picture of Jake Graydon. And you like him, too. Look! You're all red!"

"Can we drop this?" I hissed.

I had just spotted Shannen, Faith, Chloe, and Trista up ahead, and Shannen was holding almost as many flowers as I was, but hers were almost all white.

"Wow. Who're they all from?" Trista asked Shannen as we walked by.

"Pink's from Trevor. He sends one every year. And I got a white one from all my friends," she said, lifting them like a shrug. "Except Jake. He doesn't do flowers."

Annie and I exchanged a smile, and I could hardly contain my smug glee.

"He does flowers for some people," Annie sang under her breath. And I cracked up, this bubbly, silly joy gurgling inside of me. Shannen shot us a look, but I was ninety-nine percent sure it was because we were being weird, not because she'd heard Annie.

I rounded the corner, expecting at every moment to see Jake. Should I say hello? Smile? Ignore him? Play it cool? But as I came into the front hall I found myself face to face not with Jake, but David. His eyes widened and his face paled. And then he noticed the flowers.

"Oh," he said. "Hi."

It was the first time he'd said anything to me in over a month. My spirits surged with hope.

"Hey, David!"

"Looks like you're having a good Valentine's Day," he said flatly.

"Oh, these? Yeah, they're probably from some loser freshman or something," I said, waving the flowers around like a Fourth of July sparkler. "No biggie. How are you?"

"Fine." He looked away.

"Good!" I replied brightly.

"Yeah, well . . . see ya." He ducked his head and skirted around me. "Hey, Annie," he muttered as he passed.

I let out a breath and leaned sideways against the brick wall. My heart couldn't take this many emotional shifts so early in the morning. "Well. That sucked."

"Don't worry," Annie said. "He'll be all right."

"Yeah. But will we ever be friends again?" I asked.

Annie lifted her shoulders. "Probably," she said. "Unless you start going out with your 'secret admirer,'" she added, tossing in some air quotes. "Then all bets are off."

ally

That afternoon there was a pink slip on my desk in Spanish class. For the past two weeks all the juniors had been getting called to the guidance office to talk about college applications. Looked like it was my turn. As I strolled into the office, my heart instantly sank. Hammond Ross was sitting on the couch in the waiting area, slumped back with his legs splayed. He sat up straight the moment he saw me.

"I'm here for Mrs. Porter," I said to the secretary.

"She'll be with you in just a sec, hon," she replied as she typed frantically on her keyboard. "Have a seat."

I looked over at the couch. If possible, Hammond sat up even straighter, then shifted his bag to the floor to make room for me. Fabtastic. I walked over and dropped down next to him.

"Hey, Al. Happy Valentine's Day," he said.

"Yeah. You too," I replied flatly.

"Got any big plans?" he teased.

I blew out a sigh. "No."

"Looks like you got a lot of flowers there." He leaned forward as if to see them better, his hands folded between his knees. "I'm impressed a Norm would spring for something like that."

"How do you know they're from a Norm?" I snapped.

He laughed. Like anything else was inconceivable. Imagine if he knew they were from his best friend.

"Come on, Al. Who's the lucky guy?"

"I don't know, Ham. They're secret admirer flowers," I said in a condescending tone.

"Huh." He dropped down against the back of the couch

again. "When you get a bunch like that, I guess you don't notice one more."

I turned and looked him in the eye for the first time, my heart pounding blood through my veins at an alarming rate. Hammond's dark blue eyes danced happily, like he was oh so proud of himself.

"So, it was from you."

He shrugged and looked away. "Maybe. Maybe not."

"Have you forgotten that you have a girlfriend?" I said through my teeth, feeling warm and conspicuous and like I wanted to be anywhere but there.

"So?" he said, grinning at me. "Didn't matter the last time."

"You are such a pig!" I blurted.

The secretary looked over at us with that expression of impatience that half the faculty wore every day.

"I'm just kidding!" Hammond replied at a half whisper, like I was being so immature. "Calm down."

"I am calm," I said. "But just so we're clear, that night was a mistake, okay?"

A slight, embarrassed blush rose up onto his cheeks, and I instantly felt bad for being so blunt.

"Whatever," he said. He slumped down on the couch and crossed his arms over his chest, looking like a petulant kindergartner. "I was just trying to be nice. I figured no one would send you flowers, and I didn't want you to walk around school all day feeling all pathetic."

"Well, guess what? I did get flowers. So you didn't have to take pity on me," I shot back.

Mrs. Porter walked out of her cubicle with another student and sent him on his way. I was out of my seat, clutching my bag and my carnations, before she could even say my name.

"And if you want to be nice to me, how about you stop acting like I don't exist when you see me in the halls?" I said, looking back at Hammond. "I'd appreciate that a lot more than a flower."

He shook his head in exasperation, still staring straight ahead, but I could tell by the increased blotchiness of his face that he'd heard what I'd said. Maybe, just maybe, I'd finally gotten through to one of them.

ally

I sat in history class the following afternoon trying desperately to stay awake, my eyes crossing as I retyped Mr. Lewis's notes from the board and into my laptop. Outside, snow swirled and the wind whistled past the windowpanes. I was just about to let it all lull me to sleep when I saw my phone light up out of the corner of my eye. It was inside my bag but sticking out of the interior pocket just enough for me to see the screen. I glanced at the back of Mr. Lewis's balding head. He hadn't turned around in at least fifteen minutes, so enthralled was he with his own musings and getting every word of them down on the board. I snatched the phone into my lap. My heart started to pound, and suddenly I was wide awake. The text was from Jake.

Will any1 notice if I start snoring?

I glanced over my shoulder at him. He smirked and flashed his phone at me under the desk. How had he even gotten my number? I texted quickly, my fingers trembling.

IDK. How loud do u snore?

His response was immediate.

IDK. Sleep over some time and u can tell me.

I laughed out loud and slapped my hand over my mouth. Chloe turned around and shot me a reproachful look, her perfectly pink lips pursed. That was Chloe for you. Captain of the Manners Police. I loved how she didn't feel the need to acknowledge my existence unless she was silently telling me what to do.

"Something funny about the war of 1812, Miss Ryan?" Mr. Lewis asked.

"No," I squeaked.

"Good. Then let's get back to it," he replied.

My phone lit up again.

Busted!

I smiled and texted back.

Tnx 4 the flowers.

What flowers?

LOL V funny.

I have no idea what ur talking about.

I froze. It wasn't possible, was it? It had to have been him who sent the secret admirer flowers. He drew the shield and sword. No one else would have—

Gotcha!

I bit my tongue to keep from laughing. We texted for the rest of the class period. I found out his birthday was coming up in March. I told him that mine was in May. He confessed that his favorite snack dip was hummus. I told him mine was pineapple salsa. I asked if he really liked Hammond or was just taking pity. He said Hammond was cool when he wasn't licking his own reflection in the mirror. That earned him another laugh and me another lip-purse from Chloe. Toward the end of the period, Jake sent another text.

Ready 4 big game 2nite?

Valley High is going down! U coming?

Will b there cheering 4 u.

I blushed so hard I thought I might pop.

Cool.

When the bell rang, I tucked my phone away and closed my laptop. My pulse raced as I wondered what to do next. Clearly Jake and I had just taken our relationship, whatever it was, to some new level. Should I go talk to him? Was he going to come talk to me? Maybe just a smile over my shoulder and—

But then Jake walked right by me and over to Chloe and Faith, without so much as a nod. My heart fell. Apparently, the text fest hadn't changed a thing. But then why had he started it? What was the point? Was he really just that bored? Maybe he spent every class period texting someone, and he'd simply run through his entire address book.

As I lifted my bag onto my shoulder and started for the door, I loathed myself for getting so excited. Just before I got to the hallway, my phone lit up again. It was from him.

Same time tomorrow?

My heart, all of a sudden, was back from its trip to my toes. I texted back.

I'm in.

jake

The gym was packed. I'd been to a lot of Shannen's games last year, but I'd never seen it like this. One side was all yellow and purple, the other all maroon and gold. And everyone was screaming. Including me.

"Let's go, Shannen! Get the ball!" I wanted to yell for Ally, too, but I was surrounded by my friends. Still. I couldn't take my eyes off her.

The girl was effing good. Even better than I'd thought. All night she'd been hustling—taking shots when they were good, passing off when she was double-teamed, stealing the ball, getting in her player's face when she was on D. She didn't stop. I'd never seen anyone play so fierce in my life.

It was beyond hot.

"Come on!" Hammond shouted, leaning forward. "Don't let them hog the ball!"

"Let's go, Hill! Let's go, Hill!" the Idiot Twins shouted. They were shirtless behind us, their chests painted with tiger stripes, each wearing a huge burgundy frizz wig. Every time they cheered, the crowd cracked up.

The fans around us joined in the chant. "Let's go, Hill! Let's go, Hill!"

Time was ticking down. Only fifteen seconds left on the clock, and we were down by one.

"Come on, Shannen!" Chloe cheered politely.

"Yea, go," Faith said as she texted on her phone. She lifted a fist at shoulder level. "Whoo."

Hammond and I rolled our eyes at them.

"Ohmigod yes!" Trevor shouted suddenly.

"Go, Ally!" Todd added.

Suddenly the entire Orchard Hill side of the bleachers was on their feet. In the two seconds Hammond and I had taken our eyes off the court, Ally had somehow stolen the ball and was now sprinting toward the basket. I jumped up. One of the Valley players chased after her, probably intent on fouling her, but Ally was too fast. She made a perfect layup. The crowd went nuts. The scoreboard clicked. We were up by one with four seconds left. The whole team surrounded Ally, hugging her and slapping her hands. She nodded but didn't smile. The game wasn't over yet. She was all business.

Did I mention she was beyond hot?

Valley called a time-out and everyone relaxed into their seats. The cheerleaders jogged onto the floor to start a chant.

Faith finally looked up from her phone. "What happened? Did we win?"

"Not yet," Hammond said patiently. "They get one more shot."

"God. This game takes forever," she complained.

Chloe gave her a sympathetic pat on the knee.

The whistle blew.

"This is it." I had to stand up, because everyone in front of me did. The whole crowd was on its feet as two Valley players lined up at the end of the court. With only four seconds left they raced to the key. Coaches screamed, parents wailed, cheerleaders shouted. The taller girl passed it off to the lead scorer, and Shannen raced forward to get in the girl's face.

"Three! Two!"

The girl lifted her arms to take her shot, her eyes focused on the basket as if Shannen weren't even there.

"One!"

The shot went up. Shannen jumped. She reached. Time froze. And then, her fingertips just grazed the bottom of the ball, sending it sailing off the court.

"Yes!"

The timer buzzed, and the Orchard Hill bleachers emptied out onto the court, surrounding the team. Everyone was jumping up and down, hugging, screaming, crying. I was looking for Ally, hoping to congratulate her in the mayhem, when suddenly Shannen was in my arms.

"Did you see that?" she yelled.

"That was awesome!" I replied.

"We're going to Jump, right? Did Hammond drive?" She slung her arm over my shoulders, tugging me through the crowd. Hammond had scored an Explorer for his birthday, so he pretty much drove everywhere now. He'd been worried he wasn't going to get a car, but apparently his parents were selling their shore house after this summer to pay for his college, so now they felt like they had spending money again or something.

"Yeah. Let's find everyone."

My eyes scanned the gym, still looking for a glimpse of Ally. Finally I found her, standing over by the door, grinning at her mom. Dr. Nathanson and Quinn were over there too, Quinn bouncing around in her cheerleading uniform like a toddler on too much Kool-Aid. I guess the high of a big win canceled out whatever negative feelings she had about Ally. Then a couple of guys from the basketball team—Marshall Moss and Chad Lancaster—went over and gave Ally these big bear hugs. Marshall practically swallowed her into his varsity jacket even though she was covered in sweat. A lump rose up in my throat. What was that all about?

"Jealous?"

I blinked. "What?"

Shannen stood in front of me, her arms crossed over her

jersey. "Want me to go invite her to Jump?" she asked sarcastically, nodding over her shoulder at Ally and her growing entourage. Her friend Annie was over there now too, plus Dorkus Drake, though he was hanging back looking pouty.

"What? No. What are you talking about?" I said.

She rolled her eyes at me. "You *so* like her. Why don't you just admit it already?"

"I was looking for Hammond and Chloe." I spotted them standing next to the bleachers. "There they are. Let's go."

"Yeah. Sure you were. I have to hit the showers first," Shannen said, clearly irritated. "I'll catch up with you guys."

I watched her jog toward the door, which also gave me a chance to check if Ally and Marshall were holding hands, or worse. But they weren't. Which was good, at least. Ally turned and followed Shannen toward the locker room, and her family went out to the lobby to hover and wait—Marshall and the rest of them included. A surge of envy nearly knocked the wind out of me as Marshall yucked it up with Ally's mom. Marshall and those guys got to be close to Ally—to help her celebrate after one of the biggest wins of the year. And I—just because of where I lived and who my friends were—couldn't.

jake

"Where the hell are we going?"

"Have you learned nothing yet?" Shannen asked, turning around to walk backward so she could face me. "When I'm in charge, you don't get to know till you know!" A freezing cold wind whipped her hair in front of her face. She and Faith giggled and walked ahead again, looping their arms together. Hammond cursed under his breath. I kicked black snow from the curb onto Fourteenth Street and got cursed at by some crazy dude on a bike.

It was fifteen below outside. No one should have been out in the city—on foot, on a bike, or at all. But for some reason, we had let Shannen talk us all into driving in and going to Paddy B's, this one bar in the Village that Cresties had been going to since the dawn of time because they didn't card. All of us except Chloe, who had some big family event tonight. I didn't get what the big urge was to hit Paddy B's all of a sudden. We'd been there before Christmas, and we could have gone again when it wasn't cold as a witch's butt cheek.

And now, after an hour of playing pool and drinking beer, we were out on the street again, following Shannen to do who knew what who knew where. Only the Idiot Twins had stayed behind at the bar, wanting to finish a game of darts with a couple of NYU dudes who had challenged them. We were supposed to swing back there and pick them up after we completed Shannen's latest mission. Whatever it was.

Shannen and Faith suddenly stopped in front of a brightly lit window. They peered inside, clutching each other, standing on their toes.

"Holy shit. It's him," Shannen said.

Faith doubled over laughing. "Oh. My. God. Come on. Let's go in!"

Hammond looked up from the turned-up collar of his coat. He stared at the sign, which read FIFTH AVENUE GOURMET.

"Oh, shit," he said.

"What?"

But he was already following the girls through the door. Why couldn't anyone answer me? I grabbed the still-closing door and tromped into the warm shop. Shannen had her cell phone out and was holding it up as if to take a picture as Faith strode up to the counter.

"Mr. Ryan?" Faith said with a gasp. "Oh my God! Is that *you*?"

My heart took a nosedive. Mr. Ryan? As in—?

The man behind the counter was tall, slim, graying, and stunned. He wore a white shirt, a stained black apron, and a matching visor. He was getting paler by the second. Ally's father. I was looking at Ally's father.

"Hello, Faith . . . Shannen. How are you girls?" He looked at Shannen, who was still holding up her phone. "Are you—is that a camera phone?"

"No," Shannen said, waving her phone around. "I just can't seem to get any bars in here."

My fingers clenched into fists at my sides. Suddenly I realized what she was doing. She was taping this onto her video card. And he had no idea.

"Hi, Mr. Ryan," Hammond said, walking up to the counter. "Sorry to surprise you like this. Shannen didn't tell us where we were going," he said through his teeth, staring Shannen down.

"What? I didn't know he worked here," Shannen said. Her acting was completely believable. "Do you *actually* work here?" she asked, training her phone on Mr. Ryan.

"Well . . . yes. I do. I have . . . for about a year now," Mr. Ryan said, looking suspiciously at the phone. "Chloe's father was kind enough to give me a job while I get back on my feet. I've been trying to get my old job back."

"Yeah? And how's that working out for ya?" Shannen said, leaning her elbow on the countertop and keeping the lens trained on him. "I mean, it's gotta be tough after you cheated dozens of people out of, what, millions of dollars?"

His lips clamped together, and he looked like he was about to hurl. "It . . . it wasn't like that," he said. "It's complicated. You kids couldn't understand—"

"Well, why don't you try explaining it to us?" Faith said snottily.

He slipped his visor off. Bowed his head. Mopped his brow with the back of his hand. "I . . . I didn't . . . I never meant to . . ."

That was it. I couldn't take it anymore. "All right. That's enough."

Shannen whirled around, surprised. It was like she'd forgotten I was there. I grabbed the phone out of her hand and exited camera mode.

"What's your problem?" Shannen asked.

"Excuse us, sir," I said, clamping my arm around Shannen's shoulders. "We were just leaving." I dragged Shannen out of there, feeling her tense under my arm.

"I just wanted to say thanks a lot, Mr. Ryan," Faith said behind me. "If it wasn't for you, my parents wouldn't be getting divorced."

Unbelievable. This was why we'd come into the city? To torture Ally's dad?

"Faith, I'm so sorry," he replied. "I didn't—"

"Whatever."

We were back out on the cold sidewalk, but my skin was so hot I didn't feel the chill anymore.

"What the hell was that?" Shannen shoved me away from her with both hands. "You don't get to throw me around!"

"What were you doing in there, Shannen?" I demanded. "You can't just ambush somebody like that."

"Why not? He ambushed us when he stole all our money!"

"He's right, Shannen," Hammond said, joining us. "That was not cool."

Shannen rolled her eyes. "Of course you guys would defend Ally's dad."

"What the hell does that mean?" Hammond blurted.

"Are you forgetting what that guy did to us?" Shannen said, ignoring his question. "So what if seeing us made him feel bad for five minutes? I feel bad every fucking day of my life thanks to him!"

"She's right. He deserves it," Faith put in, shoving her hands into the pockets of her white coat. Her nose was all red and her eyes watery, but I couldn't tell if it was from the cold or because she was upset. "I can't even believe Chloe's dad would give him a job."

"Not to mention a place to stay," Shannen said, looking up at the apartments over the deli. Another stiff wind nearly blew us all off our feet. "What a traitor."

"He's not a traitor," Hammond spat, turning up the collar of his coat again. "He saw a friend in trouble and helped him out. Any one of us would do the same for you."

"Yeah, Shannen," I said. "You of all people know that it's not all black and white when it comes to friends."

Her eyes flashed, and she glared at me. We both knew I was walking a fine line, talking about the Hammond/Chloe/Ally situation right in front of the others. But I was right. I knew I was.

"What I don't get is, why tonight?" Hammond asked. "Chloe spilled back before Christmas. Why the sudden motivation to come find him?"

Shannen shrugged. "Oh, I don't know. Something happened after the game last night that inspired me," she said, looking me right in the eye.

"What's that supposed to mean?" I asked. Was she doing this because she thought I liked Ally? Trying to remind me that the Norm wasn't worthy because her dad worked in a deli? How shallow did she think I was?

"Whatever. I'm over this conversation," Shannen said. "Let's get the hell out of here."

She turned around and grabbed Faith's hand, speed walking down the street. Hammond and I looked at one another, sighed, and followed. All I could think about for the rest of the night was the look on Mr. Ryan's face when he'd seen Faith. He looked scared. Like he was watching his life pass before his eyes. I knew the feeling. I'd seen Ally's dad. I knew right where he was. Where he worked, where he lived.

The question was, what the hell was I going to do about it?

Okay. Ally Ryan just texted all through French class.

So?

So!? Who is she texting?

I saw her hanging out with Marshall Moss at Starbucks last night.

No. Seriously? She just broke up with David Drake.

Um, that was, like, a month ago.

I bet he's the one who sent her all those flowers.

David?

No. Marshall. He seems like the romantic type.

Not possible. Marshall was still going out with Kristie Murphy on Valentine's Day. He got her those gold earrings and then she dumped him?

So, wait. In the last month Ally Ryan has had David Drake, Marshall Moss, and some secret admirer all over her?

Yeah.

I thought she was supposed to be unpopular.

ally

Quinn twirled across the stage in a sequined pink leotard and huge, graceful tutu, her arms perfectly turned, her hair perfectly bunned, her feet perfectly pointed. Everyone in the audience applauded as she finished her circuit, my mom more enthusiastically than anyone. I checked my watch and sighed. When was this thing going to be over already?

My mother looked at me and clucked her tongue. But what did she expect? I'd never been a dancer, I'd never been remotely interested in dance, and yet here I was, sitting through a three-hour-long dance recital just so I could catch Quinn in one group number and one solo? Was this really how she thought I wanted to spend my Saturday? I couldn't even believe this was where *she* wanted to be right now. But she'd said that Quinn had asked her personally to come, and she couldn't turn her down. I guess the two of them were getting closer or something. Which of course completely wigged me out. I mean, it was sad that Quinn's mother had passed away and all, and I'm sure it was nice for her to have a mom-type figure here watching her performance. But why did it have to be *my* mom?

Okay, that was selfish and immature. But still. I didn't like where this was headed. It felt way too blended-family. If I wasn't step-freaked before, I definitely was now.

Of course, it wasn't like I had anything better to do. Annie was working. David was still avoiding me. Marshall and the guys from the basketball team were going to a Knicks game tonight and spending the day in the city. And Jake was not an option. Today was his birthday. I'd texted him to wish him a happy birthday that morning, but so far, no reply. He'd probably gotten his license and a brand-new car and was now out with Hammond and the twins and Shannen doing something Crestie. Something I couldn't be a part of.

As soon as the lights came up at intermission, I was out of my seat. The vending machines were calling my name. If I was going to make it through the second half of this thing, I was going to need caffeine. And sugar. Preferably in the form of chocolate.

"What is with your attitude today, Ally?" my mom asked, coming up behind me as I popped the top on an ice-cold can of Coke.

"Sorry. I just . . . why am I here again?" I asked.

My mother sighed and leaned back against the light blue cinder block wall. The recital was being held at some regional school a half hour from home, and I wondered if every school in North America had some kind of cinder block wall somewhere within its structure.

"You're here to support Quinn," she said.

"Right! Right." I took a slug of my soda. "And why am I supporting Quinn again?"

"Ally," my mom said in a warning tone.

I stepped away from the soda machine so the shaggy-haired skater dude behind me could get his fix—solidarity, brother—and stood next to her.

"What? I'm serious. Quinn and I aren't even friends. She doesn't care if I'm here or not."

"Well, that's kind of the point," my mother said. "Gray and I were hoping we could all hang out so you two could get to know each other better."

A knot tightened in my chest. That sounded ominous. "Why?"

"Because, hon. Gray and I have been dating for six months now," she said. "It would be nice if we could all feel comfortable getting together. It would just make things . . . easier."

Yeah. For you. But what about me? And what if my dad ever came back? What was she going to do if he walked in on some cozy family tableau of us and the Nathansons playing Scrabble in front of the fire?

Not that the condo had a fireplace, but still.

"So? What do you say? Can you give me one Saturday?" my mother asked.

I rolled my eyes. "Fine." I straightened up when I saw Gray looking for us in the noisy crowd. "There's your main squeeze now."

She shook her head at me, then waved her hand to summon him. Gray saw us and started to cut through the milling parents and dance teachers and siblings. At least he was wearing a button-down shirt buttoned up all the way today. No chest hair to be seen. I took a big swallow of soda as he approached.

"Hello, ladies," he said, giving my mom a kiss as he joined us. I looked away. "Enjoying the show so far?"

"Yeah. It's great," I said flatly. "She's a natural."

My phone suddenly vibrated. My heart leapt into my throat, and I yanked the phone out of my jacket pocket. It was a text from Jake.

Thnx 4 bday wish. Sry been out w rents all day.

I smiled and texted back.

No prob. Get ur license?

Yep. Am official driver.

"She acts, too," Gray was saying proudly. "In fact, next weekend I'm taking her down to Long Beach Island so she can audition for this local theater group. If she gets the part we'll be, living down there all summer."

Suddenly I was feeling very perky. Between Jake getting back to me and this, my "attitude" was doing a complete 180. "Really? That's great. You have a house at the shore?" Which you will be moving to? For eight to twelve whole weeks? Sayonara, dude! So much for spending quality time together. I don't know why I was surprised. Every Crestie family had a house on LBI. We'd even had one, before. This was the best news ever.

"Yep. Quinn can't wait to get down there," he said, putting his arm around my mother. "In fact, I was thinking . . . if we do end up relocating for the summer, maybe you two would like to come with."

I nearly dropped my phone. My mother looked at me hopefully. Clearly this was something they had already discussed.

"What do you think, Ally? A whole summer at the beach?" my mother said brightly.

Um, I thought it sounded like my own personal version of hell. Living with Gray and Quinn like we were a family? Would I have to share a room with the little sugarplum fairy? And would my mother be sharing a room with Gray? Vomit.

Plus, Hammond spent the entire summer down there. And Chloe and Faith and the Idiot Twins. If they all still had their houses after what my father had done.

But then . . . did Jake's family have a house down there? It made sense. They went to Sunday night dinners. They belonged to the country club. Jake's mom was clearly a joiner. Had she gone so far as to buy in to the LBI market so she could summer with the other Cresties? Who knew? But even if he didn't have a house down there, he'd definitely be visiting Hammond. Everyone always brought down friends to stay for the weekends or even for full weeks at a time.

"I think . . ."

My mother's eyes were sort of pleading. And I'd just promised to drop the attitude. And suddenly I was having visions of me and Jake hanging out on the beach, going waterskiing on the bay, sharing a seat on the Ferris wheel at Fantasy Island. . . . There was something magical about the idea. About summer. About being away from home, away from here. Even though some of his friends would be around, there was that idea that anything could happen. That all the rules could be broken. Because it was summer.

"I think it sounds great," I said.

"Yeah?" My mother seemed surprised.

"Yeah," I said. The lights in the lobby started to flash, signaling the beginning of the second act. "Come on. Let's go before someone takes our seats."

I saw my mom and Gray exchange a happy look as I walked in ahead of them, and my stomach turned, but less violently than usual. Yes, I was going to have to deal with them being all coupley all summer. And probably having Quinn all up in my grill trying to give me girly makeovers and drag me off to Sur La Plage for daily shopping sprees. But there would also be Jake.

And lots of possibility.

jake

I blew out the candles on my cake. Actually it was two cakes. One was shaped like a one, the other like a seven. Every year it was the same. My mother baked a cake in the shape of the number of the birthday and bought exactly that many balloons. Every year we took a family picture with the cake and the balloons, and every year that picture was framed and nailed to the wall in my mom's craft room by the following afternoon. There was one wall for mine, one wall for Jonah's. Every year it was the same, and every year she acted like it was all insanely exciting.

But it was her thing, so I went with it. Besides, between my multiple groundings and all the tension about grades and SATs lately, it seemed like a good idea to just chill.

"Did you make a good wish?" my mother asked, squeezing my shoulders from behind.

"Yeah," I replied. I hadn't made a wish since I was ten.

She plucked the candles from the cake, and my father moved in with the cake cutter. He hacked off a huge chunk and slapped it on a plate for Jonah.

"Looks like we're going to have a lot of leftovers," he said.

"I don't know why you didn't want to invite your friends over, Jake," my mother put in as my father jammed the knife into the cake. I smirked, wondering what his plastic surgery patients—the ones who trusted their faces and thighs and boobs to his delicate hands—would think if they could see him going to town on this cake.

"I just didn't feel like it," I said. Then, because my mother looked stricken, I added, "I just wanted to hang out with you guys."

That immediately cheered her up. What I didn't tell her was that I had a plan for tonight. A birthday present to give myself. And it didn't involve my friends.

"Here you go, Jake." My father handed me a piece of cake. I wasn't remotely hungry.

"What about presents?" I asked. There was no pile of wrapped gifts at the end of the table like there usually was. We all knew I was getting a car. That's what Crestie kids got on their seventeenth birthdays. It wasn't like I was going to pout if I didn't get one, but I knew my mother well enough to know that if everyone else on the Crest was going to be getting a car, she would be physically unable to buck the trend. I'd been hinting about wanting a Jeep Wrangler for months. Now I was curious to see if my parents had gotten me what I wanted, or if my mother had decided that a Jeep wasn't upscale enough for her son to be driving around town.

"Presents?" My dad looked at my mom with a fake frown. "Did we get him any presents this year, Linda?"

"Not that I can recall, Ted," she said. "I feel just horrible. How can we have spaced on such a thing?"

"You guys," I said as Jonah snorted a laugh. "Come on."

"I know. Why don't you take these and go to the mall?" my father suggested. He tossed me a set of keys. "Get yourself something good."

The Jeep logo stared up at me from the key chain.

"Shut up," I said.

My parents grinned. I dropped my cake and ran out the front door. Sitting in the driveway was an army green Jeep Wrangler with a removable hard top. It was so clean it shone under the full moon.

"Happy birthday, kid," my dad said, ruffling my hair.

I ducked away but then hugged him. Then my mom. "Thanks guys. This is insane. You didn't have to do this."

"Take her for a spin," my dad said.

"I'm coming!" Jonah announced.

"No. No way," I said, stopping him as he tried to get into the passenger seat.

"Come on!" he protested.

"I'll take you out tomorrow, Jonah, I swear," I said.

"Mom!" he whined.

"Jonah, it's his birthday," my mother said. "He told you he'd drive you around tomorrow."

Jonah's head drooped, and he moped back into the house. "Fine. But I'm eating all your cake."

"Go crazy, dude," I replied. "Thanks, guys," I said again. Then I jumped into the car and shoved the key into the ignition. The rev of the engine rattled my lungs, and my fingertips sizzled. It was official. I was free. I could go out whenever I wanted to. Drive to the mall. Drive to the shore. Drive anywhere I wanted and take along, or not take along, whomever I wanted.

Suddenly my phone rang. My heart stopped. Was she psychic? I fumbled it out of my back pocket and looked at the screen. The call was from Shannen. Oh. I answered.

"Hey," I said.

"Did you get it?" she asked.

"I did. Army green. It's fucking awesome," I replied.

"Then get your ass over here and pick me up. I have to get out of here."

"Your dad?" I asked, holding my breath.

"He's not home yet, but they had a huge fight last night, so I'm expecting round two."

"I'm sure it'll be all right. Maybe it won't even happen."

"Yeah, right. Why aren't you in my driveway yet?"

I felt a twinge of guilt and tried to ignore it. "I can't. I've got some stuff I gotta do."

"Stuff? What stuff? It's your birthday."

"I know. I just . . . I gotta go. I'll call you later."

"Jake. You better not —"

I ended the call and silenced my phone. I felt guilty for bailing on her, but right now she was not the person I wanted to see. She could handle her dad when she needed to. And if not, she had four other houses she could run to. My parents were still standing there, arms wrapped around each other against the cold, their breath making steam clouds in the air. I lifted my hand in a wave and pulled out of the driveway. It felt weird to be driving by myself. No parent or instructor telling me to stay to the right, slamming their feet into the floor as if there were brakes there. My heart was pounding as I made my way slowly down Vista View Lane and put my blinker on at the bottom. My skin felt alert, and the hair on my neck stood on end. My hands were actually shaking.

This was what freedom felt like.

I drove slowly up Harvest toward Twin Oaks Drive. Parents were just getting home from work. A couple of kids played basketball in one driveway. Someone was taking his garbage to the curb. Every time something moved in my peripheral vision, I flinched, but I tried to sit back and look cool just in case anyone saw me out their window. In two minutes I was there. I pulled my car into the driveway in front of the huge brick house and took a deep breath as I cut the engine.

My maiden voyage. No accidents. I got out of the car feeling as if I'd just come home from some kind of crusade. My knees were shaky as I strode up the steps and rang the bell. Every inch of me was on fire with nerves. The door whipped open. Dr. Nathanson stood in front of me, confused.

"Jake?"

"Hi, Dr. Nathanson. Sorry to interrupt," I said. "Is Ally here?"

His brow creased, but he smiled. "Uh, sure. Come on in."

I'd never been inside Quinn's house before. It was decorated all country-style, with plaid and leather and flowers. There was a fire going in the living room, which we passed right by. As we got closer to the kitchen I heard someone laughing, but it wasn't Ally. When we came around the corner, I saw Ally's mom and Quinn at one end of the table, cracking up over Chinese food containers. Ally was at the other end, poking her food with chopsticks.

"Ally. You have a visitor." Dr. Nathanson still sounded surprised. I guess he wasn't used to people dropping by for Ally. But she had texted me that she was going to be here, and a guy had to do what a guy had to do.

She looked up and her whole face changed. It completely lit up. That reaction made me feel happier than I'd ever felt in my whole life.

"Hey," I said. "Wanna go for a ride?"

ally

"Mom?" I said. "Can I?"

My mother set her fork down. "Ally, we're guests of Gray and Quinn's tonight."

"I know, but—"

"It's my birthday," Jake interrupted.

"Oh. Happy birthday," Gray said.

"Thank you, sir," Jake replied with a nod. "Anyway, I just got a car, and I thought maybe Ally and I could go get some coffee or something."

My mom raised one eyebrow. I guess she didn't buy the coffee story. But what did she think I was gonna do? We were just going to go for a drive.

"Please, Mom?" I stood up and reached for my coat. "It's his birthday."

My mother exchanged a look with Gray, and I bristled. Was she consulting him on parenting decisions now? God, now I really had to get out of there. From the corner of my eye, I saw him nod and shrug. I held my breath.

"Fine," my mom said. "You can go."

"Thanks! Bye, Gray! Bye, Quinn," I said as brightly as I could.

"Just drop her at home before ten, please!" my mom shouted after us as we headed for the foyer.

"I will! Thanks, Mrs. Ryan!" Jake called back.

I was kind of glad he'd made a point to say her name. She was, after all, still Mrs. Ryan. Apparently she needed some reminding of that.

Outside, I jumped into the brand-new Jeep with its dealer plates and had barely even inhaled that new car smell before he'd whipped out of the driveway so fast the tires squealed. He slammed on the brakes and swallowed.

"Sorry."

"It's okay. Let's just get out of here," I said.

He hit the gas and we were gone. I had wanted out of there so badly that I actually felt like we were on the run. Once again, Jake was my white knight. I closed my eyes as he took a right and drove farther up the hill. I guessed he really had been lying about the coffee. We were not headed downtown. I felt a skitter of excitement and apprehension. Where, exactly, was he taking me?

"What was going on back there?" he asked.

"That? That was a nightmare," I told him. I looked at his profile. His perfect, handsome profile, and suddenly it hit me. I was in a car alone with Jake Graydon. Who cared where he was taking me? It was his birthday, and he'd gotten a car, and he'd come to me. Not one of his random hook-ups, not one of his friends, but me. I was actually talking to Jake again. Saying words instead of sending texts. And it felt normal. Comfortable. Exhilarating, but not at all awkward. And suddenly I wanted to tell him everything. "My mom's trying to make me bond with Quinn. I think my mom and Gray are getting serious."

"Wow. That's . . . that sucks. Right?"

"Yeah. I guess. I don't know."

He made a left, and suddenly I realized where we were going. The country club. More specifically, the lake at the country club. I hadn't been there in forever, but I knew no one went there during the winter unless they were going to park in the dirt lot by the boathouse and make out.

Suddenly I couldn't breathe. I pressed my sweaty palms into the thighs of my jeans, feeling light headed. We were both silent until Jake pulled into the deserted lot facing the wide-open lake. He put the car in park, but didn't turn off the engine. He kind of slumped back against the seat and looked out at the water.

"So," I said. "Happy birthday."

"Thanks," he replied. "Sorry about just coming over like that. I didn't think—"

"That you'd be interrupting the pseudofamily dinner from hell?" I asked.

"Yeah." He took a deep breath and ran his hands up and down the steering wheel. He glanced at me tentatively. "Hey, have you heard from your dad at all?"

Another car was driving up the road, its headlights flashing in Jake's side mirror. It turned and parked at the other end of the lot, the couple inside probably wanting their privacy.

"Nope," I said, my heart heavy. "It's like he doesn't even remember we exist. He didn't even call on my mom's birthday or anything. I have no idea where he is." I let out a short laugh. "How bizarre is that? I don't know where my father is." There was a long moment of silence. Jake chewed a bit on his bottom lip. There was something weirdly tense about him.

Jake said, "Do you think he'd come back if he knew? I mean, if he knew your mom and Mr. Nathanson were . . ."

My heart squeezed. "I don't know. Maybe. I have all these daydreams about it. Like I'll walk out of school one day and he'll be standing there and he'll hug me and ask me where she is. And then I'll tell him all about her and Gray and we'll run into the school together and catch them, like, kissing in her office or something and my dad'll freak out and punch Gray in the face and tell him to stay away from his wife. It's all very dramatic."

Jake laughed and I blushed.

"I know. It's stupid." I shook my head, looking down at my hands. I'd never told anyone about that daydream before.

"It's not. I get it."

"Anyway. That'll never happen. I guess I just have to get used to the idea of my mom and Gray. Together."

Tears filled my eyes and I stopped. I felt like an idiot. "I'm sorry. You don't want to hear this crap," I said. "It's your birthday."

"No. It's fine," he replied.

I took a deep breath, gazing out at the placid surface of the water. Across the lake, the window wall on the ballroom of the country club glowed with yellow light. A thousand memories of late-night parties with my parents, of sack races by the lake on summer Club Day, of swimming races in the pool with my friends, suddenly flooded my mind. My heart was full of all the things that I'd had to give up. Things that, clearly, I was never going to have again.

"I really never thought I'd be back here."

Suddenly Jake's fingers closed over mine. My heart completely stopped. He turned his hand so that it was under mine, our palms touching, and laced our fingers together. Every nerve ending in my body was in that hand.

"Ally."

He said my name almost like a plea. I looked into his eyes.

"I know," I said simply.

And then we kissed.

And it was just as amazing as I'd always imagined.

jake

Sunday at noon I rang the doorbell at Shannen's house. It was the only time I could be sure that both she and her dad would be awake and in semidecent moods. I knew Shannen was going to be irritated about last night, but I figured a ride in the new car and breakfast at Jump would win her over. And I also kind of wanted to talk to her about this whole thing with Ally's dad. After last night, I felt even guiltier about keeping the secret. Was Shannen going to tell Ally? Did she still have that video? If someone was going to tell her, it had to be done right. And I had a feeling that if Shannen did it, it wouldn't be done right. I'd been avoiding talking to her about it up until now, not wanting to deal, but if Ally and I were going to be . . . whatever we were going to be, then not dealing wasn't an option. A decision had to be made. Shannen and I were going to figure this out. Today. But as I waited for someone to answer, I started to get nervous. What if her dad was already drunk? Or had a serious hangover? I hated dealing with him when he was pissed. I was deciding between ringing again and getting back into my Jeep when the door whipped open. Shannen stood there in sweats, scowling at me.

"Hey," I said with a smile, lifting my keys. "Wanna go for a ride?"

She crossed her arms over her chest. "Oh. So now the birthday boy suddenly decides I'm worthy?"

My arms fell to my sides. "Come on. I told you I had stuff to do last night."

She let out a short laugh. "Stuff. Good one."

What was that supposed to mean? "Look, it's totally nice out. We can go to Jump and get those bialys you like."

She narrowed her eyes at me and put her hand on the door. "I already ate." Then she started to slam the door.

I reached out and stopped it, my hand flat on the surface. "Wait."

"What?" she snapped.

"I don't know why you're so mad—"

She went to close the door again. I blocked it with my foot this time.

"But I just have to ask you something," I said, feeling desperate. Like I had some kind of ticking clock behind me.

"What?"

"You're not gonna show that video to Ally, are you? The one with her dad?" I asked.

She laughed. "You are unbelievable."

"What? I just . . . don't think she should find out that way," I said, my face hot. "Think about it. If you were her, would you want to find out that way?"

She narrowed her eyes again, still holding on to the door. "No. I wouldn't."

"Good, so just . . . don't. I think if he wants to see them, he'll go see them. It's none of our business."

As I said the words, I suddenly felt very confident about them. It didn't matter that I knew what I knew. It wasn't my place or Shannen's or anyone else's to tell Ally. This was her family's thing. If we got involved, things would just get messy. As long as I could ensure Shannen would stay quiet, I knew I could keep my mouth shut too. We'd just wait it out, and eventually Ally's dad would come around and get in touch. He'd have to, right?

"Fine," she said. "I won't tell her anything." There was something hard and final about her face as she looked at me. "Are we done here?"

I moved my foot out of the way of the door, feeling lighter

somehow. Shannen wasn't going to tell Ally, which meant I didn't have to tell Ally.

"You sure you don't want to go for a drive?"

She rolled her eyes one last time and slammed the door in my face.

Do you have a date for the prom yet?

What? It's over a month away. Why? Do people already have dates?

Um, yeah! Josh Schwartz asked Melissa Ferreti in homeroom this morning, and now everyone's asking everyone. Connor Shale's going with Shannen Moore . . . Chad Lancaster asked Lisa Rinaldi. . . .

Ohmigod. Who am I gonna go with?

Has Jake asked anyone yet?

Ohmigod. Jake Graydon is my dream date.

Well, maybe you should ask him.

Please. And be that pathetic?

If you don't do it, someone else will. That boy will be snapped up before third period.

Ohmigod. This is so stressful. I'm going to the nurse.

If you do, you might miss your chance. And then you'll be stuck at the dance babysitting some dude from St. Mark's who you don't even know just because you're vague Facebook friends and there was no one else left.

I loathe the prom.

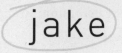

jake

I grinned to myself when I heard her footsteps coming down the hall. She started to pass me, and I reached out and grabbed her wrist.

"Jake! What are you doing?"

"This."

I pulled her to me and kissed her, cupping the back of her head with my hand. Ally giggled and melted into me, her whole body melding with mine. Two seconds later, though, she pulled away.

"We can't do this. We're so gonna get caught." But her hands were on my chest and she was blushing like crazy. She bit her bottom lip, and I almost died.

"No one ever comes into this hall at lunch," I said, glancing at the door to Barry's Custodians Only closet. Ally looked up and laughed.

"This is kind of our place," she joked.

"Where it all began," I joked back, tugging her to me with my arms around her waist. It wasn't exactly true. It had begun at my house that day back in August. But it was those detentions that had forced us to actually talk. That was where I'd really started to like her. Not just daydream about her. I leaned in and touched my lips to hers, giving her a long, slow kiss. When I broke it off, her eyes stayed closed and her head tipped back.

"You really want to go back to the cafeteria?" I whispered, tucking her hair behind her ear with my fingertips. I could practically hear her heart pounding. Or maybe that was mine.

"Mm mm," she said, shaking her head.

"Good."

So we stood there kissing without a single breath for air, until the bell rang and we finally had to wake up.

My palms sweated as I clutched my number two pencil. Time was running out. I could feel it. I stared at number thirty two, willing it to just tell me the answer.

Baseball player's chocolate bar. Baseball player's chocolate bar. It wasn't a Baby Ruth. That didn't fit. Who the heck else had a chocolate bar?

"Done!" Annie rang the bell and dropped her pencil. She shoved her completed crossword across the counter for me to envy. "Read it and weep."

I moaned and slapped my book closed. "I suck!" I said, head in hands.

"This is true," Annie replied with a matter-of-fact nod. "Why are you even here? Shouldn't you be, like, cheering for your man at the lacrosse game?"

I groaned again and stood up straight, stepping aside so Annie could ring up an elderly lady who had a basketful of discount toilet paper.

"First of all, I don't have a man. And secondly, since I don't have a man it would be kind of odd for me to attend the lacrosse game and cheer for him," I said, leaning back in front of the second register, which was closed.

"I see. Verboten boyfriends can be difficult that way," Annie said.

She handed the woman her change and gave me a hesitant look as the lady moved toward the door. "So, listen, there's something I feel like I should tell you, but I'm not sure if I should tell you."

My heart thumped with foreboding, and I stood up straight. "Well, now you obviously have to tell me."

She took a deep breath. "Okay, but I'm not entirely sure what it means."

"Annie, what?" I demanded.

"I was at the *Acorn* today and Shannen came in to talk to Chloe," Annie said, tugging her laptop out of her bag, which was behind the counter. "Of course I tried to listen in, as I always do, but they were whispering, so it was hard to hear everything."

My throat prickled. "What did they say?"

Annie opened her computer. "I typed up what I heard," she said, glancing at the screen. "Shannen said something about 'that night we went to Paddy's.' Then she said something I didn't hear, and then Chloe flipped out. She said, 'What? How could you do that? You promised me you wouldn't do anything—'"

"What were they talking about?" I asked.

"I don't know," Annie said. "But then I distinctly heard Shannen say, 'Jake made me swear I wouldn't tell Ally.'"

I felt like the floor had just dropped out from under me. Shannen and Jake were keeping secrets from me together? Secrets Chloe knew about?

Annie looked up at me, her eyes wide with apology. "Should I not have told you?"

"No. It's good. It's fine," I said, my mind reeling.

I saw a pair of headlights flash in the parking lot. Jake was there. Perfect timing, as always.

"He's here," I said.

Annie glanced over her shoulder out the window. "You should just ask him about it," she said confidently. "Maybe it's nothing."

Right. Somehow I had a hard time believing that.

"Yeah," I said. "Maybe I will." But I found I couldn't move. Jake honked the horn and waved me out, grinning.

"Or just forget about it," Annie said. "I feel bad that I just ruined your night. Just go and have fun."

"Yeah," I said, grabbing my jacket off the end of the counter. "Yeah. Okay. Thanks, Annie."

Outside, a misty rain fell from the dark April sky. I popped open the door of the Jeep, and Jake grinned at me. He had a streak of dirt on his face, and the entire side of his uniform was caked in mud. My whole body responded to his gorgeousness, but my heart felt sour. Why was he keeping secrets from me? And with my former best friend/current worst enemy?

"Wow. Rough game?" I asked, trying for a light tone.

"You should see the other guys."

He pulled out, and within fifteen minutes we were parked in the country club lot again. He leaned over to kiss me, but I couldn't kiss him back.

"Hey. Is everything okay?" he asked.

I looked into his light blue eyes. I didn't want to do this. Didn't want to sit here and pretend that everything was fine. Try to kiss him with all these questions whirling around in my mind.

"No, actually," I said, shifting in my seat.

"What is it?" he asked.

"It's just . . . Annie overheard something today," I said. "A conversation between Chloe and Shannen."

Jake swallowed. "Yeah?"

"Something about Paddy's and about how Shannen promised you she wouldn't tell me . . . ?"

Jake turned completely away from me, staring out the windshield. "Oh."

"Yeah, oh. What were they talking about?" I asked.

"That's all they said?" he asked, still not looking at me.

"That's all she heard," I replied, feeling even more suspicious.

Jake sighed and gripped the steering wheel. His hands kneaded it like it was bread dough, his knuckles turning white.

"Jake, you're scaring me," I said. "What the hell is going on?"

"I just . . ." He looked me in the eye, and for a long moment he said nothing.

"Just what?"

"I didn't want you to know about Paddy's," he said, turning away again. "I mean, I've seen you at a couple of parties, and you never drink. I thought . . . I guess I thought you'd think I was a loser for going to a bar or something."

Relief flooded through me, and I laughed. "Is that it? I don't think you're a loser."

"You sure?" He looked at me sheepishly.

"Please. I'd think you were a loser if you drank and drove or got so messy drunk you barfed on my shoes or something, but I'm not gonna judge you for going there and hanging out," I said.

Jake smiled almost sadly and looked down at his hands.

"You're really cool, you know that?"

I smiled, my face warming pleasantly. "Thanks."

He looked up at me again, and we finally kissed.

"I couldn't stop thinking about you the whole game," he said.

"Me neither," I replied, even though it didn't make sense. I pressed my mouth against his and wrapped one arm around his neck, trying to pull him closer to me.

"Ow!" He cursed and leaned away.

"What?" I asked, breathless.

"Stick shift. Knee. Not good," he said, wincing.

I laughed. "Toughen up, Graydon. Is this how you act on the field?"

He smirked and leaned in to kiss me. "No. I just wasn't expecting to get injured *after* the game."

I sighed and dropped back in my bucket seat, looking through the windshield at the surface of the lake, which was pockmarked by the now rapidly falling rain. This "date" was not going well at all.

"Sneaking around does have its drawbacks," I said.

"Yeah. But it's kind of fun, too," he said, reaching for my hand.

I sighed, lacing my fingers together with his. "It kind of sucks, though. That we can't tell anyone."

"You told Annie, right?" he said.

"Well, yeah, but—"

He lifted his shoulders. "So, there you go."

"But wouldn't it be cool if we could, I don't know, go to a movie or something?" I asked.

"Movies are overrated," he replied, reaching for me. His eyes went to my lips.

"Jake—"

He sighed and sat back again. "Ally, I thought we were good with this."

"I know," I said, looking at my lap.

"If my friends found out about us, they'd just try to break us up," he said, running his one clean hand over my hair. "I don't want to deal with any more of their crap. I just want this."

He leaned in and kissed me, and any longing for anything else melted away. He was right. If the Cresties found out about us, they'd start torturing me all over again. And I'd kind of been enjoying the not getting tortured these past few months. Ever since Shannen and I had faced off after the pool annex incident, she and the rest of them had basically left me alone. And considering the not-so-thinly-veiled threat Shannen had issued that day, and the bluff I'd issued back, that wasn't really a boat I felt like rocking.

But the prom was coming up. And it may have been a stupid fantasy, but I wanted to go with Jake. I had a whole daydream of him in a tux and me in some gorgeous dress, walking into the dance together and everyone stopping to stare. In a good way, of course. Why couldn't I have that? Why did everything have to be so screwed up?

"You okay?" Jake asked.

"Yeah. I'm fine," I said, forcing a smile even though my heart was so heavy it was tugging down on the corners of my mouth.

Maybe I'd just work a double shift the day of the prom. Earn money instead of spending it on a dress and a ticket and a limo. Save up for next year's prom.

When maybe, just maybe, things would be different.

jake

I was standing outside my English classroom, cramming for the test I was going to have to take in three minutes, when Trevor and Todd came bouncing up to me out of nowhere.

"Dude, dude, dude! Did you ask anyone to the prom yet?" Todd asked, slapping my shoulder and squeezing it. Hard.

I flinched, still clutching my copy of *The Odyssey* in both hands. My thoughts instantly flashed on Ally, and my cheeks flared. "No. Why?"

"Cool! Because I just asked Jennifer Dell—"

"And I asked Kiersten Staples—"

"And they said they won't go unless Carrie Ann Sullivan has a date too."

"So will you ask her?"

I stared at them. "Who?"

"Carrie Ann Sullivan!" they said in unison. Todd leaned toward my ear. "She's the sophomore on varsity lacrosse. The one with the black braids and the huge—"

My blush deepened and I nodded. "Right. Carrie Ann Sullivan." I swallowed hard, my brain full of thoughts of Ally. What would she think if she could hear this conversation? Probably that we were all disgusting pigs.

"I don't know, guys." I looked down at my book and tried to concentrate.

"Come on, man! If you don't ask her, we don't have dates," Trevor said, bouncing up and down in his destroyed Chuck T's.

"Why won't they go without her?" I asked.

"Who knows?" Todd said, throwing up his arms. "Some stupid

girl code? They're like BFFs or something, and they all want to go."

"What's tripping you up man? The big boobs or the hot legs? Why is this even an issue?" Trevor added.

I took a deep breath. The thing was, it wasn't like I could go to the prom with Ally.

Whatever we were doing, we'd decided to keep it a secret. For a very good reason. But I couldn't not go to the prom. Everyone was going. We were getting a limo together, and we were going to all drive down to Hammond's house on LBI after. It was going to be sick. I couldn't miss it. Ally couldn't expect me to miss it. And if I couldn't go with her, I didn't really care who I went with.

"All right, fine," I said. "I'll ask her."

"Yes!" the Idiot Twins cheered, chest-bumping each other. They turned toward me, thrusting their chests out again, but I shook my head.

"No. I'm good."

"Thanks, man," Trevor said, slapping me on the back. "You won't regret it."

The bell rang, and I turned to walk into my English class, feeling tense and nervous and sick. I told myself it was just because I was about to fail my English test, but I knew that wasn't it. Even though what I'd just promised to do made perfect sense, I had a feeling that Trevor was wrong. Somehow, I was going to regret it.

jake

I pulled my Jeep into the parking lot at the elementary school and took a spot at the back. There were a few other cars in the lot and at least twenty people playing touch football in the sun out on the Little League baseball field. I spotted Ally right away. She was laughing as she tried to tag Chad Lancaster, but he dodged her outstretched fingers and scored, spiking the ball near the backstop. All his friends gathered around him, cheering.

What the hell was I doing here? These guys weren't gonna want me here.

I glanced at Ally again. She hadn't seen me yet. I could just bail. Say something came up. Tell her I was having a psychotic break when I'd texted yes after she'd asked me if I wanted to come.

What if my friends drove by and saw my car here?

I gripped the steering wheel tightly, then got out of the Jeep. I was not going to let my friends dictate what I could and couldn't do. Just being here didn't automatically mean that me and Ally were a thing. I could have driven by, seen the game, and asked to join. Besides, Shannen hadn't spoken to me since my birthday, and she was the one who would have given me the most shit if she saw me. Eff that.

A couple of the guys spotted me as I walked over. Everyone stopped playing. Yeah. This was a mistake.

"Jake! You came!" Ally shouted, her smile huge.

Or maybe it wasn't.

She jogged forward and stopped in front of me. "Hey."

"Hey."

Was I supposed to kiss her? Hug her? I wanted to, but not with everyone staring at us like this.

"Hey, guys. Jake's on my team," Ally said, turning to her friends.

"What? No way," Chad said, palming the ball.

Here we go. Out with the Crestie.

"You've already got twelve," Jessica Landry said. "He's on our team."

"But, dude, you have most of the guys," Marshall Moss argued. He had dirt all up the side of his sweats and T-shirt. "Your team is stacked."

"What, like guys are somehow better at this?" Ally joked.

"Uh, yeah," Marshall joked back.

She shoved him and he shoved her back, laughing. Okay, so they weren't throwing me out, but I did not like this crap between Ally and Marshall.

"I'm on Ally's team. She invited me, so that's where I'm going," I said.

"Whatever," Chad said, tossing me the ball. "We'll whoop your ass anyway."

"Yeah." I laughed. "We'll see."

Ally grinned as we took the field together. "You came," she said again.

"You thought I wouldn't?" Now that I was here with her, the idea that I'd almost bailed seemed impossible.

"No. I'm just glad you did."

I smiled back. I was glad too.

So, Chad's team did whoop our asses, but it was fun. An hour later we were all dirty and sweaty and clamoring for our Gatorades and Snapples. Ally and I dropped down onto the rickety wooden bleachers and leaned back on our elbows as a few of the other guys messed around on the old jungle gym.

"Having fun?" Ally asked me, tilting her face toward the sun.

"Yeah." All I could think about was where we could go after this. Where could I take her in the middle of the day so that I could kiss her?

"Apparently Cresties and Norms can get along," she joked.

I felt a twinge of apprehension in my chest and shifted my weight. Somehow this suddenly felt like a test. "Yeah. I guess so."

"Jake! Nice game." Marshall walked over and slapped my hand.

"Thanks," I said.

"So, I heard you're going to the prom with Carrie Ann Sullivan," he said with a grin. "Nice."

I almost choked on my Gatorade.

"What?" Ally blurted.

I shot Marshall a look of serious, painful death. Ever so slowly, I capped my drink, put it down, and turned to look at Ally. My heart pretty much stopped. She looked like I'd just run over her mom with my Jeep. Crap. I already felt guilty for lying to her the other night when she'd brought up the Paddy B's thing. Now this.

"You asked someone to the prom?" she said.

"Oh. Oops. Sorry, man," Marshall said, backing off.

Yeah, sure you are, buddy.

"Why didn't you tell me?" Ally asked.

"Can we talk about this somewhere else?" I said, getting up and tugging her away by her arm. She followed me over to a huge oak tree a few yards away from the bleachers. Ally leaned one hand against the trunk and looked down at the ground, kicking the dirt with her toe.

"What's wrong?" I asked.

"Are you serious?" she asked.

"Ally, come on. It's not like we could go to the prom together," I said.

"Right, because it's okay for you to slum it with us Norms out here, but God forbid a Crestie take a Norm to the prom. The whole world might collapse in on itself," she said sarcastically.

"You know that's not what I meant," I said.

She shook her head, staring past me. "I just can't believe you're going with someone else."

"What'd you want me to do, stay home?" I asked, my face screwing up in disbelief.

"That's what I'm doing," she shot back.

Oh. Shit. "Well, I can't. Everyone's going. And if I don't go, it's going to look—"

"Who cares how it looks?" she demanded. Then she stared at her feet again. "Do you, like, *like* this girl?"

"No. I don't even know her," I replied quickly. This had to get me some points. "I only asked her because the Idiot Twins wanted me to."

"So, you're taking some sophomore you don't even know to the prom," she said flatly.

God. I couldn't get anything right in this conversation.

"Why? Would it be better if I asked someone I already hooked up with?" I blurted.

Ally's jaw dropped. Yeah. That may have been the wrong thing to say.

"I have to go," she said, storming past me.

Her pissed-off exit caught the attention of the guys, and some of them shot me looks. Great. Just great. Now they were going to kick my ass.

Ally grabbed her duffel bag from the bottom bleacher and speed walked toward the parking lot. Marshall took off at a jog after her, and I was left there facing Chad and the rest of the guys, who were all standing by the bleachers with their chins out like they were ready to rumble.

"Chicks," I said dismissively.

They didn't laugh. It was time for me to go. Over in the parking lot, Ally got on her bike and took off. Then Marshall got on his and took off after her. What the hell was going on with those two?

"Thanks for the game," I said. "I'll see you around."

Then I walked toward them, forcing a couple of them to move sideways so I could get through, just so they'd know I wasn't intimidated. But the whole way to the car I kept waiting for one of them to jump me from behind or something. I didn't breathe until I was safely inside my Jeep.

"Dammit," I said under my breath as I started the engine. I slammed the heel of my hand into the steering wheel and sat back, unable to get the picture of Ally's hurt face out of my mind. I knew it was a bad idea, coming here. It had just turned out to be a bad idea for reasons I hadn't even considered.

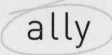

ally

Now that spring had officially sprung, I was on my bike every day after dinner, riding around town as the sun went down, enjoying the warmth. I felt like I'd been trapped in that teeny-tiny condo for months, and it was so good to get out and breathe. I loved the air this time of year, all moist and pungent with the scent of wet grass and new flowers and fresh mulch. Everywhere I rode people were mowing their lawns, landscaping crews were digging up old shrubs and putting in the new, kids were breaking out their baseball gloves and staging games in their yards. I couldn't believe how fast the year had gone by. Couldn't believe how differently it had turned out from how I had imagined.

I popped the curb at the center of town and rode into Veterans' Park by one of the side paths. Technically bikes and skateboards and scooters were not allowed in the park, but the rule was never really enforced unless there was a pack of kids ignoring it and making a lot of noise in the process. I rode over to the nearest bench and leaned my bike against the end. As I sat down to take a breather, the old-school gaslights that lined the path automatically flickered to life.

What was I going to do about the prom?

All I had to do was stop moving and the topic I'd been diligently avoiding popped into my head. I hadn't talked to Jake since he'd told me—well, Marshall had told me—about Carrie Ann Sullivan. Hadn't answered his texts or his calls. Had completely avoided him in the halls. Had even hidden from him in the stock room at CVS until Annie had buzzed me to tell me he had given up and gone home. For the past week it seemed like Jake and Carrie Ann were together everywhere, along with the Idiot Twins and their dates. And they were always giggling, flirting, making plans. It all made me want to throw something hard at them. It didn't even matter which one of them it hit. I wanted all of them to suffer. By Friday Carrie Ann and her little friends were eating lunch with Jake and the Cresties at their table in the quad, and I had made one huge decision.

I was going to that damn prom. And I was going to look hotter than Carrie Ann Sullivan could ever hope to look. And Jake was going to regret not asking me.

All I needed was a date.

I leaned back against the bench and shoved my sweaty hair behind my ears, my heart rate returning to normal. I was just about to get up and pedal home when Marshall rode his bike into the park from the far corner. I lifted a hand in a wave and sat back to wait. We'd bumped into each other a couple of times on our rides—usually he was on his way back from Chad's or riding around with one of his friends—but this time he was alone and he didn't look to be in a rush.

"Hey, Ally. Thought you might be here," he said, his bike chain clicking as he stopped in front of me. He was wearing a gray hoodie and blue basketball shorts, sweat beaded his hairline, and his cheeks were ruddy from exertion. "What're you up to?"

I narrowed my eyes as I looked up at him. The sky was turning pink overhead, and a few birds chirped in the flowering trees. The idea hit me in a rush. Marshall was cute. And nice. And definitely tall enough to not be dwarfed by me in the pictures.

"Are you going to the prom?" I asked.

He removed his hands from his handlebars and tucked then under his arms. "Um, yeah, I guess."

"Got a date?" I asked.

"Nope."

"Anyone you're dying to go with?" I asked.

His brow knitted and he laughed. "Um, nope."

"Then, do you want to go together?" I asked. "As friends?"

He looked down at me for a moment, considering. Not that I thought he would jump at the chance to squire me around in a tux or anything, but was it really that difficult a question?

"You know what? Forget it," I said, embarrassed. I got up and grabbed my bike. "It was a stupid idea."

His hand closed around my wrist. "No, wait. Sorry. I was just processing." He released me and tucked his hands away again. "Sure. That sounds cool. Let's . . . go to the prom."

"Yeah?" I said happily.

"Yeah."

We grinned at one another as the sky rapidly darkened around us. "Cool."

Huh. That had been a lot easier than I'd thought. Just like that, I had a date. Not the one I wanted or the one I'd been daydreaming about. Not a romantic date, but a date. And it was going to be fun. Really. Lots and lots of fun.

Did you hear? Ally Ryan's going to the prom with
Marshall Moss.

See, now, those two make sense. He's cute, they're
both juniors and basketball gods. Sense.

Please tell me you're not still upset that Jake Graydon
asked that sophomore.

But she's a total braindead! And she's not even pretty.

But she is known for her . . . talents.

Come on. That cannot be the only reason he asked her.

Why not? Does Jake Graydon have some hidden depths
all of a sudden? He's a slut, she's a slut.
That makes sense.

I thought he was better than that. Wasn't there some
rumor that he and Ally were, like, a thing?

Please. She is way too good for him.

Seriously.

If he'd gone there, I might have reconsidered
the hidden depths.

But he didn't go there.

No, he did not.

And he didn't go here either.

No. He did not.

Sigh.

jake

The prom was even lamer than predicted. The theme, first of all, was *Twilight*, voted on by the mousy losers on the prom committee who apparently thought they couldn't get any unless they got it from a dead guy. All the decorations were black and red. There were movie posters of some pale, scrawny dude staring out from every corner. The DJ sucked, the food was lame, and there were chaperones everywhere. Carrie Ann, who had practically jumped my bones when I'd asked her to come with me, had spent the entire preprom party at my house downing wine coolers after not eating all day so she could look hot in her dress—which she told everyone at the party. Now she was on the dance floor with her friends and the Idiot Twins while I sat at our table, watching. Good times. Meanwhile, Ally was here with Marshall Moss, who she was obviously going to hook up with later. They'd barely stopped touching each other all night. Even now, they were out in the middle of the dance floor dancing to some Black Eyed Peas song. No reason to be touching for a fast song, but they were. Holding hands while they bounced around with their friends.

She looked happy. Which made me want to punch someone. Preferably Marshall Moss.

"Hey, Jake! Having fun?" Chloe perched on the chair next to mine.

Ally had just thrown her arm around Marshall's neck. I tore my eyes away. Chloe looked at me knowingly. She was wearing a short white dress that was half-angelic, half-sexpot. Low cut, but not form fitting. I bet every guy in the room had thought about tearing it off once or twice. But that was the point of a dress like that, right?

"You like her, don't you?" she said.

I swallowed, busted. My knee-jerk reaction was to deny, deny, deny, but then I decided, screw it. I was too pissed off to care anymore. "How'd you know?"

Chloe shrugged and took a sip of her sparkling cider. "Shannen was babbling something about it a while back, but I didn't believe her."

"Why not?" I asked.

"I don't know. I just didn't see you two together," Chloe said, gazing past me at Ally. "I mean, I'd never seen you talk or anything, but then I guess you did do that detention together. Was that where it all happened? Like some kind of prison romance?" she joked.

I laughed. Why was she being so cool about this when it had been drilled into my head over and over again that Ally was untouchable? "No. I don't know when it happened. It's not like it matters."

"Why not?" She took another sip of her drink, smiling at Hammond as he passed by with a couple of guys from the team. "Doesn't she like you back?"

There was an uncomfortable knot in my chest. "I don't know. I thought she did. But now—"

We both looked at the dance floor. "Marshall Moss? Oh, please," she said. "Who would want Marshall Moss if she could have you?"

I narrowed my eyes at her. "What's with you? I thought you hated her."

Chloe took a deep breath. She leaned forward, her elbows resting on the table, her posture as straight as ever. "The truth is, Jake, that was never me."

"What?"

Chloe nibbled on a strawberry, then placed it down on her plate, her expression chagrined.

"I never hated Ally," she said with a sigh. "It was just that Shannen and Faith and Ham were so crazy adamant about how we should freeze her out . . . I just went along."

"Really?" I asked. I had wondered about that the night of her birthday, when she'd said she wished Ally were there. And she had kept the secret about Ally's father way before any of the rest of us had been forced to start keeping it. "So all this time . . . you would have been hanging out with her."

Chloe lifted her shoulders, then sat back in her chair again. "She was my best friend. It wasn't her fault, what her dad did. It all seems so long ago now, anyway." She touched her hair and sighed, then leaned her chin on her hand. "It's exhausting sometimes, isn't it? Caring so much about what other people think?"

She glanced over her shoulder at Hammond, who was laughing loudly over something one of the guys had said. I blinked. There couldn't actually be trouble in Chlammond-land, could there?

"Whatever." She sat up straight again. "The point is, I think you should go for it."

This was unbelievable. Chloe, the girl who every other girl at this school worshipped, the person who could turn around opinion of Ally Ryan with a snap of her fingers, didn't hate her. Even though she was the one person who had a good reason to. Not that she had any idea about that.

I felt guilty, suddenly, knowing something she maybe

should have known but didn't, and looked away.

"What're you losers talking about?" Shannen asked. She dropped into the chair on my other side and grabbed some grapes off the fruit plate. The skinny strap on her black dress fell down her arm, but she made no move to fix it. Her face was sweaty, and her hair was all messed up.

"Whether or not Jake has the guts to ask out Ally," Chloe said matter-of-factly.

Shannen's gaze flicked to me. She dropped back in her chair violently. "I knew it. I *knew* it!"

I clenched my teeth. "Oh, so now you're talking to me?"

It had been two months of dead silence from her. Ever since the morning after my birthday. Not a single word.

"Come on, Shannen. What's the big deal?" Chloe asked, lifting her slim shoulders. "Aren't we getting a little old for this whole Norm-Crestie thing?"

"That's not what this is about," Shannen shot back.

Chloe sighed and dusted off her fingers. "Then what is it about?"

Shannen stared at her. I could tell it was right on the tip of her tongue. She wanted to tell her about Hammond and Ally, and she was probably drunk enough to do it.

"Shannen," I said in a warning tone.

She looked at me, startled, as if she were just waking up.

"You know what? Fine," Shannen said, shoving back from the table. "You want to go out with her? Go out with her."

"Shannen—"

She grabbed her bag and rolled her shoulders back, taking a deep breath. "No. I'm serious, Jake. I'm done. If you want to go slumming, that's your problem."

Then she turned and walked off to the bathroom in a huff.

"Don't listen to her. She's drunk," Chloe said.

"I know," I said with a sigh.

"So? Are you going to ask her out?" Chloe asked, leaning forward on the table to better see Ally.

"I think it's too late for that," I said.

"Why?"

"I fucked up," I told her, toying with some of the silver vampire-fang confetti that was all over the table. "It's a long story, but . . . I think she kind of hates me now."

"So, make her not hate you," Chloe said.

Like it was that simple. "How?"

"You need a grand gesture," she told me. "The big romantic moment. Girls live for that stuff." She got up and touched my back lightly, picking up her little round bag with her other hand. "You'll figure it out."

"But what about—"

"Everyone else?" she said with a smile. She lifted her arms casually. "Look at them. Do you really care what they think?" She looked at the guys, who were sneaking sips from a flask, then almost spitting the drink out their noses from laughing so hard. "Or them?" We glanced at the girls, who were dancing and gossiping at the same time, laughing behind their hands at some chubby girl's dress. "Maybe we should both stop caring what they think." Then she turned and sauntered off toward the bathroom after Shannen.

Ally was still dancing with her friends, carefree and happy and so gorgeous I could have died from wanting to be with her. A grand gesture. What did that mean exactly? All I knew was, I had to figure it out. Because I couldn't spend one more second feeling like this.

jake

"Coach! Can I get into the supply closet? A couple of us want to kick a ball around after school today, and I need guards."

"Sure thing, Jake. I like the initiative," Coach Martz said, getting up from his desk. "It's not everyone who starts practicing for soccer season in May."

"Yeah, well. You know me," I replied.

"I do at that." He got his keys from the top drawer of his desk and lumbered past me out the door.

My heart pounded like I was doing something wrong, even though I knew I wasn't. It probably wasn't going to work out anyway. If I were on the outside of this, I'd tell myself not to get my panties in a twist.

Coach opened the door and flicked on the light, which blinked a few times before dimly illuminating the room. Long metal shelves lined either side of the closet. They were packed with everything from bins of tennis balls to forgotten fencing equipment to boxes of ancient trophies no one cared about anymore.

I glanced at Coach Martz. Was he going to hang out and wait for me? Crap. This whole thing was pointless if he did. Then his cell phone vibrated. He whipped it out and checked the screen.

"Take what you need and lock up after yourself," he said. "I gotta take this."

I let out a sigh of relief and ducked inside. There was a bin of shin guards and knee pads just inside the door. When I heard Coach's office door close, I turned toward the back of the closet. I had spotted it one day last year when Hammond and

I had been in charge of rounding up cones and nets for soccer drills. I hadn't even realized what I was looking at then. Now I just hoped it was still there.

On the second highest shelf, right under the trophies, was a long, thin box marked DANCE POMS. I shoved it aside, and there it was. A blue plastic bin with a piece of masking tape stuck to the side. On it, in pencil, someone had scrawled "rings and pins."

I held my breath. Images of Indiana Jones flashed through my mind. But when I popped the top, no light shone out at me. There was no choir of angels. Just a ton of pins and tie tacks in plastic baggies. Plus three velvet boxes.

I opened up the first one. It was big, with a maroon stone and a football on the side. The second was a gymnastics ring. There was only one left. I took a breath, pried it open, and slowly smiled.

Score.

ally

"Happy birthday, dear Ally! Happy birthday to you!"

My mother set a strawberry shortcake down in front of me at the table, and it was alight with seventeen birthday candles. I looked at the small crowd gathered around me—Mom, Gray, Annie, and Quinn—and I missed my father so much I could hardly breathe. Ever since arriving home from my driver's test—which I had gleefully passed—that morning, I had been on edge, waiting for the phone to ring. But nothing. Nada. Zip. Where was he right then? Did he even realize it was my birthday? Did he even care?

Mom looked at me sadly, and I knew she knew what I was thinking. She'd gone to so much trouble, with the dozens of colorful balloons, the spaghetti dinner, the colorful paper plates—I hated for her to think I wasn't happy. So I put on a big grin, took a breath, and blew out the candles. When they all went out with one blow, I thrust my arms in the air, mugging for Gray's video camera. Just like I was supposed to.

"Yay! You got your wish!" Quinn cheered.

Too bad I'd forgotten to make one.

I pushed myself up from the table, and my mom gave me a kiss and a squeeze. "I'm so proud of you, hon."

For what? I wanted to say. *Making it to the ripe old age of seventeen?*

But that was just the acerbic, annoyed, abandoned-daughter part of me talking. So instead I said, "Thanks, Mom."

"Are you gonna open your presents?" Quinn asked. My mom gave her a quick squeeze, which caused a twinge in my heart. Every time I saw evidence of how close those two were getting, I wanted to hurl. But at least Quinn had gotten nicer as a result. That was something. If I was stuck with her for the entire summer, I was better off with this version of her instead of the stony-silent version.

"Sure." I headed for the living room area while my mom whisked the cake away to cut it.

"So, what did you wish for?" Annie asked. "And don't give me any of that 'if I tell you it won't come true' crap."

"I hope you didn't wish for the bigger room at the shore house, because that's mine," Quinn said, dropping onto the couch.

"Quinn!" her father scolded. "Just for that I should give Ally the bigger room."

246

"What? No! Daddy!" Quinn sat forward, whining up at him.

"It's fine. I don't need a big room. I'm planning on getting a job and working as many hours as humanly possible."

"You go, party animal," Annie said.

I smirked. "Don't worry. When you come down to visit I promise to party."

"Really!? I get to come visit? Yay!" She threw her arm around my neck. "So? What did you wish for?" Once she got on topic, she rarely got off until satisfied.

"Nothing," I said, lifting my shoulders. "I forgot."

"Well, what were you thinking about right before?" Quinn asked as her father turned his camera on me again. "World peace? Cuz that would be nice."

Of course it would, future Miss America. I tried to conjure up a good lie, because I wasn't about to tell her I'd been thinking about my father, but then the doorbell rang.

My heart fluttered, and I looked at my mother across the room. She froze with the cake cutter half inside the cake. Did her stomach suddenly feel like it was going to drop out of her body too?

"I'll get it!" Gray announced, slapping his viewfinder closed.

"No!" my mom and I blurted.

But he was already at the door. I turned around slowly, holding my breath. Was my father really here? Had I somehow wished him to my doorstep? My blood rushed so loudly in my ears I couldn't even hear Gray at the door. It was like trying to eavesdrop on the lifeguards from the deep end of the country club pool—which used to be Faith's and my favorite summertime activity.

Finally, Gray returned, with our guest at his heels. For the first time since returning to Orchard Hill, I was disappointed to see Jake Graydon.

"Hey," he said.

Tears stung my eyes, and I looked down at my feet. I breathed in slowly and let it out in one, long breath.

Don't be a baby, Ally. You had to know it wasn't going to be him.

"Sorry. Is this a bad time?" Jake asked.

A bad time? Was he kidding? What the hell was he even doing here? The last time I'd spoken to him I'd taken off on my bike near tears. What about that encounter screamed, "How about you crash my birthday party?"

"No! Of course not!" my mother said brightly. I wondered how she was going to explain our random outburst to Gray later. And why was she being so nice to Jake? But then, I hadn't told her about the prom thing. I'd just acted like going with Marshall as friends was all I'd ever wanted, because the truth was too humiliating. "Come on in, Jake."

Jake's face was all hopeful. Like, for a second he forgot to act cool. And I kind of liked that. He was wearing a light blue crew-neck sweater and jeans, looking way too handsome for words. There was a small, wrapped box in his hand with a yellow bow on it.

"Actually, I can't stay," he said. "I remembered it was your birthday, and I . . ." He looked down at the present, then thrust it at me awkwardly. "Here."

I took the gift in both hands, at a loss.

"Well? Open it!" Annie said.

"It's okay if you want to wait," Jake said.

Of course that made me want to open it right away. I yanked

the paper off, and inside was a maroon velvet box. Maybe he was trying to bribe me with diamond earrings. Get me to forgive him by dropping his father's cash on jewels. He was a Crestie, after all. I pried the box open, planning all the witty, sarcastic things I would say when I shoved the contents back in his face.

My jaw dropped. Nestled inside the box was my championship ring. The one I should have been awarded my freshman year. It had a burgundy stone in the middle with ORCHARD HILL HIGH SCHOOL etched in an oval around it. One side was decorated with a tiny basketball with my first name stamped above it. The other side had the year and the inscription JV CHAMPS.

"Ohmigod," I breathed.

"What is it?" Quinn asked, standing on her toes to try to see.

Gray was filming over my shoulder. I shrugged away from him, toward Jake. "It's my championship ring," I said. "Where did you get this?"

"They still had it in the sports supply closet," he said with a shrug. "It's no big deal."

But his face was all blotchy, and I could tell he was trying not to smile over his job well done. I dislodged the ring from the slot and put it on. It fit perfectly. My chest filled with ten thousand different emotions. He'd remembered. That conversation we'd had all those months ago. He'd remembered, and he'd found my ring for me.

"Jake, this is—"

"It's nothing," he said. "You should have had it then. I just . . . got it to you." He looked around at my hovering guests and ducked his head toward mine. "Can I talk to you for a sec? Alone?"

My heart pounded in my ears. "Um, sure." I looked at my mom. "I'll be right back."

We went outside. He held the door open and everything. I was trying to figure out what I was supposed to say, when he just started talking.

"I'm sorry. About the prom," he said, looking at his feet. "I shouldn't have asked that girl."

"It's okay," I heard myself say. It wasn't okay, but it was one of those moments where it felt like it was, because this moment was so good.

"Did you . . . I mean, are you . . . with Marshall Moss?" he asked awkwardly.

I scoffed, toying with my ring. "Marshall? No. We just went as friends."

His eyebrows shot up. "Really?"

"Really." I was grinning from ear to ear.

"So, then . . . you wouldn't want to . . . I mean, would you maybe want to, I don't know, go to the movies or something?" he asked.

Somehow my grin widened. I knew he was thinking about that day in the car when I'd been talking about actually going out in public. "A movie would be cool."

"Yeah?" he said hopefully. Happily.

His smile was huge. My heart was floating.

"Yeah."

He reached out and took my hand. "Happy birthday, Ally."

"Yeah," I said. "I think it kind of is."

june

Okay, what the hell am I gonna get Shannen for her birthday? Doesn't she have, like, everything?

Do you think Jake Graydon is going to take Ally Ryan to the party?

Wait, what? Are those two a thing now?

Uh, yeah! Didn't you hear? They totally went to see the new Christian Bale on Saturday night.

Unbelievable. A Norm snagged the unsnaggable Crestie.

Whatever. Ally Ryan's reascension was inevitable.

Why?

Because. She's Ally Ryan.

ally

The Monday morning after my first official date with Jake, I basically air walked into school. He'd held my hand throughout the entire movie, even when his arm went dead on the armrest. (He spent ten minutes afterward surreptitiously trying to shake out the pins and needles.) I figured that when the movie was over he'd drive us right up to the lake again, but he didn't. We grabbed some ice cream at Scoops and walked around town for a while, and then he'd driven me home and kissed me at the door.

Which was so delicious it just made me wish we had gone up to the lake. But there was time for that. We were together now. And we both had our licenses. We could go to the lake whenever we wanted. A thrill went through my body at the very thought. Me and Jake. Together.

I was still grinning when I came around the corner into my locker hallway, but my smile quickly died. Shannen and Chloe were waiting for me.

Okay. This meant one of two things. Either they had heard about my date with Jake and were here to tell me to back off, get a life, and find a Norm boyfriend. Or they'd heard about my date with Jake and were here to surrender. I honestly didn't know which it would be, but I lifted my chin and walked right by them, pretending not to care.

"Here to invite me to another nonexistent party?" I asked, turning my back to them as I spun my lock.

"Sort of," Shannen said.

"Not exactly," Chloe corrected.

"Here."

Shannen shoved a thick square black envelope in front of my face. It was tied with a silver grosgrain bow. Intriguing.

"What's that?" I asked, popping open my locker.

"It's an invitation to my birthday party," she said.

"It's a party, but we promise it exists," Chloe said, moving into my line of sight by leaning back against the locker next to mine. She plucked the envelope from Shannen's hand and held it out to me. "And we also promise it's being held exactly where the invitation says it's being held."

My stupid heart all but stopped. An invitation to Shannen's birthday was huge. Her mom threw the sickest parties this side of Manhattan, and Shannen only ever invited her one hundred closest friends. The parties were so legendary, she'd had to have bouncers outside the country club for her thirteenth and had hired more for her fourteenth after some sixth graders had managed to sneak in through a kitchen window. People cried over not getting invited to Shannen's birthday. They had their moms call her mom and beg.

And here was an invitation all for me. I tore my eyes away from it and yanked my chem book out of my locker.

"No, thanks."

"What? Everyone wants one of those," Shannen said, incredulous.

"Call me crazy, but I don't," I said, turning to face her. "Not from you."

Shannen sighed and took the envelope back from Chloe. They exchanged a patient look that made me want to stomp on both their toes and run. What would they do if I actually tried?

"If this is about the going away party, I told you. That was

Faith's idea," Shannen said slowly, crossing her arms over her chest.

"And we didn't know the cops were going to be there. I swear," Chloe said, her green eyes serious.

I believed that Chloe didn't know about the cops. If she had, she would have stopped it. The girl knew when to draw the line. She understood the difference between what was right and what was wrong. Shannen, however, had known. She was probably the one who had called them. For her it wasn't about right or wrong. It was always about how much she could get away with.

"Ally, look . . . we know about you and Jake," Shannen said, looking at the floor briefly. She tossed her bangs out of her face as she met my eyes again. "If you're going to be with him . . ."

"Then you're going to be with us," Chloe finished.

I looked from one face to the other. Chloe seemed so sincere. Almost hopeful. It always seemed to be this way with her. Like she wanted things to be different. Like she felt bad about the way the other Cresties were treating me. But Shannen was a different story. She'd been messing with me from day one.

"Just like that," I said, looking at Shannen. "One date with Jake and all of a sudden you want to hang out with me."

Shannen lifted her shoulders. "He's my best friend."

I felt like a knife had just twisted inside my chest. I was her best friend not that long ago. She should have been doing this for me, but instead, I was the outsider—the one being grudgingly brought in to the group by association.

Jake held some serious power around here, and he didn't even know it.

"So. Will you come?" Shannen asked, holding out the envelope again.

"I'll think about it," I said, snatching the invite and shoving it into my bag.

Shannen scowled. She wasn't used to being turned down or put off. "Well, think fast. I need to do table arrangements by the end of the week, and my table is, obviously, the most important. So if you want to sit with Jake, I need to know you're coming ASAP."

Sitting with Jake. The thought sent a thrill through my heart. Okay. I had to think about this for a second. Shannen's party was an event we could actually go to together. It might even make up for the whole prom fiasco. The image of Jake arriving at my door to pick me up, wearing some stunning suit, looking all coiffed, was insanely alluring. All I wanted was to be with him, and this was another chance to do that. Besides, if they really cared that much about Jake, they wouldn't mess with me—his date—while he was standing right there. Right?

"Okay," I said, closing the flap on my bag and snapping it shut. "I'll come."

Shannen smiled. "Good."

Chloe actually hugged me. "We're going to have so much fun!"

"Yeah. Definitely."

I forced myself to smile back and hoped for the best. But if this invite turned out to be some kind of joke, all bets—and bluffs—were off.

jake

Ally looked amazing. She was wearing this short black dress with skinny straps and a colorful sash thing right under the chest that tied in a bow in the back. And her hair was up with that curl grazing her neck. At some point tonight I was going to push that curl back and kiss that part of her neck. I was practically salivating at the thought of it.

"I like you in a suit," Ally said, looking me up and down. I'd bought a new light-and-dark-blue striped tie for the occasion.

"Thanks. I like you in a dress," I replied.

She blushed and looked down at her knees. "Thanks."

We were standing right outside the open double doors to the country club's main ballroom. Inside the music was pumping. A couple of girls walked by us, coming back from the bathroom, and shot us odd looks. I didn't remotely care.

Ever since Shannen had told me she was inviting Ally, I'd been wondering why. Was it some kind of apology? Or was she trying to say she was going to accept her now that we were together? But tonight, I didn't care. I was just happy that Ally was here.

"Hi, hon! Hello, Jake."

Ally's mother came up behind us with Dr. Nathanson. Both of them were all dressed up. Shannen's mom had invited a few of her own friends, too, including Mrs. Ryan. We said hello, and Ally gave her mom a serious look.

"Are you sure you want to do this?" Ally asked her.

My heart gave a thump. I knew she was referring to that Sunday dinner when my mom had helped humiliate hers.

"Ally, we went over this. Danielle invited me, and she has been a good friend," Ally's mother said. "I've decided to just . . . rise above." She shook her hair back and smiled.

"Okay," Ally said. "We'll see you in there." Ally took a breath and stared through the doors after her mom and Dr. Nathanson. The room was dimly lit, strobe lights flashing, dozens of heads bobbing around in a sorry excuse for dancing.

Over the music it was all screeches, squeals, laughter.

"So. You ready for this?" she asked.

I reached for her hand. It fit perfectly inside mine. "Ready."

She grinned, and we walked inside. Together. Over our heads was a huge arc of black, pink, and silver balloons. The party had a fifties theme, which was Shannen's mother's idea. Vintage record albums dangled from the ceiling, there was a huge, illuminated jukebox behind the DJ, and all the waiters and waitresses were dressed in leather jackets or poodle skirts.

"Hey. The music didn't come to a screeching stop," Ally said, pretending to be confused.

"Yeah, and no one's staring at us," I replied, playing along.

"Wanna dance?" she asked.

"Not even a little bit," I said.

She wiped her brow. "Good. Let's get something to drink."

I squeezed her hand as we walked down the steps and around the dance floor. I really liked this girl. Really a lot.

"Ally! Hey!"

Chloe appeared out of nowhere wearing a pink dress with a long skirt. Hammond was right behind her, wearing a pink tie of course.

"You look amazing! Love the dress."

Ally smiled. "Thanks. I like yours, too."

I greeted Hammond with a hand slap. Chloe hooked her arm through Ally's and tugged her toward the bar. According to the old-school soda-shop signage, they were serving smoothies, milkshakes, and sodas. Unlike Mr. Appleby, Shannen's mom wasn't about to be serving us alcohol.

"I'm so happy you're here," Chloe said. "This whole rivalry thing was getting exhausting, no?"

Ally's brow creased. I bet she was wondering how Chloe could just act like it was okay to forget about the pranks and the yearlong cold shoulder. But that was Chloe. She never wanted to talk about anything unpleasant. I'd tried to explain to Ally about the conversation I'd had with Chloe at the prom—about how Chloe had never wanted to keep her out—but I think it came out all wrong. It was hard to tell her without letting her know I'd been talking about how much I liked her. And without making Shannen look bad.

"I mean, it's not your fault, what your father did," Chloe said, placing her tiny purse on the bar. "I just want the whole thing to be over so we can all be friends again."

Ally glanced at Hammond, who looked away. My skin heated and I loosened my tie a bit. No one knew that I knew about the two of them, and for the millionth time, I wished I didn't.

"What'll ya have?" James Dean, aka the bartender, asked.

"Two milkshakes. Strawberry," Chloe ordered. "Still your favorite?" she asked Ally.

"Yeah." She looked uncomfortable. I was going to have to get her away from Chloe and Hammond soon.

"Don't worry about us," Hammond joked. "We'll take care of ourselves."

"Like the independent men you are?" Chloe replied with a smile.

"I'll have a Coke," I told James Dean as he left the milk-shakes under the mixer.

"Sprite," Hammond put in.

Once we all had our drinks, Chloe lifted hers in a toast.

"So, Ally, what do you think? Friends again?"

Ally glanced at Hammond. He sipped soda through his straw and pretended not to notice.

"Sure," Ally said. "Friends."

We all lifted our glasses and clinked. When Chloe came away with a pink milk moustache, Ally smiled, and I knew she was finally relaxing. It made me relax too.

Until I saw Shannen staring us down from across the dance floor, all smoldery in a slate gray dress and major eye makeup. What was she thinking? And why did she look so pissed off?

ally

It was going well. Really, really well. Chloe barely left my side all night, which meant Hammond was there too, but he and I mostly ignored each other. Shannen had invited Jessica and some of the other girls from the basketball team, so whenever Chloe hit the dance floor I still had people other than Jake to talk to. Aside from a few glares from Crestie girls—I wasn't sure whether the glares were because I was there or because I was there with Jake, but I didn't care—no one seemed to notice me.

Except Jake. Jake noticed me a lot. His hand was always in mine or on my back. Once he even sort of tickled his fingers across my neck and over my shoulder before giving me a squeeze. Every time he touched me I felt gorgeous and like I was the only girl in the room. Nothing else that had happened for the past ten months mattered at all. Jake and I were together.

But every now and then, I'd look at Chloe and feel a twist of guilt in my stomach. She was being so nice tonight. And acting relieved. As if this was the night she'd been waiting for as much as I had. What was she going to do if she ever found out what I'd done?

I decided to try not to think about it tonight. Tonight was

supposed to be fun—a new beginning. There was always
tomorrow for worrying obsessively.

Finally, after what seemed like an hour at the table making small talk and munching on appetizers, the DJ flipped on a
slow song. Jake leaned back in his chair and eyed me tentatively.

"You wanna?"

I felt a pleasant stirring throughout my chest and all the way
down to my toes.

"Sure."

We got up, and he followed me to the dance floor. Everyone
was either pairing off or vacating the area. I saw Shannen dancing with Josh Schwartz over by the DJ, and gave her a quick
wave. She smiled back and lifted her hand from behind Josh's
neck. I hadn't had much of a chance to talk to her tonight, other
than to say "happy birthday." She was so busy greeting all her
guests and mingling with everyone.

"I'm probably going to have to dance with Shannen at some
point," Jake said, following my gaze as he slipped his arms
around my waist.

I swallowed hard, trying not to blush at his closeness, but
my heart was pounding in every pore, reverberating through
every tiny hair on my arms and along the back of my neck. "She
is the birthday girl," I agreed.

"So you don't mind?" he asked.

"Nah," I said casually.

Jake titled his head. "Huh. I was kind of hoping you were the
possessive type."

I laughed as we turned in a tight circle. "Okay then," I said,
tightening my grip on his neck. "No dancing with anyone else.
Tonight you're all mine."

Jake smiled but looked me dead in the eye. "No. From now on."

My heart skipped. "What?"

"Yours," he said simply, "from now on."

ally

"All right, everyone, if I can have your attention, please!" the DJ announced. We were all sitting at our table at the top of the dance floor, having just finished our dinners. Everyone quieted down gradually as Shannen and her parents joined the DJ at the front of the room. "Shannen's mother has put together a little video for the birthday girl's big day, and she'd like to share it with us!"

A big screen scrolled down from the ceiling as Shannen hung her head, blushing and laughing. I looked at Chloe and grinned as Faith and Hammond rolled their eyes. Shannen's mother did this every year, splicing together old family photos and videos and embarrassing Shannen. It was a time-honored tradition.

"I hope she still has the naked cowgirl picture in there," Trevor said excitedly, crunching on some ice cubes.

"And the naked firefighter one," Todd added.

"Shannen sure liked to play naked dress-up as a kid," Trevor said with narrowed eyes.

"Is there anything the birthday girl would like to say before we get started?" the DJ teased, holding the microphone out to Shannen.

She took it with a smile and looked over at our table. "Just . . . enjoy the show!"

Everyone applauded, and someone in the back of the room let out a sharp whistle. The lights dimmed and the screen flickered to life. Jake slipped his arm around the back of my chair, and I cuddled into his side. He was all warm and smelled of spicy crisp soap. In that moment I felt entirely safe and was filled with a buoyant sense of possibility.

Yours, Jake had said. *From now on.* Every time I thought about it, my skin tingled.

The video started with a close-up shot of a white tiled floor and a wet leather boot. Then, suddenly, the camera swung upward and I was looking at a gleaming deli counter, fluorescent lights, and what appeared to be Faith's back. I glanced at Faith in confusion. She was frozen, staring up at the screen, her eyes wide.

"Mr. Ryan? Oh my God! Is that *you?*" the Faith on the screen said.

My stomach completely dropped out of my body.

"Oh my God," Jake said, sitting forward, sliding his arm away from my shoulders.

I barely even noticed, though. Because up on the screen, larger than life, was my father. He was standing behind some deli counter in an apron, looking scared. He said something, but I couldn't make it out. The blood was rushing too loudly in my ears.

"What is this?" I mumbled.

Jake looked back at me. "Ally—"

Behind him, on the screen, my dad looked at the camera. "Are you—is that a camera phone?" he said.

"No," Shannen's voice replied. The picture whirled for a moment before refocusing on my dad's face. "I just can't seem to get any bars in here."

"What the fuck is this?" Hammond said from across the table.

People were starting to turn around and stare at me, but I couldn't tear my eyes away from the screen. My heart was pounding so hard I thought I might actually pass out. Where was this taken? When? Why was my father working at a deli?

I looked over at the parents' table, trying to find my mom, but she wasn't there. At least, I couldn't see her. Then there was a commotion on the dance floor. It was Shannen and her mom. Her mother had a serious grip on Shannen's arm and was talking through her teeth, gesturing up at the screen. Shannen gave an exaggerated shrug, like she had no idea what was going on, and just like that, I understood. Shannen and Faith had found my father. They'd taken this video without him knowing. And now, they were showing it to me—to everyone—to humiliate me. Shannen hated me so much she'd sabotaged her own mother's birthday tradition just to mess with me.

"Hi, Mr. Ryan," Hammond said on the video. He walked into view and shot the camera an annoyed look. "Sorry to surprise you like this. Shannen didn't tell us where we were going."

My face burned and tears stung my eyes. I looked at Hammond—the real Hammond—sitting across from me at the table. He turned his back to the screen, made a tent with his hands, and covered his nose and mouth, gazing back at me guiltily. My heart felt like it was melting under a hot iron. He knew where my father was. They all knew. Why hadn't they told me? Were they all too busy laughing at poor Ally Ryan behind her back?

"What? I didn't know he worked here," Shannen said up on the screen. "Do you *actually* work here?"

God, she was so condescending. So awful.

"Well . . . yes. I do. I have . . . for about a year now," my dad said. "Chloe's father was kind enough to give me a job while I get back on my feet. I've been trying to get my old job back."

I pushed back from my chair. I was going to throw up. I could feel the bile rising in my throat. On the dance floor, Mrs. Moore was accosting the DJ, trying to get him to stop the video.

"Yeah? And how's that working out for ya?" Shannen asked my father. "I mean, it's gotta be tough after you cheated dozens of people out of what, millions of dollars?"

A wave of laughter quickly shot through the room, then petered out. I pushed myself out of my chair.

"I have to get out of here," I said to Jake.

"Ally, wait—"

"It . . . it wasn't like that," my dad said. "It's complicated. You kids couldn't understand—"

"Well, why don't you try explaining it to us?" Faith shot back.

"How could you do this to me?" I said to Faith. "What's the matter with you?"

Faith opened her mouth. She actually looked remorseful. On the screen behind her, my dad rubbed at his brow. "I . . . I didn't . . . I never meant to . . ."

I started to turn away, my legs shaking so badly I could hardly even stand. That was when I spotted my mother. She was standing in the doorway with Gray, having just come back from the bathroom or from outside. Her hand was over her mouth, and she looked like she was about to pass out, burst into tears, or worse. I had to get to her.

"All right. That's enough."

I froze. The room—the tables, the balloons, the waiters—everything in front of me tilted. That was Jake's voice. And it was coming through the speakers. Slowly, I turned around to look at the screen. The camera whirled, and there he was, clear as day. Jake reached out, took the camera, and the screen went black.

My whole body started to shake. He had been there. Jake was there. He'd seen my father. He'd seen him doing a minimum-wage job in a dirty apron getting humiliated by a bunch of kids. Everyone in the video had been wearing winter coats, which meant it was taken over the winter. Jake was there. He'd known for weeks and weeks where my father was. And he hadn't told me.

The lights came up. Every single set of eyes in the room was trained on me. I looked down at Jake. He looked like he wanted to die.

"You knew?" I said, my voice trembling. "You knew?"

"Ally, I—"

"Don't attack him," Shannen said, crossing the dance floor. "He was just along for the ride."

"Shannen!" her mother hissed.

Shannen ignored her and kept coming. She had this evil look on her face. So self-satisfied. So happy.

"How could you do this?" Chloe asked, standing up from the table.

"She deserves it, Chloe, trust me," Shannen said.

I took a step back, but my legs were so weak I almost went down. I caught myself on the back of someone's chair. Jake got up and reached for me, but I batted his arm away. My vision was blurred by tears. I didn't know what to do, who to yell at, which way to go. All I knew was, I'd just seen my dad for the first time in two years. He was alive. He was working somewhere nearby. Yet he'd never bothered to contact us.

And everyone I knew had this information months ago.

"No. No. There was no reason for you to do this," Chloe said, shaking her head. She turned to me. "Ally, I'm so sorry. We—"

"She hooked up with Hammond," Shannen said.

I closed my eyes. Gasps everywhere. I couldn't take much more of this. My heart and brain were still trying to process seeing my dad—being betrayed by Jake—and now this? Why? Why was she doing this to me?

"What?" Chloe said.

"The night she moved away," Shannen said.

Hammond looked queasy. "How did you—"

"I walked in on you guys. I saw everything," Shannen said. Then she turned to Chloe again. "She's been lying to you all this time. They both have."

Chloe's shoulders curled. "Hammond? You didn't."

"It was nothing, Chlo," he said, getting up. "It was a million years ago. We just—"

"Stop." Tears sprang to Chloe's eyes. She turned and shakily started for the door. I automatically went after her.

"Chloe. Wait. Let me—"

She whirled around.

"Don't," she said quietly through her teeth. "I can't believe you'd do this to me." She looked away for a moment, her chin trembling. "And all this time I've been defending you. . . ."

"Chloe, please."

She took a deep breath and looked around, taking in the

rapt audience. Chloe hated scenes, and here she was, smack in the middle of a huge one.

"I have to go," she said, drawing herself up straight. "Do *not* follow me."

And she was gone. Watching her retreat, my fingers curled into fists. As I turned to face the dance floor, I knew that everyone at all twenty tables was now focused, again, on me. What were they thinking? Did they feel sorry for me because of the video, or did they think I'd gotten what I deserved? Did they think Shannen was nuts for making a spectacle out of her birthday party, or were they just loving the drama? I looked around my table, where my former friends all sat, every last one of them except Shannen and Jake avoiding my gaze. He looked tortured. She looked devilishly happy.

And something inside me snapped. She was waiting for me to turn on my Payless heels and run, but she was about to be disappointed. I was not weak. I was not the girl who crawled away from scandal in the dead of night. That was not me. Not anymore.

"Ally, honey." It was my mom, standing just behind me. "I think it's time to go."

"No," I said firmly. "No. Shannen got to say what she wanted to say. Now it's my turn."

I looked Shannen in the eye and smiled through my tears.

"Wow. You really showed me, didn't you?" I said loudly enough for everyone to hear. "But guess what? I'll get over this stupid prank." It wasn't just a prank. It was way more than that. And at the moment, it didn't feel like I would ever get over it, but she didn't need to know that. "The person you really just hurt was Chloe."

There was a flicker of doubt in Shannen's triumphant eyes, but it passed. "I didn't do anything. I just told her the truth."

"The truth. Interesting," I said. "I've got a piece of truth I could share right now, too, right?" I glanced past her at her parents for good measure. "Actually, there are a few interesting facts I could spill right now if I wanted to."

Shannen's face drained of color. She was terrified. Well, let her be. After everything she'd done to me this year, she deserved to feel like shit for two-point-five seconds. And then the two-point-five seconds were over.

"But I won't," I said, "because even though I'm a Norm now, I'm a better person than you'll ever be."

Shannen swallowed and looked away, probably still seeing her life flash before her eyes. I turned to face Jake. He stared back at me, a million emotions in his eyes, but all I could think about was how he'd betrayed me. He'd known all along where my father was. All those times we'd talked about it, all the sob stories I'd told about how my dad hadn't called, about how I didn't know where he was, and Jake knew. I'd trusted him, and he'd kept this huge, life-altering secret from me. I felt so stupid all of a sudden I wanted to cry.

"Ally—"

The very sound of his voice brought a sob into my throat. "No," I croaked. "You don't get to talk to me." I took a deep breath and looked him in the eye. "Have a nice summer, Jake."

I turned around and looked at my mother. Her eyes were sad, confused, but I could tell she was determined to hold it together. I took a deep breath and swallowed back all my emotion.

"Come on, Mom," I said clearly. "Let's get out of here."

jake

The DJ started up the music again. I guess he was trying to distract everyone from what had just happened. But for a long moment, no one moved. Except Shannen. Her mom dragged her out onto the patio, closed the door, and went ballistic. Then Hammond got up and went after Chloe. And soon, people started to file onto the dance floor.

"Are you okay?" Faith asked me, standing up.

I blinked. "What the hell just happened?"

"For whatever it's worth . . . I didn't know Shannen was going to do that," Faith said. She sighed and looked toward the door where Ally had disappeared. "She must hate Ally even more than I knew."

I swallowed hard. Shannen came in from the patio and stormed toward the lobby. I felt a surge of rage so fierce I had to move.

"I'll be right back." I went after Shannen. I caught up with her in the lobby as she was about to shove her way into the bathroom.

"Shannen!"

She stopped and turned around slowly. Her whole body was tense with anger.

"What the hell is the matter with you?" I blurted, barely containing my fury.

Shannen laughed and looked away, shaking her head. She crossed the marble floor until she was standing right in front of me. She didn't look guilty at all. Or sorry. She looked defiant. "I did what I had to do."

"What? What does that even mean?" I spat. "Why did you even invite her here? Just so you could humiliate her?"

"Kind of, yeah," she said matter-of-factly.

My eyes narrowed in disgust. "Who the hell *are* you? That was brutal, Shannen, even for you."

"Well, maybe if you hadn't been lying to me for the past six months, I wouldn't have felt the need to be so brutal," she snapped.

"Lying to you? What are you talking about?" I asked.

"I saw you, okay?" Shannen blurted. "I saw you and Ally kissing on your birthday."

I shook my head, trying to process how that was even possible. How it mattered at all right now. "What are you talking about?"

"On your birthday!" she said, throwing her hands up. "You get your dream car, and instead of coming to pick me up—your best friend—you drive over to the Nathansons' house, pick up Ally Ryan—a person you claim to not even like—and spend half an hour grinding on her in the parking lot."

I felt like I was going to hurl. "How did you—"

"I followed you!" she spat. "I wanted to know what you had to do that was so important you'd diss me, so I took my mom's car and I followed you. I was parked on the other side of the parking lot the entire time you guys were fogging up your windows."

I took a couple of steps back and sat down on one of the velvet couches near the wall, feeling weak. My brain struggled to make sense of what she was saying, but it couldn't. "So that's why you did all this? Because I ditched you on my birthday? Because I lied?"

Shannen laughed bitterly and looked across the room toward the door. "I tried everything to keep you away from her," she said, almost like she was talking to herself. "But none of it worked. Not asking nicely, not freezing her out with those stupid practical jokes, not telling you about her and Hammond, not telling you we couldn't trust her." She looked at me and narrowed her eyes. "No matter what, you still wanted her. You still *had* to be with her."

"I don't understand," I said. My brain was so fogged over I could hardly see. "If you're mad at me for being a bad friend or whatever, get mad at me. What did Ally Ryan ever do to you? And don't give me that line about her dad or this stuff about Chloe and Hammond. That's bullshit, and you know it. What did *Ally* do to *you?*"

Tears suddenly sprang to Shannen's eyes, shining along her lashes. Instantly, my heart stopped. Shannen never cried. Ever.

She looked me in the eye and spoke. "Don't you get it, Jake? She went after you."

ally

How could he do this to us? How could he just leave us and not let us know where he was? How could he be so close that my old friends could find him and yet never even try to come see us?

I sat in the backseat of Gray's silver Land Rover as we wound our way down the lane leading away from the country club, staring out the window at the thick trees. For months I had tried not to think about my father too much or for too long. Because I knew that if I did, I would sink into this black tar pit of self-pity and sorrow and anger. But now there was no keeping my head above the surface. I was sinking, and sinking fast.

He'd left us to go work at a deli. For Chloe's dad. Chloe and her father and mother had known all along where he was. Every time I thought about it, a wave of embarrassed heat crashed over my body. They knew. They all knew. Everyone but me knew everything about my life.

Even Jake. Jake, who never knew my dad before. Never knew us. Didn't really know the history, could never really understand how it felt. Jake Graydon had met my father without my even knowing. And to him, he was just some deadbeat dad working in a deli with a smear of mayonnaise across his dingy apron.

I bit my lip and tried not to cry. It would be way too obvious in the dead silence that currently reigned inside the car. Neither my mother nor Gray had said a word since leaving the club. Not that I could blame them. What were you supposed to say when you'd just seen a horrifying video of your girlfriend's not-ex husband?

"Where was that?" Gray said suddenly, quietly. His tone was pondering, as if he'd been brainstorming this whole time. "That deli. Was it in the city?"

"Gray, I don't think we should talk about this right now," my mother said firmly.

"But don't you want to find him, confront him?" Gray said, taking his eyes off the road for a moment to glance at my mother. "You finally have a lead."

My mother shot him a silencing look, and that was it. Gray focused again on the road. As much as I had started to like Gray, I felt like he shouldn't be there right then. I couldn't wait to get back to the condo so my mother and I could be alone and,

I don't know . . . throw things, talk, cry, whatever. Mom took a deep breath.

"You know what? I think it's good that we're getting away this summer," she said, in a voice that was slightly too loud and chipper. She turned in her seat and looked at me. "You'll get a job down the shore, make new friends, take up surfing again. You can put all this drama behind you and just have some fun. I think we all need a fresh start."

I just stared back at her. What was she going to do? Ignore the fact that we'd just seen my dad? That we, with one phone call to Mr. Appleby, could find out exactly where he was? Was she just going to try to go ahead with our lives as if nothing had happened? Besides, the very idea of living down at the shore with pretty much every Crestie family who'd just seen me utterly humiliated made me want to jump out of the car and run for the nearest airport.

Plus, there was that whole revelation about me and Hammond. Sooner or later, she was going to have to ask me about that. Which was, let's face it, the very last thing I ever wanted to talk about with my mother.

Shannen had really overachieved on this one.

"I don't want to go anymore," I said, my voice low.

"What?" my mother said.

"I don't want to go," I repeated. "Do you really want to spend the summer with those people?"

"We don't have to spend any time with them if we don't want to," my mother said naively.

"Right." I leaned forward between their two seats. "Hey, Gray, where's your house again?"

"Between the Schwartz's and the Ross's," he said, shooting

my mother an apologetic look. "But we have a whole acre between houses—"

"Yeah." I slumped back again. "I'm out."

"Ally, we are not going to let your father ruin our summer plans," my mother said. "When he left, I made a promise to both of us that I would not make my life decisions based on him anymore, and we haven't. We're not going to start now."

I bit down on my tongue. Didn't she get it? This wasn't about him. It was about them. The Cresties. Shannen and Faith and Chloe and Hammond and the Idiot Twins . . . and Jake.

Just an hour ago, I had thought everything was perfect. I had thought I could trust him with everything. But it had all been a lie. He'd kept this huge secret from me—him and all his Crestie pals. They'd all been laughing at me behind my back this entire time. It was clear now that if he had to choose between them and me, he would choose them. He already had, just by not telling me. By letting them keep this secret. By letting them think they were better than me.

I thought back to how hopeful I'd been when I'd agreed to go to the shore—all the things I'd imagined me and Jake doing together—and felt like a total idiot. Had he known then? On his birthday, when we'd first kissed? Had he already been lying to me? Tears of shame and misery and self-loathing stung my eyes. If I could go back, if I could rewind to the beginning of the year, I would have changed everything. Every. Last. Thing.

Gray turned into the entrance to the OVC, his headlights flashing on the elaborate wooden signage. I felt a practically primal need to be home right then. To be inside, in my sweats, under the covers, curled into a ball. To shut off my brain and be left alone for days and days and days.

"It's gonna be okay, Al," my mom said. "We're gonna figure this out."

Gray turned onto our street, his headlights flashing on the identical steps leading up to the identical doors of the identical condos. My heart caught when I saw that someone was sitting on the bottom step in front of ours. Had Jake made it here before us somehow? What could he possibly think he could say that was going to make this better?

"Oh my God," my mother said, her voice strained.

And that was when I realized that the person on the stairs was not wearing a suit and tie. He was not tall and lean and square shouldered. He was not a person I ever would have expected to see right there, right then.

It was my father.

acknowledgments

First and foremost I'd like to thank Emily Meehan for believing in this project from the beginning, and for believing in me for me. I'd also like to thank Sarah Burnes, who has been the most consistent supportive voice in my work life for the past six years. I seriously don't know where I'd be without you, Sarah. Wait. Yes, I do. Scary picture.

Huge thanks to Allison Cohen and Julia Maguire, who were the first to read the manuscript and tell me how much they loved it (much needed positivity at the time); to Justin Chanda, for seeing my vision for whatever it's worth and running with it; to Courtney Bongiolatti, who has always been so psyched about my stuff; and to Courtney Gatewood, whose gushing e-mails were a complete joy. I'd also like to thank Paul Crichton and Lucille Rettino, for believing in my work way back when, and for making me feel like my books will always be well cared for; Liesa Abrams, who said, "Why not talk to Emily?" and Krista Vossen, for the most gorgeous cover ever.

A special thanks goes out to my teachers throughout high school and college, some of who played a huge role in making me a writer. Jane Conboy, Thomas Harrington, Suzanne Montagne, Susan Gillow, Frank Cherichello, Cheryl Wall, Steve Miller, and Alan Michael Parker. Without all of you, I wouldn't be writing this acknowledgments page right now. And to any of my readers who might be skimming this: Appreciate your teachers. They are selfless and wise and can take you places you'd never imagine you could go. Use them. They like it when you do.

Thanks to my family and friends. Mom, Ian, Erin, Steph, and all the Scotts, Violas, and Donohues, what can I say? You make life interesting, fun, dramatic, and silly. Kind of like my work. Wendy, Shira, Ally, Meredith, Courtney, Jessica, Manisha, Aimee, Lynn—all the strong women in my life—thanks for always being there for me.

And finally, eternal thanks to Matt, who picks me up when I'm crumbling, reminds me I'm worth so much more than I think I am, and loves me unconditionally. You are everything. Thanks for being there and giving me our little Brady, the most precious gift I've ever been given.

Things are going to get worse before they get better.

He's So Not Worth It

kieran scott

Ally Ryan is in for one long summer
in the sequel to
She's So Dead to Us.

Daily Field Journal of Annie Johnston
Saturday, June 26

Position:

Golf cart parked across the circle from the entrance of the Orchard Hill Country Club/Shannen Moore's birthday extravaganza.

Cover:

If anyone asks, I lost a diamond earring while out on the links today and I'm checking all the carts before busting out the metal detector on the back nine.

Observations:

10:05 p.m.: Subject Chloe Appleby exits the front door in tears. Uniform: pink dress, high heels, party hair. The two lazing valets hop to attention. One reaches out to her for a ticket, which she doesn't have. Subject Hammond Ross drove her, of course. Subject Chloe starts back inside, thinks better of it, takes a step toward the parking lot, turns a heel, and almost goes down. One of the valets gamely grabs her arm and keeps her from hitting her butt. (Assessment: Subjects Chloe and Hammond had a fight. A big one.)

10:06 p.m.: Subject Hammond Ross comes barreling through the door in a panic. Uniform: Hugo Boss pinstripe suit, pink tie. Dutifully matching the girlfriend, of course. He sees the valet holding on to Subject Chloe and tears her away. She shoves him and shouts, but I can't make it out from this distance. (Note: I briefly consider firing up the golf cart and gunning it across the sea of marigolds at the center of the circle to get within hearing distance, but fear that might attract a bit too much attention.)

10:07 p.m.: Subject Chloe slaps Subject Hammond across the face so hard I can see the fingerprint-shaped marks from here. (Note: Keep the camera phone on at all times, idiot!)

10:08 p.m.: Subjects Mr. and Mrs. Appleby finally appear from inside. Subject Mr. Appleby has a few stern words for Subject Hammond, who skulks back inside. The valet has the Applebys' car for them in approximately seven and a half seconds. The Applebys peel out. (Query: What the hell did Hammond do in there?)

10:09 p.m.: Ally Ryan walks out with her mother and Subject Gray Nathanson. None of them are speaking. Ally looks like she just ate a bug. She keeps swallowing over and over again like she's trying to keep it down. The valet gets Subject Dr. Nathanson's car in approximately eight and a half seconds, and they're gone as well. (Query: WTF is going on and what does Ally have to do with it?)

10:10 p.m.: I try Ally's cell phone. It goes straight to voice mail.

10:15 p.m.: Subject Jake Graydon jogs out and looks both ways, then talks to the valets and runs a hand over his hair. He tugs out his cell phone and dials, holds it to his ear for a split second, then curses. He tries again. Same result. (Assessment: He's trying to call the same person I'm trying to call.)

10:20 p.m.: Subject Jake gives up and hands the valet his ticket. The valet gets his car in approximately two minutes. (Note: Response time is clearly slower for the children of the members than for the members themselves.) Subject Jake's taillights hesitate at the end of the long drive. And hesitate. And hesitate. Finally he turns right, headed for the crest. Headed away from Ally. (Assessment: I missed something huge. Note: Next year, get an invite to Shannen Moore's birthday party.)

ally

I had imagined my reunion with my father so many times over the past two years, I had every last detail down. I knew how many breaths of surprise I'd take upon seeing him. How long my strides would be as I raced across the distance that separated us and into his arms. I knew that he'd pick me up and twirl me around exactly three times before setting me down again, pushing my hair back from my face, and saying, "I missed you, bud."

In my mind, it had always looked like some sappy Disney movie. Him with a big, toothy grin. Me with my feet kicked up, my skirt flying. The sun was always shining and the birds were serenading us with a happy tune. It was the kind of scene that would bring tears to moviegoers' eyes everywhere.

Except I didn't actually wear a lot of skirts. And the sun had gone down hours ago. Plus, the only sound outside the car was the annoying beeping of a truck backing up. Also, it had never occurred to me that when we all saw each other again, no one would feel like smiling. In fact, the moment I spotted my dad on the front steps of the condo my mother and I shared in the Orchard View Condominium community, all I could imagine doing was shoving him as hard as I could.

"Oh my God," my mother said from the front passenger seat. Outside the window, my dad slowly rose to his feet. He was wearing pressed khakis and a crisp, white button down with varied stripes. His salt-and-pepper hair was cropped short on the sides and pushed back from his face on top. His shoes gleamed, and he wore the silver and gold Rolex my mother's father had given him on the day of their wedding. Since leaving Orchard Hill in shame and destitution two years ago, my mom had sold most of her good jewelry to help pay the bills. Apparently that plan had never occurred to my dad. "I'm not really seeing this," my mother said. "Tell me I'm not seeing this."

Her hands shook as she reached for the clasp on her seat belt.

"Melanie, just take a breath and calm down," her boyfriend Gray Nathanson said. He put the car in park and covered her fingers with his large hand. "You don't want the first thing you say to him to be something you'll regret."

"Something I'll regret?" My mother's voice sounded like it was coming to us through a tin can tunnel. "I'm not going to say anything. I'm just going to kill the bastard."

Yeah. A Disney movie this was not.

Gray said my mother's name, but she was already out of the car. I found I couldn't move; my legs had gone dead. I watched through the window of Gray's luxury SUV, as my father's eyes followed my mother's approach, and suddenly registered fear.

"How could you?" my mother screeched, slamming his chest with both hands. Like mother like daughter. My dad staggered back a couple of steps and Gray hustled out of the car.

"Wait here," he said to me, slamming the door shut behind him.

For some reason, that directive was what finally got me moving. I undid my seat belt and scrambled out onto the pavement. A couple of lights flickered to life around me, and I saw concerned neighbors peeking through the slats of their blinds. Great. I gave it five minutes before the Orchard Hill

Police Department descended on my little family reunion. As if there hadn't already been enough humiliation tonight.

"Gray? What the hell are you doing with Gray Nathanson?" my father said as I approached.

Gray had one hand on my dad's chest, holding him back as my father talked about him like he wasn't even there.

"What the hell am I—? Are you kidding me, Christopher? Where the hell have *you* been for the last two years? Who the hell have *you* been with?" my mother shouted.

"I haven't been with anyone! I've been trying to get my life back together!" my father shouted back.

"Oh really? That's funny! Because I thought your life was with us! Have you been here all this time and I've just missed you somehow?"

Gray put his other hand on my mother's shoulder. "Why don't we all just calm down, go inside, and—"

"I have a better idea. Why don't you shut the fuck up and let me talk to my wife?" my father demanded, shoving Gray off of him.

Gray finally lost his composure. His face turned purple and his fists clenched, the tendons in his neck stuck out. My heart thumped with panic. My dad was tall and toned, but thin. Not exactly the fistfighting type. Gray worked out every day and was a lot stronger-looking than my dad. If hooks and jabs started flying, my father would be toast. I had to do something.

"Dad?" I croaked.

All three of them turned to look at me. They had clearly forgotten I was there. Gray's fists relaxed. My mother's eyes flooded with tears. My dad blew out a breath, tilted his head, and said, "Hey, bud."

He even managed to smile. It was almost exactly like I'd imagined it. Except—

"No!" my mother shouted, slicing a finger through the air. "*No!* You do not get to call her 'bud.' You don't even get to *look* at her! Not after you haven't so much as called her for her birthday or for Christmas or for *anything* in the past two years! Not after what happened to her tonight, thanks to you." My mother was hysterical now, the tears streaming down her face as she blindly, haphazardly groped for my hand.

My dad's face was blank at first, then concerned. "Wait . . . what happened to her tonight?" he repeated. "What do you mean 'what happened to her tonight'?"

Nothing much. I was just completely blindsided and humiliated when Shannen Moore played a video at her birthday party for half the junior and senior class and most of my mom and dad's former friends to see. A video of her, Faith Kirkpatrick, Hammond Ross, and Jake Graydon "happening upon" my father as he worked behind the counter at a deli in New York City. Up until the moment it unfolded on the huge screen over the dance floor, I'd had no clue where my father had been for the past two years, whether he was alive or dead, whether he'd . . . I don't know . . . gotten himself a new identity and moved to Paraguay. I found out at the exact same time as everyone else in the room that he'd been slinging bologna less than fifty miles away all this time. Just making sandwiches and pouring coffee and wiping counters. Living life as if my mother and I had never existed.

Wait, strike that. A few people had known *before* me. Namely, the people in the video, who had filmed it last winter: Shannen, Faith, Hammond, and Jake.

"We are going inside now. *We* are." My mother grabbed Gray's hand as well and basically yanked us both up the stairs. She fumbled with her keys until Gray finally took them from her and opened the door. He ushered me inside ahead of him while my mother let the screen door crash behind us. She turned around and glared down at my father, who, at that moment, looked smaller than he ever had in my life. "You can stay out there and rot."

I watched my father as the door closed on his stricken, disappointed face. My mother ran to her room and slammed that door as well, leaving me and Gray alone in our cramped entryway. He put his hands in his pockets and looked out the tiny window set high in the door.

"No one would blame you if you wanted to go out there and talk to him," he said.

"Oh really? I think my mom would disagree," I replied, somehow speaking past the thick, wet paper towel that had jammed itself in my throat.

"She's just upset right now," Gray said. "But he's your father. She knows you two should have a relationship."

I swallowed hard. There was a long, skinny window of cut glass next to the front door, which you could only see through if you angled your eye just right, and even then you could only catch a sliver of the outside world. I stood on my toes and tilted my head to see my father frustratedly pacing in our parking lot. He moved out of view, then back again. Covered his face with his hands, muttered something under his breath. Finally, he turned and walked away, toward the exit of the complex, whipping out a cell phone as he went.

Just like that, he was here and then he was gone again.

"I think I'll just go to bed," I said weakly.

Gray gave me a sympathetic smile. He looked like he maybe wanted to reach out and squeeze my shoulder, and I was relieved when he restrained himself. I liked the guy, but I didn't much want anyone touching me at that moment. Definitely not a father figure touching me in a fatherly way. Not now.

I walked to my room, closed the door, and sunk down onto the edge of my bed, clutching the blanket at my sides. I was still wearing the black cocktail dress I'd bought specifically for Shannen's party and I suddenly felt like tearing it off my body in shreds. What a waste of a week's paycheck. I couldn't believe I had been so naïve. So stupid and gullible and oblivious. Less than five hours ago I'd been standing in front of the mirror in this very room, grinning at my reflection, giddily anticipating Jake Graydon's arrival so he could squire me off to the biggest party of the year. Five hours ago Jake was my almost-boyfriend. Five hours ago I was almost friends with Shannen and Chloe Appleby and Hammond Ross again. Five hours ago life was on its way to being good. It was on its way to being great. One might even say perfect.

It is amazing how in five short hours, everything completely and irrevocably turned to crap.

Pulse It

Did you love this book?

Want to get access to the hottest books for free?

Log on to simonandschuster.com/pulseit
to find out how to join,
get access to cool sweepstakes,
and hear about your favorite authors!

Become part of Pulse IT and tell us what you think!

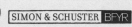

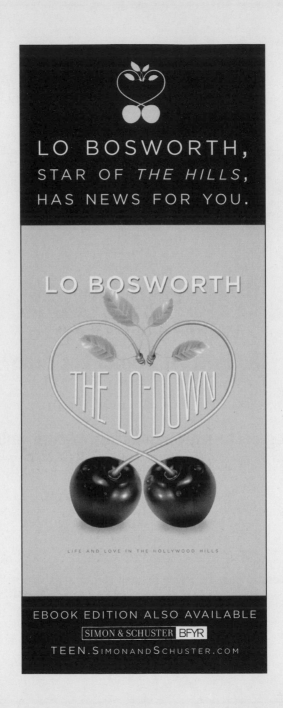

*Cara agreed to help Zoe hide out—
no questions asked.
Isn't that what best friends are for?*

Elizabeth Woods's debut novel, *Choker*, will change
everything you thought you knew about friendship.
Learn more at **ElizabethWoodsBooks.com**.

elixir

HILARY DUFF

a novel

An intoxicating new novel from

HILARY DUFF